WATERSONG

WATERSONG

CLARISSA GOENAWAN

SCRIBE
Melbourne • London

Scribe Publications
2 John St, Clerkenwell, London, WC1N 2ES, United Kingdom
18–20 Edward St, Brunswick, Victoria 3056, Australia
3754 Pleasant Ave, Suite 100, Minneapolis, Minnesota 55409, USA

Published by Scribe 2022

Typeset in Arno Pro by the publishers

Printed and bound in the UK by CPI Group (UK) Ltd, Croydon CR0 4YY

Scribe is committed to the sustainable use of natural resources and the use
of paper products made responsibly from those resources.

978 1 914484 11 7 (UK edition)
978 1 922585 20 2 (Australian edition)
978 1 950354 97 9 (US edition)
978 1 922586 44 5 (ebook)

Catalogue records for this book are available from the
National Library of Australia and the British Library.

scribepublications.co.uk
scribepublications.com.au
scribepublications.com

PROLOGUE

A long time ago, when he was a kid, he'd dreamed of drowning.

He fought hard, moving his arms and thrashing around as the water pushed him down. Excruciating pain burned in his lungs. He couldn't breathe. Through the clear water, the sunlight shifted, dancing with the ripples. The surface felt so near, yet unreachable. A woman called his name.

Shouji! Shouji!

He woke up drenched in sweat, gasping for air. The dream was vivid, and it continued night after night. Worried it was a bad omen, his mother took him to a famous fortune-teller.

The old woman sat behind a folding table covered with a black cloth in a secluded alley near Nakasu-Kawabata Station. Several lit incense sticks and a handwritten sign advertised her services.

They had to line up behind three customers who'd arrived before them. He couldn't wait to leave. The smell of incense was nauseating. The smoke made his eyes water.

When it was his turn, the fortune-teller grinned at him, revealing her uneven teeth. He flinched. His mother put her hands on his shoulders, edging him forward.

'My son has been having the same nightmare. Three times in a row.'

'That's worrying.'

The old woman reached for the boy's hand. Her wrinkled skin brushed against his as she turned his palm face up.

His mother's grip on his shoulders tightened. 'Do you see anything?'

'Yes, I see water. Too much water.' The woman furrowed her brow. 'Black, murky water. A lot of darkness.'

There was a pause.

'Your son will come across three women with the water element in their names. One of them could be his soulmate.' She closed the boy's palm. 'But if he's not careful, the water will flood. He, or someone close to him — these women perhaps — may drown.'

His mother turned pale as he stared at the age spots creeping all over the old woman's arms, wondering what they were.

'Madam, you've got something on your mind.'

'There was an accident involving a relative ...' His mother's voice was small. Shouji looked at her curiously, but she shifted her eyes away from him. 'Is there anything you can do for my son?' she asked the fortune-teller, desperate.

The old woman cleared her throat. 'I'm afraid I can't give you a definite answer, madam.' She turned to the boy. 'But your son has a kind heart, and kindness is often rewarded. With a bit of luck, he might be fine.'

MIZUKI

水月

CHAPTER 1
THE EAR PROSTITUTE

Akakawa, 1995. At a glance, the tearoom didn't look much different from the high-end cafés in Daikanyama. It was housed in an elegant, pristine-white, western-style building. But, looking closer, everything had been meticulously planned to ensure complete privacy for those inside, from the frosted-glass windows to the carefully tended garden that blocked the entrance.

Entering, Shouji saw a framed pen-and-ink illustration of a teapot hung on the wall. A pair of potted English ivies stood near the wooden front doors, which had shiny golden handles. He took a deep breath. The enthusiasm he'd felt earlier had evaporated once he'd got off the bus.

'Are you nervous?' Youko asked.

He forced a smile to reassure his girlfriend. 'No.'

'Your palm is sweaty.'

He quickly let go of her hand and wiped his on his trousers.

'Just kidding,' she said with a chuckle. 'Don't worry, Shouji. You're a good listener. I know that better than anyone. You'll be fine. Actually no, not just fine. You'll be amazing. You're perfect for this.'

He wasn't convinced, but he had to nail this interview. He needed a job to stay in Akakawa. Even a dodgy one would do.

•

Three days ago, his girlfriend had returned home earlier than usual. Youko's eyebrows rose when she saw him lounging on the low sofa in front of the television. She probably thought he should've been out there. Somewhere, anywhere, doing something …

Shouji got up. 'Have you had dinner?'

Youko shook her head. 'Not hungry.'

'Bad day at work?'

She didn't answer. After taking off her coat, she sat down next to him and hugged her knees to her chest. 'What's the show about?'

Shouji looked at the television. It was showing a family drama, but he hadn't been paying attention.

'Stop turning on the TV if you're not watching it. You're wasting electricity.'

Youko switched the television off before burying her face in her knees. She stayed quiet for a long time. He guessed today was one of those days. Shouji sighed. He couldn't cheer her up because she wouldn't tell him anything about her job. She probably felt uncomfortable discussing her kind of work. He took a deep breath and rubbed her shoulders.

The silence made the slightest sounds more pronounced: the whirring ceiling fan, the ticking clock, the rustling of leaves, and the chattering of passers-by seeping through the windows.

After Youko calmed down, she whispered, 'I'm sorry.'

Shouji gave her a gentle pat. 'It's all right.'

'You're still wearing the same clothes as this morning,' she said, staring at him. 'Were you home the whole day?'

He shifted his eyes. 'Kind of.'

'What about the job search?'

'Let's talk about it another time,' he said. 'You look tired. You should rest.'

'No,' she insisted. 'It's bothering you, so we should talk now.'

Taking a deep breath, Shouji stared at the window. Traces of water from yesterday's rain had left streaks on the glass. He'd not noticed them until now.

'I can't find a job here,' he said. 'Maybe everyone was right. I should've looked for a suitable position in Tokyo. The recruiting season isn't over. If I return now, I should be able to catch the last wave.'

She stared at him. 'You're leaving.'

'I have no choice.'

'But you do have a choice.' Her tone was flat. 'You always have a choice.'

He grew defensive. 'Look, I need a job to survive. My savings are running out. I can't rely on you to pay for everything.'

'Didn't I tell you it's fine?' Youko straightened her legs. 'I don't mind. We're a couple. We help each other. You'd do the same for me, wouldn't you?'

That was true, but … 'I do mind. I don't want to depend on you financially. It's not fair, and it's not right.' He paused and reached for her hand, squeezing it gently. 'Youko, I'm not leaving you. I'm just leaving Akakawa. We can still see each other on our days off.'

'I don't like this,' she mumbled.

Me neither, he wanted to say, but kept quiet. Instead, he looked around the room. This old, cheap apartment wasn't as comfortable as the one he used to share with Jin back in Tokyo, but he'd grown fond of it.

'Why don't you come and work with me?' Youko asked. 'I can recommend you. I'm sure they'll say yes. The pay is good.'

Shouji hesitated. 'You mean … the company also runs a host club here?' He thought of those glitzy places where young, handsome men clad in suits entertained rich, female clients. They were common in Tokyo, but he was surprised to hear they had spread to the suburbs too.

Youko gave him a puzzled look. 'What?'

'Your work …' He looked away, trying to hide his unease. 'You're some sort of high-class hostess, aren't you?'

She burst into laughter.

'Stop that,' he said, embarrassed.

Youko lunged forward and hugged him. 'You're so cute, Shouji. You wouldn't mind if I was working as a hostess?'

'I would.' He avoided her eyes. 'But you didn't listen when I asked you to stop this job you couldn't tell me about. I want to respect your decisions, even when I don't agree with you.'

She put her palms on his face, turning his head to look at her. 'I'm touched.'

He reached for her hands and pulled them away. Was she being sarcastic?

'I'm sorry. I should've told you everything from the beginning,' she said. 'My job isn't what you imagine. I don't think it's anything most people could imagine.'

He kept quiet. Go on.

'I'm a listener,' she said. 'I listen to other people's problems, letting them air whatever is eating them up inside.'

Oh. 'Something like a therapist?'

'Kind of, but not really. The place I work at looks more like a high-class tearoom than a clinic, at least from the outside. We serve an excellent range of teas too. And we're extremely exclusive. We only serve our members. Don't ask me how the company does the vetting. I have no idea. What I do know is the exclusivity comes with a hefty price tag. And to justify that fee, we guarantee absolute confidentiality and zero judgement.'

He stared at her. The more she explained, the dodgier this job seemed.

'I must never, ever disclose any conversation I've had with a client, even if my life were on the line. I wouldn't even be telling you this much if I weren't suggesting you work there.' She bit her lip. 'What do you think?'

Shouji drummed his fingers on his knee. 'Do I have to answer now?'

Youko shrugged. 'You're the one who said you really needed a job, but it's fine if you're not up for it. I'm just trying to help.'

'Hey, I didn't say I didn't want it.' It was true that he was desperate. And if, by joining Youko's company, he could understand her better, that would be a bonus. 'I'll give it a shot.'

'Good,' she said. 'I'll inform Madam.'

'Madam?'

'That's how we address the lady who runs the Akakawa branch.'

'Isn't that a bit weird? Sounds like …' He tailed off.

'A mama-san who manages prostitutes?'

He didn't want to say it, but she had. 'Erm, kind of.'

She laughed. 'In a way, it's a fitting description. After all, we're prostituting our ears.'

•

Youko opened the door and Shouji followed her into the tearoom.

'My dear!' A plump woman in a white suit greeted them from behind the counter. 'This handsome young man must be your boyfriend.'

He bowed. 'I'm Shouji Arai. A pleasure to meet you.'

'We need to talk in private,' she said to Shouji before turning to Youko. 'Sweetheart, would you mind fetching Mr Satou? Ask him to mind the counter. After that, go to the waiting room.'

Youko went through the next set of doors. Meanwhile, Madam took her time to stare at Shouji.

She was middle-aged, with curly, dark-brown hair that reminded him of a bird's nest, and she held a black pen in her right hand as if it were an extended body part. Shouji tried his best to appear relaxed while maintaining eye contact.

An older man in a black tuxedo came in. This had to be Mr Satou. Shouji bowed to him. The man bowed in return and took a good look at Shouji, long enough to make the younger man feel uncomfortable. Somehow, he looked familiar, but Shouji couldn't place him.

Mr Satou's silver hair contrasted against his black jacket. He had white gloves on, like the ones worn by taxi drivers. Everything about him was prim and proper. Shouji could picture him ironing his clothes, making sure not a single crease blighted the fabric.

Madam whispered to Mr Satou while gesturing wildly with her pen. Her nails were painted turquoise. Mr Satou nodded, and Madam whisked Shouji through the doors.

In the corridor, the two of them passed a large room. Through the huge glass windows, he could see about ten people inside. There were two long leather sofas in the middle of the room. A few people were walking around aimlessly, but most of them — including Youko — were sitting. Shouji stole a glance at her, but she didn't seem to notice.

'She can't see you,' Madam said. 'It's a one-way mirror.'

At the end of the corridor, they passed through another set of doors into a spacious room. From the front of the building, Shouji wouldn't have guessed the place was this big. With floral wallpaper and white pillars decorated with gold carvings, the tearoom was grand enough to hold a lavish wedding banquet. He counted at least thirty tables, separated from each other by curved frosted-glass panels, Victorian lace curtains, or strategically placed potted plants. Classical music played in the background. A white grand piano stood in the corner, but it looked more like part of the decoration than an instrument anyone played regularly.

Madam led him to table fifteen. The partition was designed in such a way that Shouji couldn't tell whether anyone was sitting there until he reached the table. Once he was seated, a young man wearing a similar black tuxedo to Mr Satou came in with a menu. Madam took it and dismissed him with her pen.

'Mr Arai, what do you know about this job?' she asked.

Shouji cleared his throat. 'It's to be a listener.'

'That's a good place to start. Can you imagine what kind of individual would pay for this service?'

She passed the menu to him. There were only five teas listed — English Breakfast, Earl Grey, Chamomile, Peppermint, and Jasmine White. But what was surprising was the price list. A pot was as expensive as a multi-course dinner at a high-end restaurant. Then he saw in small print underneath 'one hour' — so the price was for the listening service, not just the tea. Still, what kind of person could afford this?

'We serve high-quality tea, but some of our patrons don't even touch their cups. They don't come for tea. They pay us to listen to them. We don't judge. That's rule number one. Do you understand?'

Shouji gave a small nod.

'Let me ask you again. Mr Arai, what kind of clients do you think we serve?'

Celebrities, professional athletes, high-ranking government officials, company directors — he could imagine the kinds of people who might use this service. Individuals with a lot of money who couldn't afford their private matters to be made public. He put the menu down. It sounded strange, but he needed this job. 'Those who need our service.'

'Exactly, and they might not always be someone you'd want to be associated with in real life.' Madam tapped her pen on the spotless white tablecloth. 'I've done a background check on you. It might feel invasive, but it's necessary. We need to be careful about who we take in. After all, we're dealing with —' She paused and narrowed her eyes. 'Extremely delicate matters.'

Shouji maintained his silence, slightly nervous.

'I won't ask why you want to work here. With your qualifications, I'm sure you could find long-term employment in a good company. Youko only said you needed a job, so we'll leave it at that. But are you sure you want to do this?'

He was about to say something, but before he could, she continued: 'You don't need to answer. Wanting to do a particular job doesn't mean you're suitable for it.'

Shouji didn't know how to respond. Was he supposed to sell himself as being trustworthy? Or was he supposed to listen quietly?

'Some people think of us as an obliging friend who is willing to hear their troubles. Others see us as a therapist. But we are neither. A friend offers their opinion, and a therapist works with you to fix your problem. We're different. We respond whenever it is appropriate, but we don't give any unsolicited suggestions or views. We're not emotionally or professionally invested in our clients. We're only here to listen to their problems, not to solve them.'

She stopped and stared at him. He lowered his head as a gesture that he was following.

'Mr Arai, what would you do if a client walked over to your table, sat down, and told you he was planning to murder someone? How would you handle that?'

Shouji swallowed hard. Wasn't this hypothetical scenario a little extreme? But he decided to play along. 'I would listen to the client and offer no opinion unless asked.'

'And let him murder someone?'

As if something like this would ever happen. Most likely, he would be listening to people talk about their affairs or complain about work. This was clearly just a test. 'That would be too bad, but it's the rule of the game. We don't judge.'

Madam burst into laughter. Her plump body shook as she waved her pen around. 'That's right. You're a quick learner. I like you, young man.' She repositioned herself to a comfortable sitting position. 'Yes. Even if a client tells you he committed a crime, whatever that may be, you say nothing. We listen. We don't judge.'

She stared at Shouji.

'Our clients don't just pay us for a listening ear and kind words,' she continued. 'They pay us to keep our mouths shut. Rule number two: Nothing ever leaves your table. Let me repeat. Nothing. And I mean it. You understand?'

'Yes. No judgement, and complete secrecy.'

'If a word ever gets out, which has never happened under my watch, the company has the resources to settle things.' She wrinkled her nose. 'You don't want to go down that route. Do I make myself clear, Mr Arai?'

He nodded, trying to suppress his unease. 'Absolutely.' He wondered what kind of company his girlfriend had been working for. But at least, if he worked here, he could watch over Youko.

'This is an entirely commission-based job. You earn half of what your client spends,' she said, adopting a business-like tone. 'Having said that, there's a possibility of earning nothing if you never get picked. As time goes by, if you're good at what you're doing, you'll get regulars. Simple, isn't it? But let me assure you, it's not as easy as it sounds. Try to imagine what kind of person needs this service.' She looked into his eyes. 'Keeping that in mind, do you still want the job? Do you think you can handle this?'

Shouji paused. The job was absurd. But the pay, even if he only managed to get one client a day, was ridiculously high.

'I want to do it. I'll work hard. I won't disappoint you.'

Madam pointed her pen at him. 'Good. I love that confidence. I'll give you a one-week trial. If you give us any trouble, or if you don't manage to get any clients during this period, then it's over. You should forget every single thing about this place. Is that clear?'

'Yes.'

'We're open from Monday to Saturday. The shop is closed on Sunday, so that's everyone's day off. You'll get paid every fifth of the month.'

'Uh-huh.'

She smiled. 'All right. We'll start today.'

CHAPTER 2
THROUGH THE DARKENED GLASS

Madam led Shouji back into the corridor. He looked through the window into the waiting room. Seven people were sat on the sofas, but this time, Youko wasn't among them.

When Shouji entered, everyone looked at him, but after a few seconds they seemed to lose interest. Shouji settled on the edge of one of the sofas. He stared at the darkened two-way glass, well aware that someone on the other side could be looking at him at this moment.

'Are you new?' the young woman sitting next to him whispered.

She had a freckled face and a bony frame. Something about her made her look like she was floating. Whether it was the over-long chiffon skirt she wore or the way her body swayed, he couldn't decide.

'I joined last month,' she continued. She hadn't whispered. Her voice was just soft.

He leaned towards her. 'What are we supposed to do?'

'Nothing. Just wait until someone picks you. Try to appear friendly, maybe? Then again, we don't know what they're looking for,' she said. 'Be prepared to be here for a long time. I didn't get any clients until my fourth day.'

The door opened and everyone turned. Mr Satou came in. The atmosphere became tense, but the moment he signalled one of the women to follow him, the unease dissipated.

The woman who had just left, like everyone else in the room, was in no way remarkable. Dressed in a simple beige one-piece, she looked like a typical housewife Shouji might see at the neighbour-hood supermarket. Seeing how ordinary everyone was put his mind at ease. If they were all doing it, surely it couldn't be that bad.

'Be patient.' The floating girl glanced at Shouji. 'Your turn will come.'

•

'It's a waiting game,' Shouji told Youko as they rode the bus home.

'Don't worry, it's only tough at the beginning,' she said. 'It gets easier. Most clients are willing to try someone new, but they tend to hesitate to be the first. Give it a couple more days.'

He reached for her hand and held it. She looked at him and gave a reassuring smile. It was just a small gesture, but he felt much better.

The bus stopped, and they got off, as did an old couple. Cutting through the park, Shouji and Youko walked towards their apartment building. The old couple headed in a different direction.

'This is convenient, isn't it?' he said. 'The only bus service that passes our apartment happens to be a direct route to work.'

'It's not a coincidence,' she said. 'The company owns the apartment.'

'Really?' When they had been planning their move to Akakawa, Youko had organised their accommodation. The rent was affordable, and she had liked the apartment, so why not? 'I wonder what kind of business they are.'

'I wouldn't think too much about it. They don't like people asking questions.'

It was unlike Youko to take rules seriously, but this one made sense: after all, secrecy was part of the service.

'Since you're earning so much, why don't you move to a nicer place?' Shouji asked. It had been bugging him since he had seen the price list. 'You can afford a luxurious apartment. I get that the location is convenient, but there must be better options out there.'

She chuckled. 'I spend only a quarter of my salary on rent and bills. Sometimes less.'

'You're saving the rest? I didn't know you were so prudent.'

'Not really,' she said, shrugging. 'I donate it.'

Was that a joke? But Youko's expression was serious. 'To who?'

'Ocean conservation organisations. Sea turtles, coral reefs, things like that.'

Youko loved sea creatures. She visited Shinagawa Aquarium at least once a week, even after they had left Tokyo. But still, wasn't this rather extreme?

'Why would you do that?'

'Because it makes me happy,' she said. 'Why do men spend money getting drunk with beautiful hostesses in bars? Because it makes them happy. Why do people gamble on racehorses, or buy lottery tickets? It's not like the odds are in their favour. But it makes them happy. That's why we spend money, isn't it? To make ourselves happy.' She paused, turning to face him. 'Some women use their salaries to buy pretty shoes or luxurious handbags or beautiful dresses. I choose to spend mine on charities.'

Shouji said nothing. He didn't understand her, but fine. It was her money. She should spend it the way she wanted, and there were many worse things to splurge on.

A bicycle horn squawked at them. Shouji reached for Youko's arm and pulled her aside. The bicycle raced by, too close to her.

'Are you okay?' he asked.

She nodded, using her free hand to massage the nape of her neck.

'Tired?'

Again, she nodded. He tightened his grip. Despite working at the same place, Shouji hadn't seen Youko all day. She was always with clients, and the shop made sure everyone took their lunch break in turn, one by one. But he was pleased that now he had a better understanding of the nature of her work. It was also a relief to know that she wasn't a hostess, though he still had the impression the company was not fully above board. Her job must be so emotionally draining — he could see why she was always tired. He wanted to be more supportive. Was there anything he could do for her?

'Do you want to keep some fish at home?' Shouji asked. 'Since you love going to the aquarium so much, we could get a fish tank. It would brighten up the apartment, and you'll be able to watch the fish whenever you're at home. The other day, I saw some goldfish in the pet shop around the corner.'

'No, I don't want anything like that,' Youko said. 'It's cruel to confine fish in such a tiny container.'

'Ah …' How could he not have realised that? 'You're right.'

They walked in silence the rest of the way to their apartment. That night, he wanted her, but she turned him down.

'I'm tired,' she said, pushing his hand away when he tried to get under her shirt. 'Maybe next time.'

Must be her clients. Shouji rolled over to the other side of the bed. The spring squeaked. The bed was old, like the other furniture that had come with the apartment. Closing his eyes, he thought about his day.

He'd waited in the room, but no client had asked for him. Around noon, Mr Satou, who seemed to be Madam's right-hand man, finally called him. For a moment Shouji had got his hopes up, only to learn it was his turn to go for lunch.

Mr Satou handed him a store-bought boxed lunch and a bottle of iced green tea. Skewered meat, mixed vegetables, and rice. There was even a slice of watermelon and a small cup of milk pudding. Shouji ate alone in a small, windowless room, empty apart from a folding table, a plastic chair, and a clock on the wall. After exactly fifteen minutes — he knew because he checked the time — Mr Satou came and escorted him back to the waiting room.

'I heard you're Sasaki's boyfriend,' Mr Satou said on their way back.

'Yes.' He gave him a bow. 'I'm Shouji Arai. Pleased to make your acquaintance.'

Mr Satou narrowed his eyes and nodded. He opened the glass door and gestured for Shouji to enter.

Shouji sat idly on the sofa for the rest of the day, getting up only when he needed to use the staff bathroom, conveniently located near the door. Back in college, he'd been told more than once that he was a patient person, but even so, waiting the whole day took a toll on him.

He looked at the clock on the wall and watched the hands move. Time flowed much, much more slowly than usual. It was frustrating. He was almost convinced the second hand stopped every few milliseconds.

If this continued, he wouldn't last three days.

•

Five days later, Shouji was sitting on the same leather sofa. He'd memorised every detail of the room. From how many cushions there were (sixteen) to the number of roses on the wallpaper (two hundred and forty-eight), he knew it all by heart. He'd stared at that darkened glass longer than anything he'd ever looked at in his life.

The people in the waiting room did not interact with each other. Even when Youko was there, she wouldn't talk to Shouji.

The air was heavy. Each time Shouji entered the room, he became depressed. It felt so hard to breathe after a few hours had passed. When that happened, he got up and went to the bathroom. Splashing cold water on his face eased the discomfort a little.

Turning off the tap now, Shouji took a deep breath. Today was the last working day of the week. If he still hadn't had any clients by the end of the day, he would have to return to Tokyo. He sighed and opened the door.

In the corridor on his way back to the waiting room, he wasn't looking where he was going and bumped into a woman.

'I'm sorry,' she said before Shouji had the chance to apologise.

He gazed at her. The woman had a slender build. She wore a black top hat with a veil that hid her face. Her voice was clear and pleasant, and her deep-blue dress was elegant. An actress? That was the first thing that came to mind.

'No, it's my fault.' Shouji bowed to the woman. 'My apologies.'

She didn't say anything as he excused himself and returned to the waiting room. Youko was in there too. Knowing she wouldn't talk to him, Shouji deliberately sat some distance away from her. Unlike him, she seemed to be one of the more popular listeners, with at least one client each day. For once, he was a little jealous.

The door opened and Madam came in.

'Mr Arai,' she called. 'Can you come with me?'

Shouji got up and followed her out. The rest of the people in the room eyed him with curiosity, perhaps because Mr Satou was usually the one who came to get them. But Shouji wasn't surprised. He knew she was about to tell him he'd failed the trial.

'A client has asked for you,' Madam said when they got into the corridor.

Her words stopped him in his tracks.

She gave a pleased look. 'Wonderful, isn't it?'

Finally. Shouji greeted the news with a sigh of relief. But soon, he started to feel nervous. What kind of client would he be facing? What was going to happen now?

'I've got no idea why she selected you,' Madam said. 'She has never requested anyone new before.' She narrowed her eyes. 'Before you go in, let me give you a word of warning: please be extra careful in your conduct. The lady you're going to speak with is not an ordinary client.'

Shouji nodded, feeling the pressure increasing. He couldn't afford to fail. They entered the tearoom. Madam gestured to him to go to table number seven. He cleared his throat and went over.

'Excuse me,' Shouji said cautiously.

CHAPTER 3
THAT COFFEE-SCENTED SUMMER

The client who'd requested Shouji was the woman he'd run into earlier. She had removed her top hat and veil, revealing a lovely face that matched her gentle voice. She might not be what most people would call a great beauty — none of her features was particularly outstanding — yet everything about her looked perfectly put together. Anyone could easily grow fond of her.

She gave a reassuring smile. 'Please, take a seat.'

He did as he was told.

'Tea?' she asked, reaching for the pot. 'Are you fine with Earl Grey? Or would you like something else?'

He lowered his head. 'Earl Grey is fine. Thank you.'

'Excellent,' she said, pouring him a cup.

Shouji took a sip. He wasn't sure whether he was supposed to drink with the client, but her relaxed manner made him feel as if their positions were reversed.

'So, you're Mr Arai,' she said.

He nodded, staring at her. It was hard to tell her age. Her skin was flawless and radiant, but he could see small creases around her eyes. He had been told he shouldn't ask for his clients' names unless they offered, so he kept quiet.

'I heard you're from Tokyo,' she continued.

'Actually, I was born and raised in Fukuoka, but I studied in Tokyo.'

'I've never been to Fukuoka. What is it like?'

'All right, I guess.'

She chuckled.

Shouji inched closer. 'If you don't mind me asking, why did you request me?'

'We'll talk about that later,' she said, still smiling. 'For now, why don't you tell me more about yourself? What brought you to Akakawa?'

Probably the most common question he had encountered during his interviews, and one that had tripped him over and over. He cleared his throat before answering. 'It was a woman.'

'Girlfriend?'

Shouji nodded. 'She was based in Minato, but the company relocated her here when they opened the new tearoom and needed experienced staff.' Youko had told him all of this after his first day. 'She's also a listener.'

He thought the lady was going to ask who his girlfriend was, but she only nodded in agreement. A silence descended upon them. Shouji's mind wandered, and he recalled the day Youko had told him about her impending move during one of her visits to his apartment.

●

'What about school?' That was his second thought. His first had been: What about us? But he didn't say this.

Youko brushed her hair behind her ear. 'I'm taking a break.' Staring off into the distance, she said, 'I'm going to miss you so much.'

Akakawa was only a train ride away from Tokyo, but Shouji doubted they would see each other much if she went to live there. He reached for Youko's shoulders and pulled her closer. No, he didn't want them to be apart. 'Why don't we move to Akakawa together?'

Her eyes widened. 'Are you sure? I thought you liked Tokyo?'

'I've been here for four years. It's long enough.'

She stared into his eyes. 'What about your job search?'

Shouji couldn't answer. He didn't want to tell Youko he hadn't sent in any applications. He needed more time to figure out his career path. He hoped to be a newspaper journalist or a magazine columnist, but he wasn't sure how to get there, especially with his degree. He'd chosen in haste to major in economics and had ended up regretting it.

'I've been thinking of taking a break too,' he eventually said.

Youko narrowed her eyes.

'It's all right. I've got a lifetime to dedicate myself to work. A little break shouldn't hurt. In the meantime, I can look for a temporary job. There are convenience stores and fast-food restaurants everywhere. They always need workers.' He would be fine living anywhere, as long as it wasn't Fukuoka. Going back to his hometown was the last thing he wanted to do.

She kept quiet for a moment. 'Are you sure?'

Shouji leaned into Youko and kissed her. 'Yes, this is what I want. Let's move to Akakawa together.'

•

He had been sure then, though now he'd begun to question his decision.

'Do you have any family here, Mr Arai?' his client asked.

Another question Shouji had often encountered. 'I have an uncle who works here,' he said, carefully omitting that he'd not been in touch with Uncle Hidetoshi for years, and the last time they'd met his uncle had spoken of how much he hated Akakawa: 'A quiet, boring, small town.'

'You must have been to Akakawa often, then.'

'Not really.' Shouji tried to ignore the slight tremble in his voice. 'This is my first time, actually.'

Her eyes lit up. 'You came here, despite never having been here before because you wanted to be with your girlfriend?'

The usual response. Shouji nodded, expecting the condescending look that often followed.

She clasped her hands. 'That's so romantic.'

He stared at her. 'Don't you think it's weird for a man to follow a woman?'

'Why would it be? I'd be delighted if a man went with me to a place he wasn't familiar with because he loved me.'

Her words made Shouji blush. The past few weeks hadn't been easy. Prospective employers were often suspicious of a young man who had a 'good degree' from 'a prestigious university' — their words, not his — looking for a part-time job as a convenience-store worker or a waiter, rather than stable employment. Even when they gave him an interview, it was probably out of curiosity.

'What brings you to Akakawa?' they always asked, and when he told them he wanted to be with his girlfriend, they gave a dismissive nod. A woman following a man is fine, but a man tagging along after a woman is not. He could tell from their body language that they were judging his decision. Shouji hadn't been waiting for anyone to reaffirm his choice, but when someone finally did, it felt good.

The client with the sweet voice looked into his eyes. 'Why don't you tell me how you met your girlfriend?'

He stammered. 'It was nothing special. We're just a normal couple. We studied at the same university. I was twenty-two, and ...' He trailed off. What was he thinking? Blabbing about his personal life. 'Sorry, I ...'

'Please continue,' the woman said. 'I want to know.'

•

The summer Shouji met Youko had been scented with coffee.

He was technically still a student, though it was his last semester at Waseda and he'd completed all his assignments. The only thing left now was graduation. He should've started applying for jobs, but he'd been putting it off.

In Tokyo, he shared an apartment with another student, Jin. Both of them had majored in economics, though neither was particularly fond of the subject. While Shouji had just wanted to graduate, Jin's goal had been to sleep with as many women as possible. He had made that clear on the day Shouji had moved into the apartment, as they smoked together on the balcony.

'This is the best time of your life.' Leaning against the metal railing, Jin blew out a long stream of cigarette smoke. 'University, an unending supply of girls.'

'There will be women at your future workplace too,' Shouji said, flicking some ash.

'Maybe for you, but not for me. Once I graduate, I have to work for my father's company. He will want me to be in a serious relationship with one of his business associates' daughters.' He stubbed out his cigarette. 'That will be the end of my freedom.'

'At least you've got your whole life planned out.'

'That's what's depressing.'

Shouji shrugged, but said nothing. He would've preferred an arrangement like that. Unlike Jin, he now had to figure out what to do after Waseda.

Despite their differences, Jin and Shouji got along fine. Their apartment had two bedrooms, and neither entered the other's room. They also had a clear agreement on keeping the common areas clean and tidy. Jin did the odd weeks. On even weeks, it was Shouji's turn.

Jin was an ideal flatmate, except that he always brought home women. Yes, women. Two or three at a time. Often different faces, and none of them seemed to matter much to Jin. Not that Shouji minded, really. The women only came at night, and he was a heavy sleeper.

Shouji normally didn't talk to Jin's women. He didn't want to intrude into his housemate's personal life. But on one occasion, he made an exception.

It was early one morning that a young woman emerged from Jin's room alone, clad in a white T-shirt, her hair carelessly tied up. The sun shone on her skin as she stretched in front of the window and its warm hues coloured the nape of her long, slender neck.

He cleared his throat. 'Would you like some coffee?'

She turned to him.

'I'm making one for myself. I can make one for you too.'

The woman gave him a cold stare. She sat in silence as Shouji took out a bag of coffee beans from the cabinet.

'Unsweetened,' she whispered.

He looked at her.

'No sugar or milk,' she said.

'All right.' He nodded. 'Got it.'

Shouji took out two mugs, rinsed them, and poured the coffee beans into the grinder. The apartment was soon permeated with a rich aroma. He filled the mugs with freshly brewed coffee and placed them on the table. Then, he sat down opposite the woman.

She was thin. Her collarbone protruded from the neck of her loose T-shirt. Shouji recognised it as Jin's. He'd seen it hanging on the drying rack. The faded words printed on the chest read 'Hanshin Tigers'.

The woman lowered her head and tucked some stray hairs behind her ears. Through the gaping neckline, Shouji had a clear view of her small breasts. He was flustered, but he tried his best to act as if he couldn't see them.

She put her arms on the table and laid her head down. She looked like she was falling asleep, but then he saw that she was shaking.

'Are you okay?' he asked.

Her body trembled. She was barely making any sound, but he realised she was crying.

Shouji hesitated. What should he do? Should he try to comfort her? He glanced at Jin's room. His door was still shut. He was probably still asleep, with the other woman.

As Shouji waited for the woman to stop crying, he drank his coffee and stared at the wall behind her. Jin had pinned up some delivery leaflets: pizza, fast food, Chinese takeaway, sushi. Unlike Shouji, Jin never cooked.

By the time the woman had finally calmed down, her coffee was cold. She wiped her face with her palms and adjusted her hair. Then she returned to Jin's room without touching her drink.

●

His client chuckled. 'You're still upset about her not drinking the coffee you made?'

Shouji stammered. 'It was a waste of perfectly good beans.'

'Indeed,' she said, nodding.

She had such a pleasant way of making small gestures that it was hard for Shouji not to stare at her, but he didn't want to be rude. No matter what, he was working, and this was his first assignment. The elegant woman in front of him was charming, but he had to remember she was a client and she was assessing him.

'What happened after that?'

The woman's question roused Shouji from his thoughts. 'We met again on campus.'

Her eyes brightened. 'Tell me about it.'

●

A couple of weeks later, Shouji had spotted the young woman sitting alone in the cafeteria. He was on his way out after buying a takeaway latte. At that time, he hadn't even known her name.

Her hair was down. This time he could see it was shoulder length. She wore a faded denim dress paired with white canvas sneakers. She looked chic and stylish, giving off a different vibe. The fragility he had seen in her at their first encounter was gone. Was it the different hairstyle, or perhaps because she was in her own clothes?

He was about to leave when their eyes met. She waved at him. It would have been rude to walk away, so he went over.

'Mind if I join you?' he asked.

She nodded, cradling a cup of coffee in front of her. 'Please.'

He put down his drink and sat next to her. 'I didn't know you were a student here.'

'I seldom come. I skip a lot of classes.'

'Don't like what you study?'

'Not really.' She sipped her coffee. 'It's just, right now, studying is the last thing on my mind.' She put down her cup. 'What about you? Do you like what you're studying?'

'Not so much,' he said, 'but I'm graduating soon, so it's all right.'

She was younger than him. The strongest features of her face were her sharp eyes, accentuated with bold, dark eyeliner with winged tips. Other than that, she didn't seem to be wearing any make-up. She didn't smile much, which made her seem unfriendly.

'Sorry,' he said, 'I didn't get your name.'

'You can call me Youko. *You* for sunshine, and *ko* for child.'

That was specific. Though she did not seem to be the sunny type. 'Were you born in the summer?'

'No,' she said. 'It was the rainy season.'

'That's interesting. Why are you named after sunshine?'

'No idea. My mother chose it.'

'Your mother must love warm, sunny days.'

Youko shrugged. 'I didn't have the chance to ask. She died giving birth to me.'

Despite what she had said, her voice held no hint of emotion. It was as if she was remarking on the weather being too cold, or the coffee too sweet.

She tilted her head. 'Am I supposed to ask for your name in return?'

'You don't need to if you don't want to know it,' he said.

She pointed at his bag. 'Your keychain says S.'

'Ah, a dead giveaway,' he said. 'I'm Shouji. Shouji Arai.'

He was surprised that he was still talking to her. It was longer than he'd intended to. He wasn't good at socialising with new people, especially women. But with Youko, the conversation flowed naturally. He felt comfortable around her, though he couldn't explain why.

He glanced at her. 'What are you doing later?'

'Don't know yet,' she said.

He finished his latte and crushed the paper cup. 'I'm going back home to make myself dinner.'

'You cook?'

'Sometimes. If you've got nothing on, you should come over. Jin is away and having dinner alone is boring.'

'Is that your best attempt to invite me?' She leaned closer and whispered, 'Try harder.'

'Let me see.' He threw the paper cup at the nearby rubbish bin, but missed. So uncool. 'What about this: Let's have a Motsunabe. An authentic Fukuoka speciality, prepared just for you. I'll use beef and pork intestines. Once I add the intestines to the base soup, we'll have a rich broth. Imagine the flavours soaking into the meat, making it soft and tasty. Top it up with cabbage and garlic chives, and eat it with Champon noodles or white rice. I guarantee it's going to be the most delicious hotpot you'll ever taste.'

She smirked. 'Really?'

'Yup.' He stood and took her black canvas backpack. It was huge but surprisingly light. 'Just come over. Hotpot tastes best shared.'

'All right.' She took her bag from his hand. 'Thanks for offering to carry it, but it's almost empty. I only use it as an accessory.'

He shrugged, and they walked to his apartment.

After a nearly disastrous attempt at making the base soup — Shouji was out of the all-important soy sauce though, luckily, he found some miso paste to use instead — they ate the hotpot together on the balcony. Youko took the first sip of the broth.

'How is it?' he asked, nervous.

She gave a thumbs-up. 'It's good.'

'I'm glad.' He scooped a bowl of rice. 'I would have felt bad dragging you here if you didn't like it. But the soup tastes different from the usual one, doesn't it?'

'I can't tell. This is my first Motsunabe.'

He laughed, and she laughed too. She had dimples, and when she smiled her aloofness disappeared.

Shouji had made too much soup, so the two of them ate slowly while sharing a bottle of Junmai sake. He learned that she loved travelling solo. She told him about her backpacking adventures in Thailand, Nepal, Jordan, Indonesia, Sri Lanka, Cambodia, Turkey. But when she got to Singapore, she went quiet and lowered her head. Probably too exhausted. Or too drunk.

'It's late,' Shouji said. 'Do you want to stay over? You can use my room. I'll take the couch.'

Youko looked up. Her eyes were red.

'You know where the room is, don't you?'

She nodded. 'What about you?'

'I want to drink a bit more first.'

Shouji was tired, but he lied so Youko could rest without feeling bad about leaving the clearing up to him.

'Are you sure?' she asked.

'Yup,' he said.

The morning they'd first met, she had been crying. He had felt he had to do something for her, to save her. Was that the reason he'd told her to stay the night? He had never asked anyone to spend the night before, even the few friends he had made at university.

Sighing, he took one last sip of his sake. Perhaps he was the drunk one.

He fished out a cigarette and began to smoke. A thin crescent moon hung low in the starless sky. It had to be his imagination, but the moon in Tokyo seemed paler than in Fukuoka.

The next day, Shouji woke up to the sound of the coffee grinder. He opened his eyes and felt his whole body ache. The couch was too small for his height and he had spent the whole night curled like a prawn. If he had known he was going to be this sore, he would've crashed in Jin's room.

Getting up, he saw Youko preparing breakfast.

'I made some toast,' she said. 'Hope you don't mind me using your kitchen.'

He rubbed his eyes. 'You shouldn't trouble yourself. Let me do it.'

She laughed. 'It's just toast. Not a big deal.'

He stood awkwardly near the couch.

'Why don't you shower first?' she asked.

'Ah, yeah,' he said, scratching the back of his head. Why was he being so self-conscious?

A door opened and Jin came through. Before Shouji could say anything, Jin walked over to Youko.

'I didn't know you were here. What are you making?'

'Coffee and toast. Want some?'

'Yeah, sounds great.'

Shouji wanted to tell Jin that nothing had happened between Youko and him, but Jin didn't seem to mind. He was chatting with Youko while she buttered a slice of toast, so Shouji forgot about explaining himself.

After that night, Youko often dropped in to Shouji's apartment. On her fourth visit, they slept together. The mood was right, the timing was right — everything felt right. From then on, they often ended up in bed.

But there were also times when they sat on the floor, drank coffee, and talked for hours. He loved hearing about her backpacking adventures. Her voice was soothing, and she had a gift for telling stories. To someone like him, who had never set foot outside Japan, all these foreign countries sounded so fascinating.

He couldn't pinpoint when they became a couple. Neither of them had initiated the relationship. No explicit words were exchanged. Everything happened naturally. Friends started to refer to Youko as Shouji's girlfriend. And somehow, instinctively, he began to think of her as his.

When he was with her, time passed like water running through his fingers. He could feel it, but he couldn't stop it. Even years later, whenever he thought about that period when they were together, he always came to the same conclusion.

At that time, he had been happy.

CHAPTER 4
ONION AND WATER

Youko raised her eyebrows. 'You told your client how we met, and how we started dating?'

'Not everything,' Shouji said. He'd left out the part about how Youko and another woman had spent the night with Jin, and instead gone straight to the morning he had first noticed her, keeping the location vague.

They crossed the road and waited at the bus stop opposite the tearoom.

'I only told her the outline,' he added. No, that wasn't exactly true either. He had described their early encounters in great detail, especially the parts that he loved the most — Youko's melancholy, her aloofness, her strange fragility. The more Shouji had talked about Youko, the more he had realised how much he longed to grow old with her. 'I'm sorry, did I upset you? Was it supposed to be private?'

'Not really, but isn't it strange for her to want to know? Only friends ask those kinds of questions. Even then, most likely they're only enquiring out of politeness,' Youko said. 'Was that all? The whole time you were with her, you were talking about us?'

'Pretty much.'

'You're not doing your job then, are you? You're supposed to be listening, not talking.' She chuckled. 'Anyway, congratulations on getting hired.'

'Thank you,' Shouji said, smiling. 'I couldn't have done it without your introduction.'

'But you're not supposed to discuss what happened during the session with anyone, remember? Not even me.'

True. Somehow that had slipped from his mind. He was just so relieved that his first client had seemed pretty harmless. He had genuinely enjoyed their time together and looked forward to seeing her again.

'I know you're excited but, from now on, let's not talk about work. I don't want you to get into trouble.'

'Okay.' He hugged her. 'I'm glad I can stay in Akakawa with you.'

'Me too,' she said, and looked at him. 'In the end, did you find out why she requested you?'

'I thought we weren't going to talk about work anymore?'

Youko crossed her arms, pretending to be angry. 'Yeah, but since you told me the beginning, you need to tell me the ending.'

Shouji laughed. 'She did. She told me my voice reminded her of someone, but she didn't say who.'

'A former lover.'

'Isn't that too simple?'

'People in love are simple,' she said, her eyes elsewhere. 'Too simple.'

Shouji sensed a change in Youko's tone. She sounded off. 'What are you thinking?'

'Nothing,' she said, waving him away.

There had to be something. 'Come on.'

She glared at him. 'I said it was nothing.'

There it was again. Whenever Youko wanted to find out something from Shouji, she would insist until he told her. Yet, when it was she who was hiding something, he couldn't pry it out of her. Perhaps she had a complicated past. Fine, he could live with that. He wasn't exactly being honest with her either. Everybody has a part of themselves they never want anyone to know. Not even the people closest to them.

'Did you tell your client about Jin?' Youko asked.

Shouji shifted his eyes. 'How could I tell anyone that we met because you slept with my flatmate?'

'You misunderstand. I never slept with Jin. I didn't know him that well.'

'Then why were you there?'

'I was feeling down. A friend told me she was meeting up with one of her boyfriends, and this particular boyfriend loved to have another girl watching them doing it. I know it sounds sick, but I thought, hey, let's try it once. Who knows, I might enjoy it?'

'Fair enough, except you were wearing nothing but his T-shirt.'

She rolled her eyes. 'I was drunk and threw up on my dress. Jin lent me his clothes while mine were drying.'

'Ah.' No wonder Jin didn't seem to care about their relationship.

'Jin didn't make a fuss when I was ill in his room. He even joked to make me feel better.' She paused. 'He has a way of making others like him.'

'Yes, he's a nice guy,' Shouji said. 'But I wouldn't have guessed he was an exhibitionist. I just thought he loved company.'

'Everyone has a hidden side,' Youko said. 'It's like an onion. If you want to learn about a person, you peel off layer after layer. With each layer, you'll shed a tear. But if you peel too much, you'll be left with nothing.'

Shouji didn't think he was that complicated, but he let it slide. Their bus came and they got on. During the journey, as he stared out of the window, he thought of the conversation he'd had with Jin before he moved out.

After packing all his belongings, Shouji had gone to the balcony to watch the setting sun. Jin came out with two cans of chilled Sapporo beer and a box of cigarettes. They drank and smoked in silence. On the street, children were running around, chasing one another. A man on a bicycle rode past. He rang his bell, startling a napping stray cat.

'This is it, huh?' Jin finally said, depositing his cigarette butt into his empty beer can.

Shouji nodded. He had finished his drink much earlier. 'Are you going to get a new flatmate?'

Jin shrugged. 'I might do that, or I might go back home.'

'Give me your parents' number. Let's keep in touch.'

'Uh-huh.' Jin nodded. 'I admire you, Shouji. I wouldn't dare to move in with a girl.'

'You just haven't found the right person.'

Jin laughed. 'I don't think I'll ever reach that stage, but I'm curious. How many women did you have to date to know that Youko is the perfect one?'

'Not a lot. Nothing to brag about,' Shouji said. 'You know, I wouldn't say she's a perfect person. But she's perfect for me. Youko is different from other women I've dated. She's not just a girlfriend.'

'Then what is she? A soulmate?'

'Perhaps,' Shouji said. 'Before her, I had never thought about life beyond the next couple of months. But with her, I can sort of picture the future. Us growing old, spending time together, having a simple breakfast, going for an evening stroll.'

Jin narrowed his eyes, sighing. 'Don't take this badly, but I've had a couple of friends who told me they had found their true love. Their one and only, stuff like that. And when the relationships didn't work out, they were truly heartbroken. "I'll never recover," they'd say. But sooner or later, they found another so-called true love.'

Shouji chuckled. His friend was way too cynical. 'You sound like you've lost faith in relationships.'

'You can't lose something you never had in the first place,' Jin said. 'I don't believe in love that lasts forever. People change, and so do their needs and wants. You might think this is the life that you want. A year later, you might not feel the same. Can you be sure the two of you will stay the same? Can you predict the future?'

'I can't,' Shouji said. 'But I'd like to take the chance.'

'You're optimistic.' Jin turned to face him. 'When it comes to love, you'll always be on the losing end. Mark my words. You shouldn't get too serious.'

Shouji didn't respond. He'd said what he wanted to say.

Further down the street, a red balloon flew up into the sky. A child had accidentally let it go. For a moment, it was so near Jin or Shouji could have reached for it, but neither of them did. They saw it float up, disappearing into the clouds.

Shouji looked at the little boy who had lost hold of it, expecting him to cry. But he didn't.

Yet the episode left Shouji with a dull pain in his chest.

On their day off, Youko and Shouji hunted for cheap household items and stocked up on food. Uncle Hidetoshi was right — Akakawa was a quiet town. Yet Shouji didn't find it boring. The place had a relaxed atmosphere. It was charming. No heavy congestion on the road, no one walking in a rush. There were always plenty of seats on the buses and trains.

Or maybe it was Youko. With her, even a visit to a cramped and dusty second-hand shop was enjoyable.

She picked up a red vintage phone with a rotary dial. 'Should we get this? We've got no phone in our apartment.'

'I'd prefer something more practical,' Shouji said. 'This is cute, but hard to use.'

Youko put the phone down. They left the shop, walking aim-lessly until she tugged at his arm in front of an electronic goods shop. Rows of televisions lined the storefront behind the glass window. Colourful signs advertised various discounts.

'Let's get the phone here,' Youko said, dragging Shouji in.

'Do we need one? There's a public payphone near the bus stop.'

She turned to him. 'Absolutely. Otherwise, how will your parents call you?'

The automatic glass door opened and a smiling shopkeeper greeted them. A huge loudspeaker blasted cheery music. Shouji stood still amid row upon row of electrical appliances while Youko talked to the shopkeeper. As she spoke, she gestured with her hands. He said something, she nodded, and they walked further into the shop.

In the four years that Shouji had lived in Tokyo, he'd never received a call from his parents. And that was what he wanted. He told his mother he would call her, but only did so once in a blue moon. As for *that man*, there was no way Shouji would ever call him.

He always avoided talking about his family to anyone. But one day ...

No, not one day.

Soon. He stared at Youko's back. Soon, he would tell her about them.

She turned around and waved. 'Shouji, can you come here?'

He walked over to her. *Just not now.* He didn't want to spoil their time together by bringing up the past.

·

Shouji's client — the only one so far — laughed when he told her how he had spent a whole day looking for the perfect phone. She poured a cup of tea for him. Earl Grey, her usual choice.

'You're so sincere, Mr Arai,' she said. 'You amuse me.'

He sipped his drink. The sweet scent of bergamot blended perfectly with the bold, full-bodied black tea. There were tiny hints of sourness and bitterness that gave it an interesting flavour. According to her, the blend served in the tearoom was slightly more delicate than most traditional Earl Grey, enhancing its aromatic citrusy notes.

She brushed her hair behind her ear, revealing a gold band on her ring finger. 'Why don't you choose a name for me? It would be easier to address me.'

'Hmm … good idea.' Except he wasn't sure what to suggest. An elegant name would suit her. Perhaps something aristocratic? 'Ah. Since you always order Earl Grey, what about Lady Grey?'

'That sounds lovely, but how about a Japanese name? And I don't particularly like Earl Grey, though I don't hate it either. I prefer plain water, but it's not on the menu.'

'Maybe I should call you Mizu.' *Mizu* for water.

She paused for a moment. 'I like Mizuki.'

'All right. Mizuki then.'

A rueful smile drifted across her face. The expression was so subtle it would've been hard to catch, if not for the fact that he'd been watching her intently.

They had seen each other three times now. Mizuki came every day after lunch, looking polished and sophisticated. That day, too, she was dressed impeccably in a classic white blouse paired with a tailored beige pencil skirt. He could imagine her as the wife of a big company director, one with too much time and money to spend.

'May I call you Shouji?' she asked.

'Yes,' he said, averting his eyes to hide his embarrassment. After he had moved to Tokyo, Youko had been the only woman who'd called him by his given name. 'Mizuki, you make me feel I'm not doing a good job, as I'm always the one doing all the talking. It would be better if you would tell me something too.'

'My life is boring. You would fall asleep, listening to me.'

'Try me. The one who says her life is boring usually has the most fascinating story.'

She shook her head. 'You're good at persuading ladies, aren't you?'

'Not that I know of. I can't persuade you.'

'Let's make a deal.' She leaned forward. 'We'll take turns asking each other a question, and the one being asked has to answer honestly. No lies. Nothing but the truth. I won't be able to tell if you're lying, but I know you won't be. I trust you, and you need to trust me too. What do you think?'

'Fine with me. I've got nothing to hide.' Or rather, he was confident she wouldn't ask any difficult questions.

'And one more rule. You can't ask about names.' She bit her lower lip. 'I don't want you to get into trouble for knowing too much.'

'That's fine.' She was definitely someone connected, then. 'Who goes first?'

'Let me start.' She shifted in her seat. Her eyes brightened. 'Did you move to Akakawa because of your girlfriend, or was there something more?'

'It was because of her,' he said.

She gave him a gentle smile. 'You must love her so much.'

Shouji paused. 'I'm not sure about that. Not about my girlfriend, but love. I always feel it's too generic, too convenient, to label feelings as love. What I feel towards her is much more complicated.'

'How so?'

'There's affection, no doubt, and I feel comfortable around her. I want to make her happy and keep her away from harm. But to call it love is too simple. There's something more to it.'

She paused. 'You'll find out one day.'

'I hope so,' Shouji said. 'Mizuki, didn't you ask me two questions?'

'Did I?' She chuckled, tapping her fingers on the shiny surface of the glass table. 'It's your turn then.'

He cleared his throat. 'Have you ever been in love?'

She nodded. 'I was in love once.'

'Just once?' He tilted his head. 'Was it with the guy who has a similar voice to mine?'

'Sharp, aren't you?'

So Youko had been right. 'Why don't you tell me more about him?'

Mizuki didn't answer. Instead, she reached for her tea, took a sip, and gently put her cup down. Shouji waited for her to say something. When she finally did, she said, with a subtle smile, 'This is the first time I've talked about him with anyone.'

And she began the story of how she fell in love with a voice.

CHAPTER 5
THE WOMAN WHO FELL IN LOVE WITH A VOICE

'When I was in my early twenties, I went to New York to live with my aunt,' Mizuki said. 'I was there to study English, but the language course hardly took a third of my day. Most of the time, I was idling at the apartment. My aunt suggested I work part-time, and her friend happened to be a recruiter for a telemarketing firm.'

'You worked as a telemarketer?' Shouji asked.

She nodded. 'Yes, those pesky callers everyone hates. Not a job many people would like. Maybe that was why the company took me, even though I had no work experience.'

'What did you sell?'

'Credit cards. Mind you, at that time, not many people used them.'

•

November in New York was always chilly but, to Mizuki, the reflective glass panel on the eighteen-storey building made it seem even colder. The skyscraper never ceased to make her feel alienated. Still, being here was better than staying in her aunt's apartment. Whenever she was alone, she ended up thinking too much.

Bracing herself, Mizuki entered the building and waited for the elevator with a dozen other office workers. Sometimes, noticing her Asian features, people would try to greet her in Chinese. She didn't know the language, but neither did she feel like explaining that she was Japanese. Or rather, she just didn't want to talk.

Even when the weather was warm, Mizuki would put on her long, thick shawl. It was way too big, covering half her face, and too long, almost touching the floor, but she loved the anonymity it granted her. Her face hidden, she became an anonymous figure in this metropolitan city.

The door opened and Mizuki got in, pressing number fourteen. At times like this, she missed the elevator ladies in Japan. Pressing your floor number wasn't hard work, but having a lovely smile greeting you when you entered the lift certainly brightened up everyone's day.

•

'We take many things for granted,' Mizuki murmured to Shouji. She took another sip of her tea. 'Until they're taken from us, leaving a gaping hole.'

•

Stepping out of the lift, Mizuki walked to the telemarketers' section and clocked in with her attendance card. All the telemarketers worked in tiny cubicles in an open office segregated by low partitions. Each desk had a telephone, a stack of papers covered in names and phone numbers, and a pen for marking. Everyone was busy with their lists. Occasionally, someone would stand up and exclaim, 'I scored a deal!' and everyone was supposed to clap.

'It's to boost morale,' the manager had told Mizuki when she started. But when there were more and more days when no one clinched any deals, the absence of cheers dampened everyone's mood. Mizuki grew used to seeing new faces each week.

'No one lasts long in this job,' a girl who used to sit next to Mizuki had told her on her last day. 'This is the kind of job you do for a while, until you find a better opportunity.'

Mizuki took off her shawl and folded it, then set it aside. She looked at the thick stack of paper in front of her. As the days went by, the contact list felt more and more intimidating, given the number of people who slammed the phone down on her.

Perhaps it was time to give up. Then again, what was she worried about? They were only voices. They couldn't do her any harm.

She took a pen and a piece of paper. It was the first Monday of the month, so the list was full of new names. Mizuki glanced over them. Her list started with G: Gorski. Gortman. Gorzynski. Gosey. Gosha. Gosier. Gosling. Gossack. Gossard. Gostowski. Her index finger grazed the paper, smudging the ink. Then a name caught her interest.

Gouda, Takeshi.

The name sounded familiar. She was sure had heard it before, but when? Was he a family friend or a former classmate? Takeshi Gouda, Takeshi Gouda … Ah, wasn't that the big bully in the *Doraemon* series? Giant, yes, that was his nickname, but his real name was Takeshi Gouda.

She supposed that real people were bound to have the same name as famous cartoon characters sometimes, but it was still strange. Oh well, it could be worse. Like Nobita Nobi, though she doubted anyone would name their child Nobita Nobi.

With new-found curiosity, Mizuki picked up the receiver and punched the numbers on the keypad. She didn't have to wait long. The person at the other end of the line answered the call on the second ring.

'Gouda speaking.'

'Good morning,' Mizuki said. 'I'm Sarah, calling from HFC Marketing Services. Is this a good time to talk?'

•

'Sarah?' Shouji repeated.

Mizuki laughed. 'The manager told me not to use a Japanese name. People would get confused, he said, so he picked an English name for me.'

'But why Sarah?'

'When I came to sign the contract, his radio was playing a Sarah Vaughan number. Are you familiar with her?'

'I've heard the name, but I can't say I remember her songs. I don't usually listen to jazz.'

'I don't know much about it either, but I enjoy listening to all kinds of music. I've played piano since I was four. The usual classical stuff. My parents forced me to go to music lessons. I didn't enjoy it, but I couldn't say no.'

'You must be good if you trained from such a young age,' Shouji said politely.

She shook her head. 'I was in New York for a few years, and during that period I stopped playing. Since then, my fingers don't move the way they used to.'

'That's a pity.'

'What about you?' she asked. 'Do you play any musical instruments?'

'Not really,' he said, and paused. 'My mother used to be a professional koto player, but I didn't inherit her talent. Didn't I tell you I'm a boring guy?'

Mizuki stared off into the distance. 'Talent is just hard work and confidence.'

Shouji went quiet. Had he ever worked hard at anything? Not really. His life so far has been relatively easy.

She glanced at her watch. 'I'm sorry, it's time for me to leave,' she said, getting up. 'I'll see you tomorrow.'

He stood, too, and accompanied her to the reception area. Before she left, he told her, 'You've got to tell me the rest of the story.'

'I will,' she promised him with a smile before closing the front door.

He caught a glimpse of a black Bentley with a chauffeur on the road.

After Mizuki left, Shouji returned to the waiting room and spent the rest of the day there. As usual, there weren't any requests for him from other clients, but he wasn't worried. He had Mizuki. That was more than enough for him. With a client like her, he didn't need anyone else.

But Mizuki didn't return the day after, nor the day after that.

CHAPTER 6
THE POLITE GIANT

'Mr Arai, someone has requested you.'

Shouji nodded at Mr Satou. *At last.* He had been worried about Mizuki. Shouji stood and followed Mr Satou out of the waiting room. The older man was impeccably dressed as usual, though there was always something about him that made Shouji uneasy. They went to a table, but the person who was waiting there wasn't Mizuki. It was Madam, and next to her sat a large, middle-aged man with sleek, grey hair.

He had an old, deep scar underneath his left ear, and wore a tailored black suit paired with a grey woollen shawl. A gold Rolex circled his wrist.

The man looked at Shouji. 'Take a seat.'

His stern tone made it sound like he was giving a command. His eyes were narrow and deep, and they reminded Shouji of that man.

'Mr Arai,' Madam whispered, snapping Shouji out of his thoughts.

Shouji bowed to the man and took a seat.

'I won't take up too much of your time,' the man said. 'My wife seems to be fond of you. Please continue to take care of her. I'm glad she has found a reliable person to talk to.'

'The honour is mine,' Shouji said, finally understanding who the man was. Yet he couldn't help but be surprised to learn that the man was Mizuki's husband. The two of them had such opposite dispositions. While Mizuki was kind and gentle, her husband radiated an intimidating and oppressive air. The atmosphere felt heavy around him.

The man shifted his eyes to Madam, and she nodded.

'You can go now,' Madam said to Shouji.

Still puzzled, Shouji bowed and returned to the waiting room. A few minutes later, he was called again, this time to speak with Madam one to one.

Once he'd sat down, she pointed her pen at him and asked, 'Have you wondered why you've only been seeing one client?'

Was this an appraisal of his performance? 'I'm still new. It will take a while to receive other requests, but I will try my best to improve and work hard.'

'That's not the case, my dear. In your second week, a few clients requested you, but we had to turn them down because of your special status.'

'Special status?' Had he heard her right?

'You need to understand the situation. I wouldn't normally reveal this kind of information, but he has given me permission. Mr Arai, the person you spoke with is one of the owners of the company, and the one who is in charge of overseeing this establishment.'

'Aren't you the manager?' He had thought she ran the place.

'Me?' Madam giggled. 'I'm just a normal employee, not much different from you. I'm not even the most senior here.'

'Uh-huh,' Shouji mumbled, wondering who the head of the staff was. Could it be Mr Satou? No, it was unlikely the boss would spend his days escorting listeners to their clients' tables. Perhaps someone in the shadows? Someone he had not yet seen …

'Our owner is an important figure, and so is his wife. At his request, he wants you to serve only her.'

Shouji was taken aback. 'Why wasn't I informed?'

'It's not our practice to divulge our clients' instructions unless we've received specific permission to do so. I understand you might be concerned about how the arrangement will have an impact on your income. After all, you're earning a commission. But don't worry. There is a privilege that comes with your special status. As part of the deal, we're going to pay you the same commission as the top earner of the month.'

Now, that was way too generous.

'In exchange, please be cautious in your conduct. Recently there have been some leaks.' Madam pressed the back of her pen on the table as if crushing an insect. 'I would hate it if anyone I oversee broke our rules and the company had to deal with them. Believe it or not, I care about all of you, my lovely children.'

Shouji cleared his throat, feeling uncomfortable. 'I understand.'

But what were they worried about? Mizuki hadn't told him anything sensitive. Their conversations were not much different from those he would have had with his friends back in Tokyo. Relationships, first job, insignificant stories from the past. Who would want to know mundane things like that?

He started to wonder, could Mizuki be a celebrity? Perhaps they were worried he was going to sell her stories to the media? No, if she were someone famous, he would have recognised her. He was sure he'd never seen her face before. He would have remembered someone as elegant as her. Mizuki's husband, however, looked vaguely familiar, but he couldn't quite place him.

'The less you know, the better,' Madam said, seemingly reading his mind. 'Anyway, enough of me talking. Your client will come tomorrow, and I've been told to let you know that certain things need to be —' She lifted her pen and held the ends with her fingertips. '—*overlooked.*'

'What do you mean?'

'You'll understand tomorrow.' She swirled her pen around. 'Just remember what I told you during our first conversation. The client is not your friend. Don't try to offer your opinion or solve their problems.'

After the conversation with Madam, Shouji left the tearoom. No point in staying for the rest of the day, since he wasn't allowed to meet other clients. But Youko still had to finish her shift and Shouji wanted to go home with her, so he bought a newspaper and waited at a nearby café. He returned to the tearoom five minutes before closing time.

Youko looked surprised to see him already outside. He didn't say anything and, in return, she asked nothing.

•

Shouji felt a sharp pain in his chest. He was at a loss for words. Mizuki was wearing the black top hat with the veil again, but he could see the dark, bluish mark on her pale face. There was a cut near her temple where the blood had dried.

Mizuki was the one who spoke first. 'I'm all right.'

He felt awful for making her say those words. She was in denial, as much as he was. He was supposed to overlook her injuries, but he couldn't pretend he didn't see anything.

'What happened?' he asked in a small voice.

'I fell,' she said, her voice equally soft.

Her words pierced him. 'You need to be more careful,' he said. He tried to sound natural, but his voice cracked.

Mizuki reached for her teacup. That day she wore a long-sleeved turtleneck sweater. She had taken great pains to hide her wounds. He wondered how bad they were.

Yet here he was, getting paid to turn a blind eye. Shouji felt sick thinking about it. Mizuki said something, but he couldn't hear her voice clearly. Fragments of the childhood memory he'd tried so hard to suppress came flooding in.

•

The storage shed was dark, illuminated only by the moonlight that streamed through the ventilation window. A broken light bulb hung from the ceiling. Animal sounds seeped in through the gaps in the damp, wooden walls.

Shivering, he bit his lip so he wouldn't sob. He tried to ignore the pain from his fresh bruises. He had often hidden in the shed while playing with his friends, but it was the first time he had been there at night. Without the daylight, the place was cold and terrifying.

You will stay here until you remember, he had been told, but he didn't understand. He didn't know what had happened.

When he pressed his head to the wall at a certain angle, he could see the night sky. Not a single star was there. The crescent moon was partially hidden by clouds. He prayed that it wouldn't rain and that the dawn would come soon. He wanted it so badly he could almost imagine a sliver of the first morning ray.

Hang on, Shouji. Mother will come to get you soon, he told himself.

•

'Shouji ...' Mizuki leaned forward. 'You don't look well. Is it because of me?'

'No, I'm fine,' he said quickly. He needed to get himself together. He cleared his throat and asked, 'Are you going to continue the story from the other day?'

'That's right, I almost forgot.'

•

'If you're trying to get me to sign up for a credit card, then any time is a bad time,' said the low voice at the other end of the line. 'I'm not interested. Let's not waste each other's time.'

It was a polite rejection, but Takeshi Gouda had the tone of someone firm and in control. Knowing that if she didn't say anything, he would certainly hang up, without thinking, Mizuki said in Japanese, 'Wait a minute.'

A brief silence ensued. 'Are you Japanese?'

'Yes.' She bit her lip. Did the company manual forbid her to converse in her native language? No, it hadn't been mentioned during the training, though she was sure it would be frowned upon.

'What's your name, miss? Where are you from?'

She told him her name, and that she came from Akakawa.

'This is so nostalgic,' he said. 'I haven't spoken Japanese for a long time.'

'How long have you been in New York?'

'Long enough to make me homesick.'

'Why don't you return to Japan?'

'I've got a job; I can't leave.'

They ended up chatting for half an hour, during which time Mizuki told him she was in New York to study English, but she had too much free time, so she worked part-time as a telemarketer.

'What about you, Mr Gouda?'

'I'm a teacher.'

'You don't teach at this hour?'

'Not until eleven,' he said. 'Miss, I'm happy to talk to you, but the longer you stay on the line with me, the less chance you have of getting a new customer.'

'Even if I called my whole list, there's no guarantee anyone will sign up,' she said. 'I have an idea. Why don't you say yes? I would have one new customer for the day, and I can speak to you as long as you like.'

'Smart, aren't you?' He chuckled. 'But like I've said, I've got no intention of getting a new credit card.'

'Then I need to keep talking to convince you.'

He burst into laughter.

'Your name, is it real?' Mizuki asked.

'Hmmm. What do you think?'

'I don't know.'

'One of the great things about staying in New York is that no one realises I share a name with a Japanese cartoon character.'

'Good point.'

He laughed again. He seemed to be in a jovial mood and sounded like a kind person. Since he was a teacher, chances were he was older than her.

'How old are you, Mr Gouda?'

'Old enough no one checks my ID in the cinema.'

'Why are you always deflecting my questions?'

'Why do you keep asking difficult questions?' he teased her. 'I'm sorry, but it looks like I've got to hang up now. My next class is going to start in fifteen minutes.'

'Wait,' she said. 'Just one last question.'

'Yes?'

'Can I call you Giant?'

A brief silence. 'What do you think?'

CHAPTER 7
YELLOW BUTTERFLIES

'Have you ever fallen in love with someone before you saw them?' Shouji asked.

Youko gave him a puzzled look. 'Is that possible?'

He shrugged, passing her a bowl of rice. 'Maybe?'

Tonight's dinner was grilled eel, egg roll, salad with ponzu dressing, and miso soup. Shouji had prepared everything but the salad. Of the two of them, he was the better cook.

'I doubt it,' Youko eventually said. 'In reality, you need to be reasonably physically attracted to the other person. I'm not saying your partner has to match your ideal image, but that there has to be a baseline of what you can accept.'

He bit his lip. 'True.'

Youko put down her chopsticks. 'Hey, Shouji, what do you like about me?'

He looked at her for a long time before answering. 'It's hard to pinpoint one particular attribute. I like everything about you.'

She raised her eyebrow. 'Everything?'

'Uh-huh,' he said with a smile. 'For example, I like the way you cross your chopsticks when you use them, and the way you fold your legs up in front of your chest whenever you're watching TV, and how you always wear a T-shirt two sizes too big.'

She pretended to be offended. 'Are you insulting me?'

'I'm not,' Shouji said, and laughed. 'What I'm trying to say is, I like you the way you are. Everything about you is adorable.'

Averting her eyes, she picked up her chopsticks and continued eating.

'What about you?' Shouji asked. 'What do you like about me?'

'Uhm, everything.'

'You're just repeating my answer.'

She shrugged. He waited for her to say something, but she kept quiet. It wasn't that he needed her to praise him, but sometimes he wished she could be more reassuring.

The clatter of the chopsticks and the sounds of the two of them slurping miso soup echoed in that tiny, old apartment.

•

'It's not easy for a woman to communicate her true feelings,' Mizuki said.

Shouji tilted his head. 'Is that so?'

'When you're talking to the person you love, your mind gets muddled. You end up saying all the wrong things. Later on, when you're lying alone in bed, you beat yourself up about it: *Why did I say something so silly? I should've said this and that instead.*' Mizuki laced her fingers together. 'You make up your mind that, next time, you're going to say all those clever things you've thought about and rehearsed over and over. But then, when you see them, you get nervous and forget everything you've rehearsed.'

'Really?'

She gave him a playful smile. 'You think I'm making it up?'

'Of course not,' Shouji said, but he didn't think Youko was someone who would fumble. He looked at Mizuki. 'So, you fell in love with Giant from that one conversation?'

'Not exactly,' she said. 'I can't remember when it started, but I began to look forward to work because I liked talking to him. I wanted to spend more time together. Our conversations were the highlight of my days. I grew so familiar with his schedule that

I remembered his classes better than he did. Sometimes, I had to remind him it was time to end the call because his class was about to start.'

'Was he your first love?'

'I guess so. Or, at least, close to it.'

'What did you talk about?'

'A lot of things …' Her eyes shifted, reminiscing. 'Like, coincidentally, he supported the Yomiuri Giants. That was why he didn't mind me calling him Giant.'

'But who doesn't like the Yomiuri Giants?'

She tilted her head. 'Hanshin Tigers fans?'

'Which one are you, Mizuki? Are you with the Yomiuri Giants or the Hanshin Tigers?'

'Neither,' she said. 'I like watching baseball, but I don't care which teams are playing, or who is the winner. I just love the energy and the excitement in the field. A good game is a good game.'

Shouji chuckled. 'You say things that don't make any sense, but you explain them so well, I sort of buy your reasoning.'

'That's a relief.' Mizuki clasped her hands together. The ring on her finger was a plain gold band. Simple and understated, which gave it a quiet elegance.

'What happened to Giant in the end?' Shouji asked. 'Did you ever get to meet him?'

She shook her head. 'Neither of us ever suggested it. Maybe we grew too comfortable speaking to each other on the phone, and we didn't want to ruin this blissful existence. Or perhaps both of us were hiding something.'

'He could be old enough to be your father.'

'That wouldn't be surprising, but I was thinking of something else.'

'Such as?'

Mizuki reached for her tea. 'He could've been married.'

Her words reminded Shouji that she knew nothing about this man.

'I used to think that if neither of us said anything, we could stay that way forever,' she continued. 'That was naïve of me. One day, when I tried to call him, the line was no longer in use. I didn't really know anything about him apart from his name and that he liked the Yomiuri Giants. I didn't even know where he worked.'

'You knew he was a teacher.'

'Even that, he might have been making up,' she said, taking a sip of her tea. 'Just like now, I might be lying to you about everything. Perhaps I've told you a make-believe story.'

Had she? Unlikely. She would have to be a great storyteller to come up with something so detailed and convincing.

Mizuki gave a half-smile. 'You can't tell, can you?'

'True, but if you start doubting everything, then there would be nothing left to believe in,' Shouji said. 'Are you still looking for him?'

She paused. 'I think so, even though it's been years.'

'Uh-huh.'

'Perhaps I'm in love with the idea of waiting. It gives me a glimmer of hope,' she said. 'Sometimes, I'm not sure if what I'm doing right now is waiting or letting go. It's been so long. It's getting hard to tell them apart.'

'You must be a patient person, Mizuki.'

'Aren't you the same, Shouji?' She looked into his eyes. 'Aren't you looking for something too?'

'What makes you say that?'

'I don't know. I just sense it. From the first time we talked, I felt it within me: *This person is like me. He's looking for something.* But what you're searching for, I can't tell. And somehow, I feel that I shouldn't be asking.'

He didn't reply.

'As for me, at the end of the day, nothing might happen,' she said. 'I might never find him again. And that is fine. I'm all right with the way things are. Even though we never met, we made good memories.'

'You don't know that yet. Maybe you're close to getting what you want.'

'Positive, aren't you?' Mizuki said. 'Now it's your turn to tell me a story.'

'What do you want to know?'

'Anything,' she said with a smile. Her gaze was soft. 'Like, how did you get that faint scar above your lip?'

Shouji touched the slightly raised mark. No one had ever asked him about it, not even Youko. 'I got it when I worked part-time at a second-hand bookshop back in Fukuoka. When I opened the shutter, a metal bar fell and grazed my face.'

Her eyes widened. 'Was it serious?'

'Not really, but it was quite dramatic.'

•

A few years had passed, but Shouji still remembered the incident in vivid detail. It had been a Monday morning, and the shops around the area were about to open. Shouji was there for the first shift. He was pulling the shutter up when a huge metal bar fell on him. A sharp pain shot through his upper lip. People nearby turned and stared. Eri — his boss's daughter, who was opening the shop with him — screamed hysterically. His boss ran over to check he was okay.

'Don't worry,' Shouji said to them, wiping his lips. 'I'm fine.'

But when he looked down, his hand was smeared with blood, and so was his white shirt. As a precaution, he and Eri went to the hospital. Clutching Eri's floral handkerchief to stem the blood, Shouji worried about her. She was still sobbing, her body shaking.

Eri was older than Shouji and already at university. She studied in Tokyo, but during the holidays would return to Fukuoka to help in the bookshop. She was usually calm and composed, so he was surprised by the way she'd reacted. He wanted to console her, but he had no idea how. Eventually, the doctor told them the cut wasn't serious. At most, Shouji might get a barely noticeable scar. Eri finally calmed down.

The next day, his boss told Shouji his daughter had a fear of blood.

'My wife died when Eri was little. Hit by a truck, in front of our house.' He paused, seemingly struggling to find the right words. 'Eri saw everything. There was a lot of blood.'

•

Something about Mizuki reminded Shouji of Eri. The two of them exuded the same air of elegance and fragility, like the yellow butterflies fluttering in his mother's garden in Fukuoka. They were small and delicate, their wings so paper-thin anyone could crush them with a bare hand.

'I had my boss and his daughter worried,' Shouji told Mizuki. 'The blood wouldn't stop, but it wasn't a deep cut.'

A week later, his summer holiday ended, and so did his part-time job. On his last day, Eri gave him a poetry book as a farewell present. She apologised for panicking, and he mumbled something along the lines of there being nothing to worry about. For a moment, he wondered where the book could be. He didn't remember packing it when he moved to Akakawa.

Mizuki checked her watch.

'Time to leave?'

She nodded.

'I'll see you tomorrow.'

Mizuki got up. 'What are you going to do later?'

Shouji shrugged. 'Wash some clothes, clean up a little, have instant noodles for dinner?'

'Try to eat something healthy.'

He was smiling as he saw her out.

•

Once he'd done the housework, Shouji found that he'd run out of instant noodles.

'I'm going to the convenience store,' he told Youko.

Her eyes were glued to the television. 'Can you get me some shampoo?'

'All right,' he said. 'Anything else?'

'No, that's all.'

He put on a jacket and walked down the staircase. The night was slightly chilly and windy. Shouji shoved his hands into his pockets.

On his way down, he passed the building manager and they nodded to each other. The young woman had told Youko and Shouji that the apartment was supposed to be for single occupancy, though she'd also said, 'If you don't give anyone a reason to report you, I don't think the owner will care.'

Shouji turned towards the back of the building, where he'd parked his second-hand bicycle. Taking out a key, he crouched to unlock it. It was then that he felt a tap on his shoulder.

He turned around. A man he didn't recognise grinned down at him.

CHAPTER 8
THE PROPOSITION

The man looked like he was in his forties or fifties. His chin was covered in short stubble. He wore an oversized black suit, a slightly crumpled white shirt, and dark-grey trousers — a typical salaryman ensemble. His features were bland enough not to stand out, but Shouji was certain he'd never seen him before.

'Mr Arai, can we talk in private?' the man asked.

Shouji furrowed his brow. How did this man know his name?

'I've got a proposition that would benefit us both. I will only need ten minutes of your time. If you don't like it, feel free to turn me down and walk away.'

That sounded like a scam. 'I'm sorry, but I'm in a rush.' Shouji began to wheel his bicycle away.

The man moved to block his path. 'Ten minutes of your time, Mr Arai. There's nothing to lose, don't you agree? Or how about this: shall we head to the convenience store together? We can talk while we walk. You're on your way there, aren't you?'

Something wasn't right. 'How did you know?'

The man scratched his chin. 'I've been watching you, learning your routine. Everyone has one. Know what I mean?'

Shouji tensed. 'Why would you do that?' Could this have something to do with his work?

'Because it's in my interest, and maybe it's in your interest too.' The man mustered a grin. 'Now, am I getting your attention? Shall we talk?'

61

Shouji locked his bicycle back up and walked with the man. He needed to know what this stranger was up to.

They cut across the dimly lit park. Two joggers passed in front of them, followed by a cyclist. After that, the path was empty. The man put his hand into his pocket and took out a business card.

TOORU ODAGIRI. REPORTER.

'Which newspaper?' Shouji asked.

'None in particular. I work for myself. I go around digging for good stories and sell them to the highest bidder.' Mr Odagiri rubbed his nose. 'I hate to gloat, but I'm good at my job. I hear you're also good at your job, Mr Arai.'

Shouji sensed where this conversation was going, but he feigned ignorance in the hope that the man would reveal more information. 'What has this got to do with me? I'm hardly anyone important.'

The man laughed. 'True, you're a nobody. But your client is not. I'm talking about the wife of Kazuhiro Katou.'

Was that Mizuki? Finally, Shouji realised who Mizuki's husband was: a politician. He had seen him in the papers a couple of times. No wonder his face had been familiar.

'You don't seem surprised, Mr Arai. I take it that you know who I'm talking about. Good. Saves me the trouble of explaining. Have you met the husband? A formidable man, don't you think? Someone you don't want to mess with. But people like him are bound to have secrets, and that's what I'm after.'

Shouji returned the business card. 'I don't know what you're talking about.'

'Don't be hasty.' Mr Odagiri shoved it back. 'As I said, this is a two-way thing. I'll benefit, but you'll benefit too.'

'I don't see how I can benefit from this.' Shouji didn't want to get into trouble.

'It goes without saying, Mr Arai, that you'll be rewarded.'

He sighed. 'I don't need money.'

'Of course you don't.' Mr Odagiri flashed him a smile. His teeth were sparkling white and perfectly aligned. 'It's just a small gesture of appreciation from me. The ultimate reward is the joy and relief you'll get, knowing you've rescued a lovely lady from her troubled marriage. It's obvious he has been hurting her. The poor woman ...'

Shouji took a deep breath.

'Ah-ha,' Mr Odagiri said. 'Now I've got your attention, huh?'

Shouji didn't respond.

'Listen,' Mr Odagiri said sternly. 'I've been tailing Mr Katou's wife for months. She always has personal guards around her. She doesn't socialise, and she spends most of her time at their house, except when she's with you, of course.'

'I don't need to hear—'

Mr Odagiri cut Shouji off: 'You're her only friend, Mr Arai. Apart from you, she has no one.'

Shouji's chest felt heavy.

'I'm sure you can see that their marriage is not normal. There is something odd about them. You know that her husband is extremely controlling. I suspect he is abusing her, but I can't get close enough to her to obtain solid proof. But you can.'

The convenience store was only a few steps ahead of them. Shouji stopped walking so they could remain in the shadows. As much as he wanted to help Mizuki, it was too big a risk, and he wasn't convinced it would be that easy. He knew Mr Katou had ties with a criminal organisation. Trying to help might make things even worse for Mizuki. Shouji shook his head. 'I'm sorry, but this won't work.'

Mr Odagiri gave him a concerned look. 'Are you worried about getting into trouble? Rest assured, Mr Arai, I would keep your name out of the story.'

Shouji shrugged. He doubted it would be that simple. 'I've got no idea how I can help you. I know nothing.'

'You'll know something,' Mr Odagiri insisted. 'Sooner or later.'

'Even if she told me anything, second-hand testimony is meaningless. What you need is proof.'

'That's correct. Which is why I need you to lure her out of that place you're working at. If I could just have a moment with her—'

Shouji sighed, recalling the black Bentley that chauffeured Mizuki to the tearoom and waited outside. 'And how am I supposed to do that? You know how closely guarded she is.'

'That's something you need to figure out yourself.' Mr Odagiri smirked. 'I'll wait for your call. I have high hopes for you. You look like a nice guy. You won't be able to help her any other way — her husband has spies in the police. Do the right thing, Mr Arai.'

He bowed and disappeared into the night. Shouji stood in the dark for a long time, thinking, before eventually heading into the convenience store. The shop seemed brighter than he'd remembered. For a moment, he forgot what he had planned to get. He browsed the aisles aimlessly, looking at the colourful displays of snacks.

'Shouji, what are you doing?'

He turned around and saw Youko.

She was frowning. 'You've been gone for an hour. I was worried, thinking something might have happened.'

'I'm fine.' Shouji forced himself to smile. 'Sorry, it's silly, but I forgot what I came here to buy.'

'We've run out of instant noodles, and I asked you to get me some shampoo,' she said, 'but since I'm here, let's get some other stuff too.'

Youko went to the entrance to fetch a shopping basket. Shouji followed, but he wasn't paying attention to her. He was busy thinking about Mizuki. Someone had to help her. She had to get out of that marriage, away from that dangerous man.

Later that evening, the memory Shouji had been trying to suppress slipped into his sleep again.

In his dream, he was a small boy, crouching in his family's shed. He was crying and shivering, hoping someone would come to help him. The night was slow and cold, and the darkness knew no end.

•

Shouji woke up, drenched in sweat. His breathing was rapid. His fingers and toes were cold and numb. His own piercing cry still rang in his ears, echoing. He closed his eyes, desperately trying to calm himself. Everything was all right. He clenched his fists.

You're safe now, he whispered silently, over and over.

Focus on the moment. Inhale, exhale. Inhale, exhale. Inhale, exhale.

Slowly, his breathing returned to normal. He opened his palms, feeling the chill dissipate. He wiped his forehead with the back of his hand.

In the past, he had been too frightened to retaliate. He had said and done nothing, and he had ended up hating himself. But this time, he didn't want to make the same mistake. Nothing would change if everyone continued to turn a blind eye. He had to be brave. He would not keep silent. For Mizuki, but also for himself. This was his chance to redeem himself.

In the dark, Shouji reached for the business card in his wallet.

CHAPTER 9
ATONEMENT AND FORGIVENESS

Mizuki didn't come the next day or the day after. She didn't come for an entire week, as autumn made way for winter. The following week, Mr Odagiri stopped Shouji again while he was on his way to the convenience store.

'I did say I would try to help,' Shouji said, pulling his knitted hat lower, 'but there's not much I can do if she's not turning up. I've no idea when I'm going to see her again. Maybe she'll never return. You should consider it a lost cause.'

Rather than be disappointed, Mr Odagiri smirked. 'We're getting close. Just stick to the plan we discussed.'

Shouji was worried about Mizuki — had her husband somehow found out what they were planning and so was keeping her away? He had started to question whether working with Mr Odagiri was a good idea.

'Don't believe me? You should, Mr Arai.' Odagiri tapped the side of his nose with his gloved fingers. 'I can always sense it when a big scoop is about to come, the same way sharks can smell a drop of blood in the ocean. Mark my words. You'll see her soon. Maybe as early as tomorrow. And I'll be there, waiting.'

Shouji shrugged. Such big words, but things like instinct, sixth sense, women's intuition ... None of them was scientific. He wasn't buying it.

They went their separate ways.

•

The next day, Mizuki finally showed up.

When Mr Satou told Shouji that someone had requested him, he quickly went to the back entrance to look for Mr Odagiri. To his disappointment, the reporter was nowhere to be seen.

Shouji returned and walked to his assigned table. Mr Satou eyed him suspiciously, but the older man didn't say anything. Perhaps his cold stare was warning enough. Seated behind the partition, Mizuki held her teacup with long, gloved hands. She wore huge sunglasses, but they couldn't hide the blue-black bruises on her face.

Mizuki gave a thin smile. 'It's been a while.'

'Are you okay?' Shouji asked in a small voice.

There was a long pause before she answered, 'I guess so.'

'That's a question you can't honestly answer, can you?' He glanced around to check if anyone was watching. No one was nearby. He knew he was breaking protocol, but he didn't care. 'You're a strong woman, Mizuki.'

She looked down. 'You know that's not true.' Her voice cracked. 'I'm too cowardly to do anything, and that's how I ended up in this situation.'

Shouji paused. 'Are you really all right with this?'

'I guess so,' she said for the second time. 'Don't worry about me, I'm fine.'

He said nothing. What could he do? He was helpless.

She entwined her gloved fingers. 'You don't believe me?'

'I'll believe you if you want me to. After all, that's what I'm paid for.'

Her head hung low.

Had he offended her? Made a terrible mistake by being too direct? But why was she shivering?

No, she was crying. Tears fell on her white gloves, darkening them in patches. His chest ached. He put his hand on hers. She raised her head and pulled away.

Enough was enough. He had to help her, even without Mr Odagiri's assistance.

Shouji stood and grabbed Mizuki's hand. She instinctively reached for her coat. He led her away from their seats, hurriedly exiting the tearoom. She didn't say a word. She was probably confused. He was confused too. What was he doing? He brought her to the back entrance, which was meant only for staff. Hopefully everyone was too preoccupied to notice them. They didn't have much time.

When Shouji pushed open the metal door, the cold air greeted them. The alley was empty. It was too early for anyone to take a break. He felt relieved.

'Where are we going?' Mizuki asked.

He gathered his courage, still holding her hand. Mr Odagiri wasn't here, so he had to come up with a new plan, even if it meant getting himself into trouble with the company, even with Mizuki's husband. 'To the police station.'

Her face paled. 'What for?'

He looked into her eyes. 'For everything that shouldn't have happened but did happen.'

She pulled her hand out of his. 'Nothing happened. Let's go back. If we hurry, you won't get into trouble.'

But Shouji knew he was unlikely to get away with this, even if they returned now. And he was too worried about her. 'Let's go to the police, Mizuki. We don't have much time. You can get a protection order.'

'I don't need that.'

'This has to stop. You can't go on suffering in silence.'

'I told you I'm fine.'

Her denial frustrated him. He reached for her sunglasses and took them off. She lowered her face. Her left eye was bloodshot. The skin surrounding it had turned blue-black, and she couldn't fully open it. There was a fresh cut above her eyelid.

'Have you seen a doctor?' he asked.

She nodded. 'Our family doctor said the swelling should be gone after a couple of weeks.'

'You're lucky you didn't lose your sight.'

'It's not as bad as it looks.'

Trying to hold back his emotions, Shouji carefully peeled off her gloves and rolled up her sleeves. More blue-black marks and scars. Some whip marks. Most of her cuts looked old, but a few were fresh. The blood had just begun to dry. Shouji clenched his teeth. How could anyone do something so monstrous?

'Are you satisfied now?' she asked, uncovered. 'But let me tell you something. Going to the police will only bring problems for both of us. My husband has considerable influence. His family runs most of the big businesses around here. He has Akakawa in his palm. He will always win.'

'Don't say that.'

'I've seen so many people fail to bring him down. He always manages to silence them.'

'You haven't tried.'

'He would say I fell, or that the injuries are self-inflicted. No one would believe me. I have a family to protect. I don't want them to be harmed. You too, Shouji. You've got someone precious to you, too. Your girlfriend, remember?'

Youko ... How could he not have thought of her earlier? He'd been foolish. He was willing to take whatever came his way, but what about her? What if the company decided to go after her too?

Shouji looked at Mizuki and her injuries. No, he couldn't just stay silent. Not after what he'd seen today. He had to help her, but he couldn't compromise Youko's safety either.

Mizuki put on her sunglasses and her gloves. 'Come on, Shouji. Let's go in. It's cold outside.'

He clenched his fists, feeling paralysed.

'Please, we can't act recklessly,' she pleaded. 'We can't afford to make any careless mistakes.'

She had a point. Being rash would only endanger everyone he was hoping to protect. Reluctantly, Shouji went back in with Mizuki. No one stopped them. Whether they didn't notice, or they just pretended not to see them, he wasn't sure.

Once Mizuki and Shouji were seated, the silence descended between them. They didn't even look at each other. Both of them were drowning in their own thoughts.

Finally, she grabbed her coat and stood. 'Sorry, I've got to go.'

He nodded, even though she'd barely spent any time there. He offered to walk her out, but she declined. On his way back to the waiting room, he overheard her voice coming from one of the offices.

'Yes, I had a panic attack. Shouji took me outside to get some fresh air. I'm all right now. I will rest at home for a couple of days, and everything will be fine. Don't worry about me.'

'Are you sure he's not overstepping the boundaries?' It was Madam's voice. 'We have a strict code of conduct here, and any employees who fail to comply are disciplined.'

'No, no. Please don't blame him. He always does an excellent job. I would be upset if I caused him any trouble.' A pause. 'Also, do you mind keeping this between us? I don't want my husband to worry. You know how protective he can be.'

Madam sighed. 'Fine.'

'Thank you. I know I can always rely on you.'

'Do send my regards to Mr Katou.'

'I will.'

The conversation ended. Shouji quickly walked into the waiting room, not wanting anyone to catch him listening.

He waited there for the rest of the day, despite knowing his name wasn't going to be called. He needed to be with Youko, to be physically close to her, even if she acted as if they were strangers.

After everyone was dismissed, Shouji crossed the street and waited for Youko on a park bench. A client had requested her near closing time, so he had to wait awhile.

'What's wrong with you?' she asked, sitting next to him. 'You look upset.'

'Nothing's wrong.' Shouji buried his face in his hands before looking up.

Youko gave him a concerned look.

'I'm fine,' he said. 'Just tired.'

'Let's go back and rest. I'll cook something simple tonight.'

She reached for his hand as they walked side by side to the bus stop.

Shouji thought of a teacher he'd had in primary school. She was new to the job, bright-eyed and eager to do her work well. One day, soon after the incident, the teacher told him to follow her. She took Shouji to the quiet corner before asking about his bruises.

'What happened to you, Arai?' she asked, lowering herself to the same height as him. 'What are these marks?' She gave him a gentle smile. 'It's all right. You can tell me.'

'I fell,' he said, repeating what his mother had instructed him to say.

The first time he lied, his throat felt dry. His heart beat faster. He clenched his fists and looked down. He hated covering for that man, but he was terrified of him. And he loved his mother. He didn't want her to get into trouble.

The second time he said those words, this time to a classmate, they had become more natural. 'I fell.' He repeated the lie to different people. *I was careless. I fell*, he would say with a grin.

A stupid grin he grew to hate, and which haunted him for years.

CHAPTER 10
ONE OF THOSE DAYS

Shouji couldn't sleep that night, even though he felt exhausted. Morning came, and he was still wide awake. Youko rolled out of the bed, washed, and got dressed. After she had bundled herself into some warm clothing, he told her to head out without him.

'I'm not going to work today,' he said from the bed.

She leaned over him. Her brow creased in concern. 'Are you sick?'

'Just tired. I'll be fine after resting for a day.' He could smell her perfume: a fresh, floral fragrance.

'All right. I'll let Madam know.' Youko grabbed her bag. 'It's so unlike you to miss work.'

'Everyone has days like that.'

'Days like that ...' She repeated his words slowly and paused. 'But if you're unwell, please see the doctor. I could come with you.'

'I'm okay. I just need to rest.'

Shrugging, she got ready to leave.

He glanced at her and called, 'Hey, Youko.'

She turned around. 'Uhm?'

'Do you think there's any meaning in what we're doing?'

She looked at him. 'What?'

'Do you think we're helping our clients? That listening to them alone can be of use? Have you ever wondered if we're just encouraging them in their delusions?'

Youko crossed her arms. 'Are you okay?'

'I am,' he said. 'But, please. Answer my questions.'

She paused before taking a deep breath. 'What do you expect? We're just doing our job. We're not creating miracle potions, cure-it-all pills. Like everyone else in society, we're here to play our part.'

'What does that mean?'

'Do you want to hear what I think?' She stared into his eyes. 'Shouji, you're not clear about your role. You're letting your personal feelings cloud your judgement. You're getting too attached to your client.'

He avoided her eyes.

'Once you want to take action, or you start longing for a different outcome, this job is no longer for you. Being a listener is a passive role. You need to be kind and empathise, but at the same time to suppress your own thoughts, and that can be a lot to ask. It's not easy.'

Youko was right.

'I've got to go,' she said. 'I'll see you at dinner. Have a good rest.'

Once she left, Shouji shifted his position and looked through the open window. It was another bright, beautiful day. But he didn't remember ever seeing the sky so pale before — white, as if it had been stripped of its colour. It reminded him of a blank sheet of paper, left unwritten.

He felt uneasy.

*

At some point, Shouji fell asleep. When he woke up, it was half past noon. He showered, got dressed in warm clothes, grabbed his backpack, and headed out for lunch, wondering what Madam's reaction to his absence might have been.

She would be suspicious after what had happened yesterday. Or perhaps, she would've anticipated it. He couldn't be the only employee who'd had a meltdown. She would probably remind him of the rules and, after that, pretend nothing had happened. Business as usual.

Shouji took a deep breath and rubbed his hands. The weather had got colder, and he wondered if he should start wearing gloves. He was a couple of steps away from the bus stop when he heard an engine roar behind him.

He turned around. A black car was coming towards him at high speed. Without thinking, he threw himself out of the way, landing on all fours.

The vehicle mounted the pavement. People screamed.

The car stalled for a moment, its front wheel stuck, giving Shouji enough time to notice that all the windows were blacked out.

'Are you all right?' someone asked.

Onlookers started to crowd around him. The car reversed. It looked like it was getting ready to drive at him again. Wait, that couldn't be. Was it his mind, playing tricks on him? No, the car was heading straight at him. He had to get away.

Shouji stood up quickly. Snaking his way through the crowd, he headed into the park, which the car couldn't enter. Safer than staying on the main road.

Heart racing, he ran as fast as he could to the densest part of the park. The bushes hid him well, but he didn't want to slow down until he was sure he was safe. Shouji looked around. There wasn't anyone he could ask for help. No one jogs in the early afternoon, especially not in December. The only place with a lot of pedestrians would be the pathway towards the bus stop, but he couldn't go back to the road. He ran deeper into the park.

After he was sure he'd got away, Shouji stopped to catch his breath. He fell on the grass. His knees felt weak. He hadn't exercised for a long time, so his stamina wasn't exactly the best, and the cold weather made it harder to breathe. He was so exhausted from running. But what was it all about? That car had tried to hit him, he was sure of it. He opened his bag and took out a bottle of water, downing it in a few big gulps.

Then he recalled what Mr Odagiri had told him. The reporter was going to stake out his workplace. What if Mr Odagiri had been there, armed with a long-range camera, and taken pictures of Mizuki's bruises and cuts? What if he'd tried to get them published, but had been found out?

Shouji took Mr Odagiri's card from his wallet. He had to get in touch with him. There was a phone booth not far from the bus stop, but what if the car was still there? No, it would have left by now. Someone would have called the police. Should he go to them for help? He remembered what Mr Odagiri had said about spies. He couldn't risk it. Especially with Youko still at work. What if they harmed her in retaliation? He shouldn't be hasty. He decided to wait a little longer.

To change his appearance, Shouji took off his fleece jacket. He fished out a grey woollen scarf he had inside his bag and wore it over his turtleneck sweater. He rested under the trees, hidden by the bushes. The sun shone through the leaves, creating a contrast between the shadow and the light.

He recalled his childhood in Fukuoka. He thought of the house he used to live in, and the traditional garden surrounding the old building. His mother had a master gardener who came in every month to look after the place. The man was too old to do manual work, but he had an assistant with him. The gardener had worked for his mother's parents and many other families in Fukuoka for generations, starting as a young apprentice himself. Before he came, his mother would make a trip to a specialised confectionery store to buy some wagashi. She'd serve the traditional sweets with seasonal tea to the gardener and his assistant. After that, she would sit with the master on the front porch, listening to him talk. His mother, who used to be a professional musician, was always in tune with the changing of seasons and appreciative of nature.

Slowly, Shouji's rapid breathing started to ease. Thinking about his mother somehow calmed him down. He stared at the sky, wondering if the same paleness could be seen in Fukuoka.

But wait … What was that?

A cloud of thick black smoke billowed into the sky, rising from the other side of the park.

Shouji stood up. It came from the direction of his apartment.

His stomach churned. Could this be related? Had they assumed he had returned to his apartment? Was it another attempt on his life?

Cautiously, Shouji walked through the park towards the source of the smoke. But what if they were trying to lure him in? The thought crossed his mind, but he felt more at ease in the crowd of people drawn in the same direction out of curiosity. He could easily blend in with them.

He turned to his right and saw a middle-aged woman in a red puffer jacket.

'What happened?' he asked.

Her face grew animated. 'The apartment building behind the park is on fire.'

Shouji hurried on.

A big crowd had formed outside the old building. Blazing embers leaped and snarled, flickering and crackling. His chest tightened. The car, and now this fire. He couldn't dismiss them as coincidences.

The crowd grew larger. Shouji knew that if he wanted to get away, he shouldn't miss this opportunity. He slipped through the onlookers and headed to the phone booth on the other side of the park. Everyone's attention was fixed on the fire, but he was still nervous someone might spot him. The walk felt long.

When he finally reached the booth and closed the door, a wave of relief came over him. He inserted some coins and punched in

Mr Odagiri's number. There was a ringing tone before someone picked up.

'Mr Arai?' a man said in a muffled voice.

It wasn't Mr Odagiri. They must have got to him.

'I know it's you, Mr Arai,' the man continued. 'Good weather, isn't it?'

Shouji tried to think if he recognised the voice. Could it someone he'd never met before? But if that were the case, the man wouldn't bother to muffle his voice.

Think, Shouji. Think.

He sharpened his ears and searched for more clues. Noise ... sounds ... He could hear faint music playing in the background. A string orchestra. The tearoom? No, the song wasn't one of the usual ones. Shouji knew all of them by heart.

'Mr Arai, I know you're a good person,' the man said. 'Unlike the scum I took care of, you had noble intentions.'

His stomach knotted. 'What did you do to Mr Odagiri?'

The man took his time to answer. 'I put him back where he belongs. He's a rat, isn't he? A particularly nasty one too. Where do you think rats should be?'

'Let him go.'

A chuckle followed. 'Do you really believe that scum is going to expose the truth through the press?' A long silence ensued. 'No, that was never going to happen. Tooru Odagiri has never sold a single article. He is a scammer and a blackmailer. He sniffs out the dirty secrets of rich and famous people to extort a handsome sum, often with help from well-meaning, gullible people.'

Shouji clenched his fists.

The man continued, 'In my younger days, I used to be like you. Naïve, eager to help. Or, should I say, reckless?' The man laughed, seemingly amused at himself. 'But then I grew up. Are you starting to regret your actions now?'

Shouji cleared his throat. It was still bothering him, who the voice belonged to. 'Who are you?'

'Let's set a ground rule here. Number one, absolutely no questions.'

Shouji ignored him. 'Who sent you? Was it Mr Katou? Or Madam?'

'Mr Arai, you should stop now before my patience runs out. Do you understand?'

Shouji didn't respond. He didn't want to play by this man's rules.

'Let's cut to the chase.' The man's tone became stern. 'What happened today is the beginning. More incidents are going to come your way if you stay in Akakawa. But I am not an unreasonable man. I can understand why you did what you did, however foolish. If you leave this town and never tell anybody what you know, you'll be safe. But you have to leave everything — and everyone — behind you.'

He thought of Youko. Was she still at the tearoom, or . . .?

'Where is Youko?' Shouji demanded. 'If you dare touch her, I —'

The man hushed him. 'She's safe. She doesn't know anything, and she didn't break any rules. If you stay away from her, she'll be fine.'

'Let me see her.'

'I'm afraid that's not possible. It is too dangerous for both of you. She is not a target yet, but she could become one if the company thinks she has acted with you.'

As much as he hated to admit it, Shouji knew the man was right. *This bastard.*

'She'll be safe as long you do as I say. Go somewhere far away and don't look for her. You're still young. You'll move on.'

The man stopped talking. The music had stopped too.

'I'm running out of time,' he said, chuckling. 'Farewell, Mr Arai. I wish you a safe escape from Akakawa.'

The line was abruptly cut.

Shouji dialled the number again, but this time he couldn't connect. He tried one more time and got the same result. He clutched the phone tighter. His palms were sweaty. What should he do now?

Calm down. First, he had to reassess the situation.

Could he trust this stranger? Of course not, but also, just like the man had said, there was no reason for the company to punish Youko — she hadn't done anything wrong. If he went to her now, he might put her in more danger. As it was, she could deny knowing anything, and it would mostly be true. At this moment, the wisest move was probably to avoid drawing attention to himself.

Shouji opened his bag. He didn't have many belongings with him, and only a little cash. He wouldn't be able to sustain himself for long. He had to get in touch with Youko somehow, to make sure she was safe. Once she'd seen their apartment, hopefully she would know that something was wrong and would try to get to safety. But he had no idea where she would go. They didn't have any friends in Akakawa.

Would she return to Tokyo to wait for him there? Should he go to the train station? No, she would realise that Mr Katou's people would probably be waiting to ambush them there. If he were her, he would hide somewhere in the town, lie low for a while, but where?

What should he do now? There was nobody he could contact. Unless ...

Uncle Hidetoshi. Could he still be working at the same place?

Shouji stared at the emergency contacts listed in the phone booth. Taking a deep breath, he slotted in more coins and punched in some numbers.

'Good afternoon, Akakawa Police Station,' said the voice at the other end of the line. 'How can I assist you?'

Shouji cleared his throat. 'I'm looking for Hidetoshi Oda.'

'May I know who is speaking?'

Erm. 'Jin Fujiwara.'

'Please wait for a moment, Mr Fujiwara. I'll transfer your call.'

A string of melody played before someone picked up.

'Oda here,' a hoarse voice said.

'Uncle Hidetoshi, this is Shouji,' he said. 'Do you still remember me?'

'Ah, Shouji. What are you talking about? How could I forget you?' Uncle Hidetoshi broke into laughter. 'But why are you calling, and what's with the fake name?'

'Do you remember what you told me the last time we met? You said I could find you anytime if —'

'If you're in trouble,' he continued. 'Yes, I remember. So, dear nephew, what can I do for you?'

'I need to talk to you in person. By any chance, do you know a safe place to stay in Akakawa?'

'Aren't you studying in Tokyo?'

'No, I've graduated, and I'm here now.' Shouji tried to sound as calm as possible. 'But something has happened. I need a place to spend the night, but I don't have much money.'

Uncle Hidetoshi paused for a moment. 'I've got no idea what kind of mess you've got yourself into, but I know a cheap business hotel you could consider.'

CHAPTER 11
THE KATSURAGI HOTEL

The hotel Uncle Hidetoshi had recommended was on Akakawa's border. From the outside, Katsuragi Hotel looked like a humble establishment. It was only five storeys high and the exterior paint was no longer fresh. The architecture itself appeared dated. Shouji walked in and saw a woman in a beige kimono at the reception counter. The traditional garment reminded him of his mother. In front of her stood a small Christmas tree, a nod to the festive season.

'Good afternoon.' The woman bowed to him. 'How may I assist you?'

'He's staying here for a week,' a man answered.

Shouji turned to see Uncle Hidetoshi getting up from one of the sofas in the lobby.

For a moment, he was taken aback by his uncle's changed appearance. He was thinner and more haggard than the last time they had run into each other in Fukuoka, around six years ago.

Uncle Hidetoshi had been in town for a couple of days. Shouji was wandering aimlessly around the shopping mall after school when they bumped into each other. They had a quick catch-up over a cup of coffee — mainly his uncle talking about his boring new life in Akakawa. It was then that Uncle Hidetoshi told Shouji to contact him if he ever needed any help. Shouji thanked him, even though he wasn't sure if they would ever see each other again. But now, Uncle Hidetoshi was the only person who could help him.

Shouji was about to greet Uncle Hidetoshi when the older man gestured for him to keep quiet.

'Detective Oda, it's been a while.' The receptionist greeted Uncle Hidetoshi as she handed Shouji a form. 'Please fill in your details here.'

'Mrs Katsuragi, my apologies for imposing on you, but this young man is being targeted by a violent and persistent admirer. We're still investigating, but we'd like to keep him safe and hide his identity. Would you mind exempting him from the formalities?'

She frowned. 'I'm so sorry to hear that. It must be distressing.' She took back the form and smiled at Uncle Hidetoshi. 'I understand. We'll follow the usual procedure.'

'Give him one of the rooms on the fifth floor. That level still isn't in operation, is it?'

'That's correct, but the rooms there haven't been fitted with a television.'

'Don't worry about that.'

'Well, then ...' She took a key from her drawer. 'Please don't hesitate to contact me if you need anything.'

'Thank you for your help,' Uncle Hidetoshi said, taking the key from her.

She bowed to Shouji. 'Enjoy your stay.'

Shouji returned her bow before following Uncle Hidetoshi into the corridor. His uncle knew exactly where to go. He had probably accompanied other guests, who — like Shouji — were hiding from someone.

'Pretty convincing, wasn't it?' Uncle Hidetoshi said once they were in the lift.

'Uh-huh,' Shouji said. 'Where did that story come from?'

He laughed. 'A movie I watched recently. A psychotic fan terrorizes a young, handsome writer. A beautiful hotelier comes to his rescue.'

They exited on the fifth floor. The door to Shouji's room was directly opposite the lift.

'Why don't you tell me who you are running away from?' Uncle Hidetoshi used the key to open it. 'I see that you didn't bring any luggage. Did you leave in a hurry?'

A sudden heaviness overcame Shouji as he entered the room. What had happened came flashing back. Mr Odagiri in the shadows … the fire … and Youko's worried face before she left the apartment.

'You don't look good,' Uncle Hidetoshi said, pulling out a chair. 'Take a seat.'

The older man got his nephew a glass of water. Shouji gulped it down in a few mouthfuls.

'Better?' Uncle Hidetoshi asked.

Shouji nodded, placing the empty glass on the table. 'Thank you.'

'Tell me what happened. What are you doing here in Akakawa? I haven't seen you in years.'

'I'm sorry, I should've come to see you as soon as I arrived, but …'

Uncle Hidetoshi waved it away. 'It doesn't matter.'

He sat on the bed, opposite Shouji. Neither of them spoke for a moment.

Shouji glanced at his surroundings. The hotel room was small but adequate. It had everything he needed — a queen-sized bed, a wooden wardrobe, and a dressing table with a matching chair. There was an en-suite bathroom too.

'The woman at the reception counter reminds me of your mother,' his uncle eventually spoke. 'I bet Yurie still wears kimono all the time.'

'Uh-huh.'

'How is she now? Is she well?'

'Yes, she's healthy.' Though the last time Shouji had seen his mother was close to five years ago, before he'd moved to Tokyo.

'That's good.' Uncle Hidetoshi nodded a few times. 'Health is the most important thing for people our age.'

Uncle Hidetoshi was Shouji's mother's cousin. They used to be so close, almost like brother and sister. A long time ago, Uncle Hidetoshi had served under Shouji's father in the Japan Self-Defense Forces. He even introduced Shouji's parents to each other. But then one day Uncle Hidetoshi had a big disagreement with Shouji's father. It was more than a decade ago, and Shouji couldn't remember what had happened. But the fallout was bad enough that Shouji's mother had cut all connections with Uncle Hidetoshi.

Uncle Hidetoshi moved to Tokyo and joined the police force. Later on, he was transferred to Akakawa. Shouji pitied him. His wife had passed away giving birth to their only son, and the son, too, had died when he was around two years old. Uncle Hidetoshi was pretty much on his own in a quiet, little town. Who would've thought that, one day, Shouji would end up in Akakawa too?

'I'm in big trouble,' Shouji told Uncle Hidetoshi.

'Tell me more,' the older man said. 'Start from the beginning.'

Shouji began to recount how he'd moved with Youko to Akakawa and what she'd told him about the job, right up to the strange phone call. Uncle Hidetoshi listened intently, nodding occasionally and mumbling at appropriate times.

After Shouji had finished, Uncle Hidetoshi was quiet, seemingly deep in thought. Shouji fidgeted with his fingers. Though he felt better after sharing his predicament, the unease lingered.

Quite some time passed before Uncle Hidetoshi spoke. 'I think I understand what you're trying to say. You took this questionable job at this shady company owned by Kazuhiro Katou and broke your agreement with your employer. After that, all these incidents happened.'

'That's right.'

Uncle Hidetoshi scratched his chin. 'What makes you sure that the fire was their handiwork? Do you have any proof?'

Shouji shook his head. 'But I know it was them.'

'So, it's a gut feeling.' Uncle Hidetoshi hesitated for a moment. 'I do hope you're off the mark. Because if it is indeed Kazuhiro Katou's doing, then your life is in danger. I need time to investigate this properly.' He stood. 'In the meantime, please remain here. As long as you don't go out, you should be all right.'

'I'm not sure if I can afford to stay longer than one night.'

'I'll handle that. The hotel is cheap, anyway. Also, normally only the first and second floors are in operation, so there shouldn't be any other guests on this level. Just to be safe, though, don't go anywhere. Wait in your room until I return.'

'I still need to buy food, and I don't have any other clothes.'

'I'll ask Mrs Katsuragi to give you a simple meal, and I'll get you something to change into. Don't leave your room. Lock the door and use the safety bolt. Don't open the curtains or make any noise. Stay as hidden as possible. You got that?'

'Yes.'

After Uncle Hidetoshi left, Shouji wasted no time undressing. Despite the chilly weather, he was sweaty. Standing in the shower cubicle, he let the water gush down from overhead. It felt so good. He pumped the shampoo and worked it into his hair.

Perhaps Youko had managed to escape somewhere after she saw the apartment building on fire. She could be waiting for him in a safe place. A sense of relief slowly filled him, but it was quickly washed away. He was fooling himself. He had no idea where she was.

Shouji came out of the bathroom with the towel around his waist. He threw himself on to the bed and fell asleep, exhausted. When he woke up, his stomach was rumbling. He got up and gathered his dirty clothes from the floor. A note peeked from under the door.

Dear Shouji,
I've left some clothes and food outside the door.
Uncle Hidetoshi.

Shouji retrieved the items. A carton of instant noodles and some new clothes: two V-neck T-shirts in black and white, a mustard-coloured sweater, a pair of dark jersey pants, and a pack of briefs. Everything was too big, but he could live with that. He tore the labels off and put the clothes on. After that, he made himself a cup of yakisoba-flavoured instant noodles using hot water from the bathroom. Instant food had never tasted so good.

•

Shouji spent the next day cooped up in that tiny hotel room. Mrs Katsuragi brought him takeaway food from the convenience store three times a day. In the morning, she also thoughtfully included a cup of coffee.

Unlike Shouji's mother, Mrs Katsuragi was a woman of few words. She would knock on the door, pass him the food, and leave. Her manner was discreet, yet courteous.

But by the third day, Shouji was overwhelmed by boredom. He couldn't sleep. He was always restless, especially when night came. Tossing and turning on the bed, he listened to the distant sounds of vehicles, feeling lost, missing Youko.

This is what it feels like, being cut off from the rest of the world.

He was so frustrated that he felt like screaming, but he knew he shouldn't make any noise or cause any trouble.

To channel his pent-up energy, he did hundreds of push-ups, day and night. Pressing the cold, hard floor, Shouji exhausted himself until he collapsed. After that, he took a long, warm shower. The ritual helped to make him feel calmer, but only to a certain extent.

Shouji knew he wasn't going to last much longer. Holing up in that small room was driving him crazy. He had to get out. He had to find Youko.

Please, please, just be safe, until I can find a way to get to you.

•

On the fifth day, someone knocked on the door at around seven in the morning. It was Uncle Hidetoshi.

'Good morning,' Shouji said.

His uncle came in without returning his greeting. His breathing was heavy. The white shirt under his grey suit looked even more crumpled than last time. A black coat was slung carelessly across his arm.

'Can I get you a drink?' Shouji asked.

Uncle Hidetoshi put his coat on the bed and pulled out the chair from the dressing table. 'Don't bother. I'm only staying for a short while.' He gestured to the bed. 'Take a seat. I need to talk to you about this situation of yours.'

From his tone, Shouji knew it wasn't going to be good news.

'You've got yourself into a tight spot,' Uncle Hidetoshi said. 'When you told me what had happened, I had a bad feeling. Kazuhiro Katou and his family hold considerable power around here.'

'Was he the person behind the fire?'

Uncle Hidetoshi scratched his chin. 'Hard to say for sure, but I'm inclined to believe you might be right. Thankfully, it wasn't a big fire. No one was injured. Everyone managed to evacuate in time. From what I understand, it might have been caused by an issue with the building's construction. For safety reasons, all the residents have been asked to move out while the case is being investigated. That being said, for your safety, I would advise against returning there to retrieve your belongings.'

He tightened his fists. 'We can't let him get away with this. I want to file a police report.'

'Listen first.' Uncle Hidetoshi gave him a stern look. 'The police aren't going to do anything. They won't take your case. He has spies in every station. Even if they did, Kazuhiro Katou is meticulous. He won't let you get your hands on any evidence that might implicate him. You've got zero chance of winning against him.'

Hearing that, Shouji's throat felt dry. 'What about Youko? Where is she now? Is she with the other residents?'

'She's completely disappeared. Some people saw a young woman matching her description buying a bus ticket to Tokyo on the day of the fire.'

Should he feel relieved? The organisation had let her go, as promised, but ... 'She wouldn't leave without me.'

Uncle Hidetoshi tilted his head. 'Are you sure? Even after the fire? Where else would she go?'

No, Youko wouldn't just abandon him, no matter how intimi-dated she was. This had to be a misunderstanding — unless she had gone to Tokyo to find him.

'If she's smart, she won't have remained in Akakawa,' Uncle Hidetoshi continued. 'And you shouldn't either.'

Shouji weighed up his options. If Youko were in Tokyo, there was no question. That should be where he went next. Furthermore, Tokyo was a big city. If he was careful, the company wouldn't know if he tried to get in touch with her.

'As for your previous workplace, everything is gone,' Uncle Hidetoshi said. 'The shop was sold and razed to the ground a few days ago. What's left is an empty plot of land. I asked around about what kind of establishment it was and got a curious mix of answers. Some said it was a tearoom, a few others said it was an illegal bar. Others said it was an exclusive members' club. One person told me it was run by an underground prostitution ring. Whatever used to be there was definitely seedy.'

Shouji kept quiet, trying to digest it all.

Uncle Hidetoshi tapped his shoulder. 'Are you okay?'

'Erm …' Shouji had wanted to say he was fine, but what came from his mouth was nothing more than a mumble.

'Here's an idea. Why don't you take this as an opportunity to explore a new place? Osaka, Yokohama, or Nagoya. I've got friends in those cities. They can help you settle in. You can start afresh. Anywhere is fine, as long as it's a place you're unfamiliar with. Why not escape the dreary winter and go to Okinawa? No one would guess you'd go there.'

Shouji shook his head. 'I can't do that. I've got to find Youko. If she's gone to Tokyo, then I'll follow her there.'

Uncle Hidetoshi frowned. After a while, he took an envelope from his jacket and handed it to Shouji.

'What is this?' Shouji asked.

'Some money. It's not much, but you should be able to buy a train ticket to Tokyo and have enough to tide you over for a while.' Uncle Hidetoshi let out a sigh. 'Maybe this isn't such a terrible idea. After all, Tokyo is a massive city. You should be fine if you don't go back to places you used to visit. If you must, do it discreetly. Keep a low profile.'

Shouji returned the envelope. 'I appreciate your help, but you've done more than enough.'

'It's not a lot of money, and you need it now.'

His uncle had a point.

'If you don't want to take it, just think of it as a loan. You can return it to me the next time we meet.' Uncle Hidetoshi stood up. 'I've got to go. There's a train leaving for Tokyo at five in the afternoon. There should be plenty of seats available. Just be careful. Don't trust anyone.'

'All right.'

'When you call your mother, send my regards to her.'

'I will.'

'But don't call too early. Give it a couple of weeks.'

'Got it.'

He paused. 'And one more important thing. I think it's best not to contact me for now. There are many ears in the office.'

'I understand.'

'Oh, also ...' Uncle Hidetoshi scratched his neck. 'Today is Christmas, so Merry Christmas. That's what young people say to each other, isn't it?'

Shouji realised only now that it was 25 December.

AKAKAWA DAILY

Human Body Parts Found near Aka River

25 DECEMBER 1995

Akakawa, Japan. The police have found a severed right hand and a left foot near Aka River over the weekend. The two body parts were recovered two kilometres apart after a jogger reported seeing the hand on Saturday morning. The fingernails were painted with turquoise nail polish. The police have yet to determine the identity of the remains but they are presumed to belong to a female.

'We're still combing the area to look for any other body parts,' Chief Inspector Tanaka from Akakawa Police said. 'We're also going through missing persons reports for potential leads. Rest assured, we're working hard to solve this case.'

Initial findings suggest that the victim was recently deceased. The circumstances surrounding the death are as yet unknown.

The body parts are being sent to the forensic department to confirm if they are from the same person and to determine the cause of death and the identity of the victim. Foul play is suspected, but the police are quick to dismiss the possibility of serial murder.

'It's likely to be an isolated incident,' Chief Inspector Tanaka said. 'Akakawa is a safe town, though we should remain vigilant at all times.'

Aka River divides Akakawa in half and gives the town its name. The river is famous for the old maple trees that flank the water. Tourists and locals flock to the area in autumn to enjoy the brilliant red foliage.

LIYUN

丽云

CHAPTER 12
UNDER THE BRIGHT LIGHTS

Tokyo, 1995. Following Uncle Hidetoshi's advice, Shouji got off the train in Shinjuku and called Jin at their old apartment from a public payphone. No one answered, so he tried Jin's family home instead. Good thing the phone number was similar to his family number in Fukuoka, so he could remember it off the top of his head.

Jin finally picked up.

'It's me,' Shouji said, 'I just arrived in Tokyo. I need your help.'

'Ah,' Jin said, a little too loudly. 'Did you get into trouble?'

'Why do you ask that?'

'A few days ago, some men in suits came and asked for you.' Jin sounded uneasy. 'They didn't look like your typical yakuza, but they were not friendly.'

'What did you tell them?'

'Well, the truth? You'd left Tokyo some time ago, and we were no longer in contact. At first, they refused to leave. I had to threaten to call the police. They also gave me a business card, so I could call if you got in touch. They even offered reward money.'

Shouji paused. That was strange. Hadn't the man on the phone promised to leave him alone? 'What was printed on the card?'

'I figured you wouldn't want to deal with them, so I threw it away. It was a lawyer's office. Can't remember the name.' Jin paused. 'What exactly did you do?'

Shouji didn't answer. 'Did Youko come to see you?'

'Wasn't she with you in Akakawa?'

'It's a long story.'

'Come on. Just spill it. Did you borrow some money? Sleep with a married woman?'

Shouji sighed.

'Another thing,' Jin said. 'Recently, some strange men have been loitering near my house. Could they be looking for you?'

'Possibly. I was planning to come over to your place, but now I don't think it's wise.'

'Yeah, terrible idea,' Jin said. 'Where are you now? Are you safe?'

'Don't worry about me. I'll stay at a friend's house until I can find a permanent place.'

'All right. As long as you're okay,' Jin said. 'By the way, a girl I used to hang out with at Waseda recently returned a poetry book she said she borrowed from me, but she probably just nicked it from the apartment. It might be yours. Give me a second.' There was a brief pause followed by scuffling noises. '*The Collected Poems of William Carlos Williams*. Does it ring a bell?'

'Yes, that's mine.' That was the book Eri had given him on his last day of work at the bookshop. 'Why don't you keep it for now? I'll get it from you another day.'

'Yeah, sure.'

Shouji remembered his last conversation with Eri. She had told him she had written her number in the book. He had promised to get in touch if he ever came to Tokyo, but he never had. He felt slightly guilty. 'There is a phone number on the last page. Can you read it for me?' He took out a pen and notebook from his bag.

'Yeah, sure.' Jin did as he was told. 'A lady's writing, eh? Is she cute?'

'None of your business.'

Jin laughed, and their conversation ended there.

Shouji came out of the booth, bracing himself against the cold weather. He had told Jin he was going to a friend's place, but the truth was, he couldn't do that. He didn't want to drag more people into this mess, especially after hearing how the company had looked for him in Tokyo.

The money from Uncle Hidetoshi would be enough to stay at a cheap hotel for a few weeks, but Shouji wanted to stretch it as much as possible. He had no idea when he would secure a job. In the end, he checked into the first twenty-four-hour internet café he saw.

'How long?' the young assistant behind the counter asked.

Shouji glanced at the price list. 'Eight hours. I'd like a private cubicle with a reclining chair.'

The assistant handed Shouji a small clipboard with his booth number. Shouji went to look for his designated cube. Walking through a tiny corridor under the bright lights, he passed rows of doors with shoes in front of them.

Booth twenty-three was tiny, but the chair looked comfortable. A computer occupied most of the space on the desk. Cigarette smell lingered in the air, which made him want to smoke, but he'd finished his pack and couldn't be bothered to go out to get another. Shouji took off his watch and placed it next to the keyboard. The time showed a quarter past midnight. Shoving his rucksack under the table, he turned off the computer screen and adjusted his seat. Despite the room's size, he managed to get the chair to recline fully without touching the door. He closed his eyes, enveloped by muffled audio and the sound of people snoring.

•

Loud laughter woke Shouji in the middle of the night. He stared at the strip light on the ceiling, wondering for a moment where he was. Ah, that's right. The internet café. He checked the time. It was half past three.

Seeping through the door, the sound of footsteps came and went. Shouji tried to go back to sleep, but he couldn't. He exited his cubicle. A man in office attire came out of the cubicle next to his at the same time. Shouji followed him, guessing correctly that the salaryman was heading for the complimentary drinks.

A small table had been placed at the corner of the room, on top of which was a water dispenser, a Thermos flask, a tray filled with instant coffee and tea, and three stacks of paper cups. Shouji took a cup and filled it with water.

'Excuse me.' The salaryman he'd followed — a man in scruffy white shirt and black trousers — was standing next to him. 'You're Arai, aren't you?'

Feeling tense, Shouji looked closely at the salaryman. The man was short and round in the middle. Was he being followed? Could this man have been sent after him? 'Sorry, you are …'

'I'm Yoshioka. We were both in the journalism club at Waseda, remember?'

'Ah, yes,' Shouji said, finally placing him.

The man gave him a warm smile. 'I saw you walking in here.' He laughed. 'I happened to be looking for a place to rest, so I came in too.'

Yoshioka had been a senior member of his university journalism club. When Shouji had entered as a freshman, he was in his third year. Yoshioka dropped out shortly afterwards, so they didn't spend a lot of time together, but they did speak once or twice.

'What a place to spend the night, eh? Did you miss the last train too?' Yoshioka asked, making himself a cup of coffee.

Shouji hesitated for a moment. 'I moved out of town after graduation. I just returned to Tokyo this evening, and I haven't found a place to stay yet.'

'I see … Well, this place isn't bad. Clean and cheap. I've been here a few times. Most importantly, the coffee is free. I can't sleep without drinking a few cups. Strange, isn't it? People usually drink coffee to keep awake, not to help them sleep.'

'Uh-huh.' Shouji wasn't in the mood to chat, but he wasn't sure how to walk away without being impolite.

'Travelling, wasn't it? Where did you go? All around Japan?'

'I lived in Akakawa for a couple of months.'

'Why Akakawa? It's just a small town.'

Shouji shrugged.

'Let me guess. You got sick of the crowded city and wanted to experience suburban life but ended up getting bored to death.'

Not wanting to give too much away, Shouji ventured no opinion.

'What's your plan now, Arai?'

'I need to find a place to stay, and a job,' Shouji said. 'What about you? What do you do?'

'I'm a junior editor at a magazine publisher. We've got some travel and in-house publications. Small circulation, nothing fantastic, but the people are friendly and the office has a fancy coffee machine.' Yoshioka took a sip of his drink. 'Though, right now, it's out of service.'

A publisher? Shouji hesitated for a moment, but there was no harm in asking. 'I don't suppose there are any openings in your company?'

Yoshioka frowned a little. 'There are, but are you sure you want to work there? It's just a small company. Unlike me, you graduated from university, didn't you?'

Shouji nodded, remembering rumours that Yoshioka had had to drop out because of a family situation. 'I want to be a writer. Perhaps a journalist or a columnist. My degree is not related, so it's hard to get in.'

'I see,' Yoshioka mumbled. 'You were one of the more hard-working first years in our club. You still write? That's good. My company is always looking for part-time writers. The pay is not high, but if you can do the job well and fast, you can earn a reasonable amount.'

Shouji couldn't believe his luck.

'You can give it a try.' Yoshioka grinned. 'Also, I shouldn't say this but, if you want, you can rough it at the office until you find a place to stay. We work long hours. Sometimes, when we're on deadline, we sleep at our desks and wake up the next day to continue working. There's a cheap public baths near the building. It's convenient. Since you can doze off in an internet café, you should be able to sleep there too. I normally stay if I have to work late, but tonight, no coffee.'

Shouji looked down at his cup. Everything was happening so fast.

'Are you good at English?' Yoshioka asked.

'I'm all right. I took a few elective courses in English.'

'Great. We need people like you,' Yoshioka said. 'Follow me, I'll give you my business card. Today is Monday, so you can come to my office on Wednesday. I'll talk to my boss about you tomorrow.'

He didn't bother to correct Yoshioka that, technically, it was already Tuesday since it was past midnight.

'Say, Shouji. Are you going to the end-of-year reunion?'

'Reunion?'

'It's tomorrow in the Hotel Fountaine. You probably didn't get the invitation because you were out of town.'

Shouji tried to think of an excuse not to come. He needed to find Youko.

'Our senior editor will be there. I can introduce you to him. He's an alumnus too.' Yoshioka opened the door to his cubicle. An empty cup of instant noodles stood next to the keyboard. 'Some of the current students will be there as volunteers, including a few of our juniors from the journalism club.'

Wait. Could this be an opportunity to find out Youko's whereabouts? If she were in Tokyo, she would probably be staying with a friend, most likely a current student at the university. She had dropped out mid-year, but her friends would still be studying there. Someone ought to know her, or at least might know someone else who might know her, and an event with a strict guestlist should be safe.

Yoshioka handed Shouji his business card. Shouji didn't recognise the company name, but he wasn't in a position to be picky.

'The party starts at eight. Shall I meet you in the lobby around that time?'

'All right,' Shouji said. 'I'll see you there.'

CHAPTER 13
NAMELESS SEASON

At the reunion, Shouji's introduction to the senior editor — a small man in his fifties — went well. Or rather, it didn't go particularly badly. The man gave Shouji a cursory glance, then nodded. 'I'll see you tomorrow in the office,' was the only thing he said.

Yoshioka patted Shouji's back. 'Good job, Arai.'

Shouji stayed with him for a while, but when Yoshioka went to greet some friends, he used the opportunity to slip away. He approached girls who looked like they could be current students and asked whether they knew Youko Sasaki. None of them did. A few were unsure. Why hadn't he brought a photograph of her? Most people probably wouldn't remember Youko just by her name, but if he had a picture to show, it might jog their memory. Resigned, Shouji went to the bar and ordered an Asahi Super Dry.

'Rough night?' the bartender asked.

His face must have shown it. Shouji gave the bartender a weary smile and thanked him for the beer. Gulping it, he felt slightly refreshed.

Putting down his glass, he listened to a quartet belting out a rendition of 'Every Breath You Take'. The female vocalist was good. Her voice wasn't unique, but it was pleasant enough.

'You're Shouji Arai, aren't you?'

Shouji looked up.

A young woman smiled at him. 'Do you remember me? We both took Professor Sakamoto's accounting class.'

102

He stared at her. Sharp, bright eyes, a strong jawline, and a slightly tanned complexion, the girl wore a simple grey dress paired with black tights. He didn't remember her. 'I'm sorry, my memory isn't great.'

'I'm Liyun,' she said. 'I sat next to you once.'

Even so, nothing came to mind. Then again, she had only said 'once', hadn't she?

'You don't remember me, do you?' Liyun looked genuinely disappointed.

'Sorry.' He should have pretended that he knew her, but he wasn't in the right state of mind to entertain anyone. 'You're not Japanese.'

'I'm from Singapore.'

He gave her a vague nod.

'We never talked, so you wouldn't have noticed me.'

Another nod. 'But you know my name?' Shouji asked.

'That's because you're famous on campus.'

'Am I?' Shouji chuckled.

'You're Jin's flatmate, aren't you? Everyone talks about the special gatherings at your place.'

'Indeed,' Shouji replied in a flat tone.

'You don't seem to care what people say,' Liyun said, narrowing her eyes.

He shrugged. 'It depends who's talking.'

'What if it's me?'

Shouji kept quiet. He wasn't in the mood for a long talk, and this conversation was starting to drag. Liyun sat down next to Shouji and ordered a lychee Martini for herself. He finished his drink, wanting to leave as soon as possible. He had a strong urge to smoke.

'I overheard you asking about someone,' Liyun said.

He turned to her. 'Do you know Youko Sasaki?'

'Is she your girlfriend?'

'She is,' he said impatiently. 'Do you know anything about her?'

Liyun pursed her lips, seemingly thinking it through. Eventually, she shook her head. 'No. I don't.'

What was that? For a moment she'd got his hopes up.

The bartender came with Liyun's cocktail and she mouthed a thank you. She turned to Shouji and gestured to his empty glass.

'Why don't I buy you a drink? You can tell me about your girl-friend. It must be fate to run into you.'

Fate? He fought the urge to sneer. 'I've drunk too much, and I've got some work to do. Enjoy yourself. I have to leave now.'

She leaned forward. 'Can't you stay for a while?'

Shouji forced a polite smile. 'I'm sorry. Perhaps another time.'

'Wait. Give me your number. I'll give you a call next week.'

He couldn't believe how persistent she was. 'I'm inbetween places right now so I don't have one, and I'm *really* busy with work.'

Liyun shrugged and sipped her Martini. 'Fine. I'll let you off this time. We're bound to see each other, anyway.' And then she added, 'Never underestimate a woman's intuition.'

He didn't know it yet, but she was right.

CHAPTER 14
PHONE CALLS

Call •1 [27.12.1995 // 8.54 pm]

Jin speaking. Oh, it's you, Shouji. Where are you now? Oh wait, you shouldn't tell me in case I get kidnapped and tortured to rat you out, like in those yakuza movies. *[Laughs]* Nah, I haven't heard from Youko. Those men? No, they never returned. Perhaps they got scared when I threatened them. *[Laughs]* All right, take care. I'll let you know if she gets in touch. *[Laughs]* You're right. I don't have your number, but I doubt she will call me, anyway.

Call •2 [28.12.1995 // 9.32 am]

Mr Arai, I understand your predicament, but we can't divulge our students' personal information. It's an infringement of their privacy. Yes, I heard you, but this is the university's policy. I'm so sorry, but I can't offer any more help. Even if you speak to my superior, he'll tell you the same thing. My apologies. If you're worried about her, why not make a police report?

Call •3 [28.12.1995 // 9.42 am]

Shouji, finally you remember to call your mother. I'm fine, what about you? Did you find a job? In Tokyo? I'm so happy for you, but what about your girlfriend? Didn't you move to Akakawa to be with her? I understand. Young people usually prefer to stay in the city rather than in the suburbs. I really hope to see you soon.

Call •4 [28.12.1995 // 8.48 pm]

Yes, this is Jin. Oh, Shouji. I figured you would call again. No, I've heard nothing from Youko. Have you tried checking out all the places she used to go? *[Mumbles]* Yes, I'll call your office if there is any news.

Call •5 [28.12.1995 // 9.13 pm]

Hello. That's correct, I'm Junko. Yes, I know about you from Youko. Why are you asking me? Aren't you her boyfriend? You should be the one who knows where she is. She's been working part-time. Waitressing, I think. No? I'm not so sure then. We're friends, but I wouldn't say we're close. I've not kept in touch with her. I thought she moved in with you?

Call •6 [29.12.1995 // 9.53 am]

Mr Arai, as I've said, we can't divulge our students' personal information. I understand she's missing and you're worried about her, but there's nothing I can do unless the request comes from the authorities. No, my answer won't change even if you call again. I'm not trying to make things difficult for you. I'm just doing my job.

Call •7 [30.12.1995 // 5.02 pm]

Oh, you're Youko's boyfriend? The Chinese guy? No? I must have misheard it then.

Call •8 [31.12.1995 // 8.40 am]

Of course it's all right to call. What are you talking about? All
mothers love to hear from their children. Yes, I'm good. What about
you? How's your work? That's great. I'm glad you've found what
you want to do. I'm so proud of you. Ah, you haven't told me where
you're staying now. Hang on, let me get a pen and paper. [Mumbles]
Yes, got it. Why do you want me to keep it a secret? Fine, I won't
tell anyone. Tonight is New Year's Eve. Are you visiting the shrine
with your girlfriend? Once you can take some days off, remember to
bring her to Fukuoka. Introduce her to me. And don't forget to take
note of your first dream this year.

Call •9 [01.01.1996 // 00.01 am]

Hi Youko, it's me. I'm leaving this message from a public phone. I
can't tell you where I am because I've no idea who is going to listen
to this recording. Most likely it won't be you. [Laughs] I don't know
what I'm expecting, calling our old number, but ... I want to see you.
Youko, I ... [Sighs] I don't know what else to do to find you. I've got
no idea where you are, or what you're doing right now. I wonder if
you're all right. This year's winter is colder than usual. Be careful not
to catch a cold. [Pauses] Ummm ... I should say Happy New Year,
shouldn't I? This is the first time in my life spending the first day of
the New Year alone. [Laughs] I assure you, it doesn't feel good. Every
day I'm searching for you, but I ... [Sighs] I'm a mess right now.

•

Shouji hurried into the phone booth and closed the door. He
rubbed his hands together. His fingers were frozen. It was March
— the weather should have been warmer by now — but for some
reason, Tokyo remained blanketed by cold air.

He retrieved some coins from his pocket. He should stop leaving these random messages — he'd been doing it over and over for the past few months — but he couldn't help himself.

Before Shouji could feed the coins into the slot, the phone rang. Jolted, he picked it up.

'Youko?'

The line was silent.

'Youko, is that you? Are you there?'

No answer.

He heard a clatter, followed by sound of a string orchestra. His stomach knotted. He recognised the melody. The same music had been playing when he'd spoken to the mysterious man who'd answered his last call to Mr Odagiri.

Calm down, he thought. This time, he had to take control of the situation.

'We spoke before,' Shouji said.

The man on the other side of the line laughed. The sound was muffled, as if he had a handkerchief to mask his voice. 'Nice of you to remember me, Mr Arai, and congratulations for making it safely out of Akakawa. But I must admit I'm a little disappointed you chose to ignore my warning not to look for Youko Sasaki.'

Shouji's palms began to sweat. The man knew.

'Young, innocent love, so sincere yet so naïve.'

Shouji clenched the phone more tightly. He shouldn't let his emotion overcome him. This was an opportunity to get more information. He had to make the man talk and, hopefully, reveal something useful. 'What do you want?'

The man adopted a more serious tone. 'Mr Arai, you made light of my warning. Instead of living a quiet life in Tokyo, you snooped around looking for Youko Sasaki. Tell me, how many times have you visited the Shinagawa aquarium?'

Shouji felt a lump in his throat. He knew that too.

'What made you think that we wouldn't find out?'

He swallowed hard. 'What are you trying to say?'

'Mr Arai, I am going to give you one last chance. I owe you that.'

Shouji wondered what he could mean.

'Live your life quietly, enjoy being a journalist, and forget about Youko Sasaki. Stop leaving messages and making enquiries about her. Let go and move on. It's as simple as that. You might not remember, but you did a brilliant job of it when you were young.'

Could this man be someone he knew in Fukuoka? He still couldn't place the voice.

'Are you trying to help me or threaten me?'

The man chuckled. 'Perhaps both.'

'Who are you? Are you connected to my family? What it is that I can't remember?'

In the background, the orchestra was reaching a climax. The man laughed. 'Oh, I love this part. Beautiful rendition, isn't it? Can you hear it?'

'We've met before, haven't we? Was it in Tokyo, Akakawa, or Fuku—'

The man shushed him. 'Enough for today. I hope we don't encounter each other again.'

No, Shouji had to prolong the conversation. 'You know where Youko is, don't you?'

A long pause, enough for the orchestra to play a few bars. 'The only thing you need to know is that she is safe, and you need to move on with your life without her. None of this would have happened if you had followed the rules and hadn't been so reckless.'

Shouji hated to admit it, but there was some truth in that.

'You should stop being so weighed down by your past.'

'Are you giving me life advice?'

'There is merit in listening to your elders.'

The man laughed and hung up, but Shouji kept the receiver in his hand.

He glanced out of the telephone booth. The glass was coated with fog. He could hardly make out what was outside, but one thing for certain — he was being watched.

AKAKAWA DAILY

Teenage Girl Killed During Robbery in Swimming Pool

1 JUNE 1973

Akakawa, Japan. A 14-year-old girl was fatally wounded during a robbery at a swimming pool in Akakawa.

Umi Harada, a local teenager, was found by the building's cleaner, lying in a pool of blood, at around 8.00 am. She was pronounced dead at the scene by paramedics. According to Inspector Tanaka from Akakawa Police, her death is estimated to have occurred between 3.00 pm and 5.00 pm the previous day.

The victim is the daughter of the swimming pool's owners. At the time of the incident, the pool was closed for maintenance. It is not clear why Harada was there.

'The cause of death has been identified as head trauma,' Inspector Tanaka said in a statement to the press. 'There were signs of a struggle and the victim's valuables were missing.'

No one in the neighbourhood had reported anything suspicious.

'I didn't know there was a robbery,' said Mr Matsui, the owner of the drinks stall that operated near the swimming pool. 'Everything was peaceful until the police came this morning.'

Inspector Tanaka told the press that investigators were reviewing robbery cases around the area to see if they could be connected to the homicide. Anyone who has information that might be related is asked to contact the Akakawa Police Office.

The victim's family refused to give any comments to the press and asked for privacy.

Harada was a student at the nearby Akakawa High School. Her form teacher, Miss Kobayashi, described her as outgoing and cheerful.

'Harada was a popular student,' said Miss Kobayashi. 'She brought laughter and joy to the class. Everyone is in disbelief. She will be greatly missed.'

The school is planning to hold an assembly in her memory.

CHAPTER 15
THE ROLLING ACORN

Swirling his third glass of Cabernet Sauvignon, Shouji stared at the massive chandelier. The suspended crystal caught the light, reflecting a rich array of colours. He sniffed his wine, wondering how the hotel staff cleaned the chandelier. Perhaps they lowered it.

Lately, he'd been attending work parties at least once a week, which he didn't enjoy. Crowded places made him uneasy. Even when he knew people, he still felt like he didn't belong. Luckily, the alcohol usually made it more bearable.

Sigh. And now, he had to attend another Waseda reunion …

Just two years had passed since he'd returned to Tokyo, but he felt as if he'd been on edge his whole life.

In the end, he'd followed Uncle Hidetoshi's advice to steer clear of his previous circle. He'd mostly stopped calling Youko's friends and the student office — no one had been able to help. Perhaps part of the reason was that, just like him, she didn't socialise much. After they got together, they had spent most of their free time with each other.

Towards the end of the year, he'd finally secured a permanent job — the company had made him full-time a few months ago — and a rented apartment. He should have been more thankful but, somehow, he hated his life. On the surface, everything was all right, yet he never had anything to look forward to. The days were monotonous. He couldn't wait for everything to be over. Perhaps if God existed, he could finally ask, 'What was the point?'

Shouji glanced at his watch. 9.23 pm. He looked for Yoshioka, who had insisted that he come along. His senior was with a group of men, seemingly engaged in a lively conversation. Their banter wasn't going to end anytime soon. Shouji made his way to a quieter spot. He didn't want Yoshioka to beckon him over. Socialising was never on his agenda, unless he really had to. At events like this he would usually show his face, have a couple of drinks, and discreetly leave, though tonight he'd promised Yoshioka they would walk to the station together.

Leaning against the wall in the corner of the ballroom, Shouji gazed at the crowd and sipped his wine. It had a nice body and a strong aroma. He lifted his glass against the light, staring at the deep, ruby hue. A woman came to stand next to him.

At first, he didn't pay her any attention. But then he thought it was odd that she was standing so close to him. He stole a glance. It took him a while to remember her.

'The Singapore girl,' he muttered.

'Oh, finally.' She laughed. 'I have a name, you know.'

'Sorry, I'm not good with names.'

Leaning closer, she whispered, 'It's Liyun.'

'Uh-huh.' He was sure he would forget it again the next time they met.

'Didn't I tell you we would see each other again?'

She looked more mature than he'd remembered. Perhaps it was her classy burgundy dress. Her hair was longer too, and she had on more make-up, but her overly friendly demeanour had not changed.

Liyun gave Shouji a playful smile. 'Why did it take you so long to remember me? Did I become so much prettier you couldn't recognise me?'

He shrugged. 'Probably.'

'I'll take that.' She clutched his arm and pulled him towards the bar. 'Let's have a drink together. I was here with a friend, but she ditched me for a former classmate. He miraculously became a CEO of a public listed company.'

He reluctantly followed her. It was too early to leave, anyway. Yoshioka was still preoccupied. They took their seats at the bar. She ordered a bottle of beer.

'You like Asahi Super Dry, don't you?' she said.

Shouji knew he shouldn't drink beer after wine, but he said nothing. He'd been drinking more and more recently. Wine, beer, sake, any alcohol he could get his hands on, but nothing seemed to affect him. He couldn't get drunk even when he wanted to. The increased amount only dulled his tastebuds, making him feel bad. A good drink should be appreciated, not downed mindlessly.

The bartender came and poured two glasses of beer. Liyun raised her glass.

She took a sip and turned to him. 'Refreshing, isn't it? You don't mind me calling you Shouji, do you?'

'Uh-huh,' he mumbled. He hardly knew her, but whatever. 'Up to you.'

'How are things with your girlfriend? Did you manage to find her?'

Not his favourite topic.

'I overheard you asking some people about her earlier,' she continued.

This girl got on his nerves. If she had heard that, why did she ask whether he had found her? If he had, he wouldn't be asking around.

'You've been searching for so long. Are you sure you're looking properly?'

He wasn't. Or rather, he couldn't. He hadn't stopped looking for Youko, but beyond making some discreet phone calls to mutual acquaintances, he couldn't think of any other ways that wouldn't endanger her life and his. He had thought of reaching out to her family, but she had seldom talked about her past. He didn't know where they were. Once, she had told him she was originally from Iwate prefecture, but that was it.

•

'My parents never got married,' Youko said. 'My father left my mother when she fell pregnant. She passed away giving birth to me. There were medical complications, but also, she had always been sickly. Have I told you? She was only eighteen.' She paused, narrowing her eyes. 'I pity her. She was still a child.'

'Then who did you live with?' Shouji asked.

'My mother's older siblings. They passed me from one family to another. I was unwanted. They always said how stupid she was to get pregnant. I hated them. I studied hard so I could get into a university in Tokyo, leave my hometown for good.'

He reached for her hand. 'You did well.'

'Uh-huh.' She nodded. 'Let's not talk about this again.'

That was the only conversation they had had about her family. Did they never talk about it again because she had asked him not to? Or was it because he didn't want her to ask him about his life back in Fukuoka? Probably, both were true.

•

'Shouji, I'm waiting for your answer.'

Liyun's voice pulled Shouji from his thoughts. He gulped down his beer. He used to like Asahi Super Dry for its clean and crisp taste but, nowadays, it tasted bland and gassy.

'It's been so long,' she said. 'Don't you think she has moved on with her life?'

'If that were the case, she would have told me.'

Liyun chuckled. 'Are you sure?'

He couldn't respond. The truth was, more and more, Shouji had started to wonder if he did know Youko, and if what they'd had

had been real. He had wanted to spend the rest of his life with her, but what about her? How had she felt about him?

Liyun looked into Shouji's eyes. 'Leaving without saying a word is one way to dump someone. Some women are bad with farewells, they slip away quietly. You should take the hint.' She clapped her hands twice. 'Wake up.'

He averted his eyes. 'Direct, aren't you?'

'Just say it: "You're not nice, Liyun." I'm used to it. I've got a reputation for being blunt, and I plan to live up to that.' Liyun topped up Shouji's glass. 'Drink up. It will make you feel better.'

'I'm not sad.' He had long ago graduated from that phase.

'Actually, I'm not seeing anyone, and I'm getting old.' She drank her beer, seemingly not paying attention to what he'd said. 'Maybe we should pair up. Can I be your girlfriend?'

He ignored her.

Liyun pursed her lips, pretending to be upset. 'That's a flat rejection, isn't it?'

Shouji finished his drink. 'Some men are bad with rejections, they keep quiet.'

'Ha!' She laughed, and poured him more beer. 'You're good. You're funny.'

He took another gulp. 'I didn't see you last year.'

'I couldn't come.' She paused. 'The reunion was in September instead of December. The date happened to fall around the same period as the anniversary of my brother's death. I always return to Singapore that week.'

Her honest answer caught him by surprise. He wasn't used to such candour, especially from women. 'I'm so sorry.'

'It's all right. I mean, it's been years.' She gazed at the rows of bottles displayed behind the bar. 'He used to travel a lot. I keep on imagining he's away on another trip and, once he runs out of money, he'll return, looking more ruffled and tanned.'

'Uh-huh,' he mumbled, not knowing how else to respond. He sometimes imagined Youko returning, what she might look like now.

'Have you heard of this saying? Often, we only realise how precious something is after we've lost it,' Liyun continued, tilting her head with a thin smile.

He felt a familiar weight in his chest.

'What have you been doing?' Liyun turned to Shouji, jovial again, though he sensed it was forced. 'Did you become a CEO too?'

'I'm just a poor writer,' he said.

Her face beamed. 'You're penning the great Japanese novel?'

'Nothing as fancy,' he said. 'I write articles for magazines.'

'What kind?'

'All sorts of stuff. Travel, wine and dine, men's magazines — you name it.'

'That's a range,' Liyun said. 'I just arrived in Tokyo a few weeks ago.'

Shouji finished his drink.

'I had to return to Singapore because my mother had an operation. She's fine. It was minor knee surgery, but she kept exaggerating how much it hurt. Perhaps that was her way of saying she wanted me to stay there longer.' Liyun ordered another bottle. 'I'm taking a break right now. I haven't decided if I should finish my studies or find a job.'

'It's easier to find employment once you've graduated.'

'The kind of job I'm looking for doesn't need a degree.'

The bartender brought them a fresh bottle and this time Liyun took it from him. She poured the bubbling liquid into the centre of the glass from a higher position. About halfway through, she paused so a thicker layer of foam settled on top of the beer. After that, she poured the rest, tilting the glass at a 45-degree angle, causing the foam to rise gently. When she was done, the head was slightly taller than the glass. A perfect 3:7 ratio.

'I want to work in a record store, or a vintage clothing shop, or a small bakery,' she said. 'I'm not planning to climb the corporate ladder. I only want a simple life. A normal job, home-cooked meals, perhaps something fancier for special occasions.'

Shouji drank his beer in one go. Despite Liyun's careful handling, it still tasted bland. He stared at the residual white foam rings. Was he so drunk he no longer enjoyed his favourite drink? No, it had been a long time since he had got wasted.

They finished the second bottle, then a third. Shouji tried to leave, but Liyun ordered another one.

'This is the last, okay?' he said. 'I've drunk too much.'

She laughed. 'You're young. You can drink more.'

He grunted and let her fill his glass. She went on to tell him about her family. She and her brother had studied Japanese at a language school near their house since they were little.

'At first, there were forty of us,' Liyun said. 'But, one by one, the students dropped out. After three years, my brother and I were the only ones left. But we had fun. We always looked forward to the class. Our teacher was a nice Japanese lady who used to be an air stewardess. She married a local businessman.'

'Uh-huh.'

'My brother and I wanted to study at a university in Japan.'

Their parents had been against it, but the two of them were adamant. In the end, their parents relented.

'Can you believe it? We had never been to Japan. Thankfully, we managed to adjust to living in Tokyo. My brother even found a Japanese girlfriend, though I haven't been so lucky.' She turned to Shouji. 'Am I boring you?'

'No,' he lied. He was sleepy and he wanted to go home. 'But I have to leave soon. It's getting late.'

'Let's finish this bottle. Don't waste it.'

Not wanting to be impolite, Shouji drank, but faster.

Liyun told him about Singapore, and how she preferred the weather in Japan. 'Over there, it's always hot and humid, and you feel sticky. But there are no earthquakes. No need to stock up on food in case you get trapped in your apartment.'

He mumbled occasionally, giving appropriate responses, but largely it was Liyun who did the talking.

'Have you ever been to Singapore, Shouji?'

'Not yet.'

'You should come. It's a nice place. Plenty of things to eat.'

'I will,' he said, 'and you can be my guide.'

'It's a promise then.'

She told him which places to visit. He continued to drink. Would she notice his lack of enthusiasm? Probably. Shouji's head spun, but he didn't stop reaching for his glass. But Liyun ... She hardly touched hers. Was she not a drinker? Then why had she ordered so many bottles?

Feeling giddy, Shouji slumped on to the bar. He sank into a deep slumber and reunited with Youko. The two of them were lying on a bed in a room he didn't recognise. The light was off, but moonlight seeped through the windows.

They made love on top of the white sheets. She was under him, her breath heavy and unsteady. He caressed her hair and kissed her. His desire for her was overwhelming. He needed her. More and more — he couldn't get enough.

'Shouji,' Youko whispered his name.

Her soft voice only made him want her more. He got off her, turned her around, and saw what looked like an image of a flower on her shoulder.

'You got a tattoo?' he asked.

'Yes.' She glanced at him. 'You don't like it?'

'I don't object. It's just … unexpected. Why?'

She didn't answer. It was then that Shouji remembered he'd been separated from her. Then, this had to be a dream.

Shouji looked at Youko. She seemed so real. He could feel the warmth of her skin and hear her breathing. He reached for her and pulled her close. He didn't want her to leave. He wanted them to stay like this, even if that meant getting trapped in this dream realm eternally.

She pressed herself on him. 'Want to guess what the tattoo is?'

'I don't know,' he whispered. 'It's hard to see.'

'If you think it's an image of a flower, then it isn't. It's a heart. An open heart.'

'Why an open heart?'

She whispered into his ear. 'Well, why not?'

•

Shouji opened his eyes, squinting. Everything was bright and blinding. He felt extremely dizzy. In the distance, the familiar sound of a train came and faded away. Slowly, he began to recognise his bedroom.

He'd got wasted. He couldn't believe it. He'd been drinking a lot, but not once had he been drunk. Then again, yesterday, he'd had both wine and beer. Should have stuck to one.

Shouji felt nauseous. How had he got home? Had he inconvenienced Yoshioka? Getting up, he glanced at the mirror. He was in his boxers. Even in his drunken stupor, he'd managed to undress.

The door opened with a creak. Liyun came in, wearing an old T-shirt of his and towelling her wet hair.

Shouji's heart sank. No, this couldn't be happening.

'You're up,' she said. 'Hope you don't mind me borrowing your clothes. I tried to ask, but you were sound asleep, you wouldn't answer.'

What on earth had he done? He tried to say something, but his throat was dry.

Liyun came closer and leaned towards Shouji. He could smell his mint shampoo on her, which made him even more anxious.

'What's the matter?' She frowned. 'Say something.'

Shouji's stomach rolled. He felt sick. He could feel something rising inside him. He ran to the bathroom and retched into the toilet bowl, but nothing but saliva came out. Liyun followed behind.

She crouched next to him. 'You vomited yesterday. Your stomach should be empty.' Rubbing his back, she offered him some tissues. 'Are you all right?'

Shouji cleaned his face, Liyun watching. They returned to the bedroom. He sat on the bed and she took the space next to him. She didn't say anything, but he knew he had to address what had happened.

Taking a deep breath, Shouji tried to stay calm. 'I know this is terrible to say, but I only have a vague recollection of last night. But …' He put his palms on his knees and lowered his head. 'I'm sorry for everything.'

Her eyebrow rose.

'What I did is inexcusable,' he continued. 'I'm not saying that you should forgive.'

She clicked her tongue. 'Why are you making such a fuss? It's not a big deal. We're not kids, are we?'

'That doesn't make it okay. I'm sorry.'

'I told you, it's all right,' she insisted, laughing. 'Don't worry about that. Things happen. Hey, Shouji. Raise your head. We had fun. It's normal for drunk people to —'

'I shouldn't have taken advantage of you.'

She paused. 'What do you mean?'

'I shouldn't have slept with you. I know my apologies can't change anything, but if there's something I can do. Please, let me make it up to you.'

Liyun bit her lip. Had he said something wrong? Had he hurt her? Maybe she was expecting something more, something he

couldn't give anyone for now. Perhaps he shouldn't have said anything and just let their relationship drift away naturally. But that
wouldn't be right.

She crossed her legs. 'You said I could ask you for anything,
didn't you? That's helpful. As you know, I've got no job. I'm broke.
I've been staying at a friend's house, but she told me I need to move
out. Can I stay with you until I can afford my own place?'

Shouji hesitated. 'You want to live with me?'

'That's right.' Liyun grabbed his hands. 'I'll help out with the
housework. I cook quite well.'

He pulled his hands away. 'I don't think that's a good idea.'

'Why not? You're living on your own, and there's a spare bedroom.'

'You snooped around my place?'

'Stop overreacting. I was just taking a tour.'

'Well then, you should know I use the other room as a store-
room. It's a huge mess.'

She raised her chin. 'Then it's time to clean it up.'

He sighed. 'Liyun, it's a bad idea for a young, single woman like
you to share an apartment with me, just the two of us.'

'You'd prefer to live with an older, married woman?' She gave
him a playful nudge. 'I didn't know you had that in you.'

He sighed again. She didn't get it.

Liyun laughed. 'We've slept together, haven't we? In that case,
there's nothing to be worried about.'

Her words made Shouji feel guilty. He shook his head in frustration, but he owed it to her to make things right. And he had told her
she could ask him for anything.

'Only until you get a job,' he finally said.

She gave him a big grin. 'That's a deal.'

'And, about last night, it was a mistake. It won't happen again. In
the meantime, before we clean up the spare bedroom, you can use
my room.'

'What about you?'

'I can sleep on the couch.'

She kissed his cheek. 'Fine by me.'

'Stop it.' He pulled away from her.

Liyun stared at him.

'I'm sorry. You can live here, but let's not get too close. I don't want any misunderstandings.' He shifted his eyes uncomfortably. 'Just to be clear, I don't want to get into a romantic relationship.'

'Still not over her, huh?'

'It's none of your business.'

'Fair enough.' Liyun stood. 'You're not looking for a romantic relationship, and neither am I, so there's no need to be so uptight.' She covered her nose. 'By the way, you stink. You should shower. I'll make breakfast. After that, you can come and help me pick my stuff up from my friend's place.'

She pulled her damp hair up into a messy bun and gazed out of the window. The morning sun shone on her gleaming skin. Seeing her like that reminded Shouji of the first time he met Youko. Something inside him ached.

Not wanting to face Liyun, he lay on the bed and turned his back on her. He heard her opening the door, walking towards the kitchen. She was humming a familiar melody. 'Donguri Korokoro', a classic children's song his mother had taught him.

An acorn rolled over and over,
He suddenly fell into a pond.
A loach came and said,
'Hello, little boy, let's play together.'

At times like this, he felt like he had forgotten something important.

CHAPTER 16
SHE MUST HAVE BEEN A CAT IN HER PREVIOUS LIFE

After helping Liyun pick up her belongings, Shouji lied that he had to return to the office. She didn't say anything, even though it was a Saturday.

Shouji reached his office around noon. The lift didn't run at the weekend, so he had to climb the staircase to the fourth floor. The sunlight flooded in through the dusty glass windows, hurting his eyes and giving him a headache. A loud bang jolted him. The noise came from the construction site across the road. Shouji gripped the handrail tighter. His balance was still slightly off. Opening the door to his office, he cursed himself for getting so drunk.

The entire floor was quiet and dark. Taking off his winter coat, Shouji dragged himself to the worn-out sofa near the entrance. He threw himself on it, dropping the briefcase he'd brought along just for show. He felt exhausted, but he knew he only had himself to blame.

Shouji heard someone press the switch. The light turned on. He got up and saw Yoshioka, still wearing the same clothes as yesterday. He was limping. A dark patch stained his shirt's left pocket.

'You look awful,' Yoshioka said. 'Are you so drunk you forgot today is Saturday?'

Shouji laughed. 'I should be saying the same to you.'

Yoshioka pulled up a chair on wheels and sat in front of Shouji.

'I missed the last train. I wanted to walk home but, in my drunken stupor, I headed to the office instead.' He scratched his overgrown stubble. 'I probably spend too much time in the office. This place feels more like home than my own apartment.'

'You're crazy,' Shouji said. Their office wasn't exactly near the reunion venue. 'How long did it take?'

Yoshioka laughed. 'Less than three hours.'

'Not bad.'

'I can't feel my legs. They've turned to jelly.' Yoshioka gave Shouji a long, hard look. 'What are you doing here on a Saturday?'

Instead of answering, Shouji asked, 'Do you know how I left the party?'

'Not really. You told me you wanted to walk to the station together, but when I looked for you, you were gone. I figured you were too tired and left first.' Yoshioka glanced at Shouji. 'Why are you here? You've clearly been home, showered, and changed.'

Shouji shrugged. 'I had to leave my apartment and couldn't think of anywhere else to go.'

'You spend too much time in the office too.' Yoshioka paused. 'Did something happen? No one comes into the office on a weekend for no particular reason.'

Shouji stared at the stain on Yoshioka's shirt. The dark red colour made it looked like dried blood, but it was probably red wine or meat sauce. 'I was so wasted last night I brought home a cat.'

'A cat?' Yoshioka repeated loudly. 'What kind of drunk brings home a cat?'

Shouji sighed deeply. 'This kind?'

'Interesting. Tell me about it.'

An image of Liyun came to mind. Her damp skin gleaming in the morning sunlight. She had a peculiar way of walking, as if she were avoiding invisible booby traps.

'She's a strange cat,' Shouji finally said.

'If it's a rare breed, you should sell her to a pet shop. Problem solved.'

Shouji rested his head against the back of the sofa, feeling more and more exhausted. Yoshioka moved to sit next to him.

A few minutes passed before Yoshioka said, 'You look troubled.'

'Do I?'

'Yeah.'

Shouji thought of Liyun, and then of Youko. If Youko were here, how would she react? She probably wouldn't forgive him. Even he couldn't forgive himself.

All he wanted was to see Youko again. Even if she was going to swear at him for cheating on her, even if it would take him forever to earn back her trust, he would put up with anything. If only he could find her.

But what if she had never returned to Tokyo? Perhaps she'd been waiting in Akakawa. No, that couldn't be true. Shouji took a deep breath. Was there nothing more he could do? Apart from Uncle Hidetoshi, who had specifically instructed him not to contact him, was there no one else he could reach out to?

Of course, there was also Mizuki. But he had brought enough trouble to her. When he'd reached Tokyo, he had considered trying to contact her, but the more he'd thought about it, the more he realised the best thing was probably to stay away. Every time he thought of Mizuki, he felt a tremendous amount of guilt.

'If there's anything you want to talk about, I'm all ears,' Yoshioka said.

Shouji hesitated. He didn't want to bother his senior, but he had exhausted all his other options. 'Remember I used to live in Akakawa?'

Yoshioka nodded. 'What about it?'

'The reason I had to return to Tokyo was that I'd tried to help a female friend leaving an abusive marriage. Her husband was a politician with considerable influence. But instead of saving her, I ended up with people wanting to kill me.'

Yoshioka's eyes widened. 'That's serious. Are they still pursuing you?'

'I can't be certain, but I like to think that they eventually gave up.'

'You seem relaxed for someone with a noose around his neck.'

Shouji forced himself to laugh. 'It's been two years. I used to be anxious, but not anymore,' he said. 'There's just one thing. I often wonder about that friend. Most probably, she's still stuck in that marriage, though I do hope that she managed to get away somehow.' Even as he said the words, he couldn't help dismissing it as a feeble attempt to make himself feel better about his helplessness.

Yoshioka took a long sigh, seemingly thinking hard. 'You want to meet up with her?'

'Not necessarily — I don't want to put her in danger again — but I'd like to know how she is doing. She's not someone just anyone can easily get information about, but you might know …'

'The wife of a politician, did you say? I'm going to bet she was an ojou-sama,' Yoshioka said. 'Why don't you tell me her name? I'll ask my contacts.'

'I don't have her real name.'

'Just give me whatever information you do have. What about the husband?'

'His name is Kazuhiro Katou.'

'Ah.' Yoshioka was silent for a moment. 'The Katou family, eh? I'm sure I can find something.'

'I really appreciate it, but please be careful. These people are dangerous.'

The older man sneered. 'I did a few years as a crime correspondent. I've played with fire. No big deal.'

'Like eating the expired wagashi in the pantry?'

They both laughed, recalling one occasion when Yoshioka had to go to the hospital because of a terrible stomach ache. He had stubbornly finished up a box of Fujiwara confectionery past its sell-by date. A client had sent it as a gift, but somehow the bag had lain unclaimed and unopened for more than a month.

Shouji turned to Yoshioka. 'I'm sorry to impose on you. I should do this on my own, but I don't know how. I feel so useless.'

'What are you talking about?' Yoshioka said, nudging him. 'It's perfectly fine to ask for help. It doesn't mean you're weak. It shows that you're wise and brave. You don't need to do everything alone.'

'Uh-huh.'

The conversation ended there, and the office was once again still. Distant chatter from the construction site nearby filled in the gap. A man shouted that lunch break was over.

'I'm going to leave soon,' Yoshioka eventually said. 'You should go home too.'

Soon, the workers' voices vanished, swallowed by noises from heavy machinery.

•

Shouji stared at the scene in front of him. Cardboard boxes stacked on top of each other filled the living room. Hardly any space left to walk.

Liyun came out of the kitchen and greeted him cheerfully. 'You're back. I've made dinner. I cooked some Peranakan food. I hope you like it, but if you prefer to stick to Japanese cuisine, let me know.'

Shouji walked past her into the spare bedroom. All his stuff was gone, replaced with a futon, a coffee table, and some cushions. She'd even put up a white curtain patterned with tiny roses, which looked oddly similar to one in the apartment he used to share with Jin.

'What is this?' he asked in a flat tone.

'Kind of messy right now, but I should be done by tomorrow. Oh, since you don't have any curtains, I went to buy some,' she said. 'You're so strange, Shouji. How could you not have curtains? Anyway, I wasn't sure if the size would fit, so I only bought them for this room. After I've finished unpacking, I'll get more for —'

'Liyun,' Shouji cut her sentence. 'Did you pack away my things without asking?'

'You were busy. I didn't want to bother you.'

He clenched his fist. 'This is the first and last time I'm going to say this. Do *not* touch my stuff.'

'Hey, I was trying to be helpful. I didn't have any bad intentions.'

'Who cares about your intentions? The road to hell is paved with good intentions.'

Liyun looked startled. Shouji felt his heart race. He was surprised by his anger.

'I'm sorry, I ...' His words trailed off. He sighed in frustration and went to his room. How on earth had he ended up in this situation? He threw himself on the bed. Agreeing to let Liyun stay here had been a grave mistake. He made a mental note to talk to her tomorrow. This arrangement wasn't going to work.

•

Shouji woke up in the middle of the night. His room was dark. He dragged himself over to the light switch, then opened the window.

The road was empty. Streetlights shone on the asphalt. He looked up. A faint, waning moon hung in the sky, accompanied by dim stars. He thought he'd seen the same view in the past, back in Fukuoka.

'Hello, there,' Shouji whispered. 'We meet again.'

The cold night wind blew into his face, returning his greeting.

His stomach growled. The alarm clock showed 2.41 am. Shouji stretched and went out of the room. If his memory served him correctly, he had some instant noodles stashed somewhere in the kitchen.

It was only after he turned on the lights that he remembered the mayhem from earlier. Luckily, Liyun had put the cardboard boxes to one side. Otherwise, he would have tripped over them.

Shouji went to the kitchen and saw some dishes on the table, sealed with plastic wrap. Pork stew, stir-fried vegetables, spicy pickled vegetables. The rice cooker was on so the rice was warm. Liyun had even written a note that read 'Eat Me'. He chuckled. Who did she think she was? Alice in Wonderland?

Without wasting any time, he tore the plastic wrap off and began to eat. He was so hungry he couldn't be bothered to heat the dishes. But even though the food was cold, it was delicious. The pork belly meat was tender and flavourful, cooked using tamarind juice. The stir-fried vegetables had dried shrimp in them. The pickled vegetables went well with the rest of the dishes.

After the satisfying meal, a guilty pang crept into Shouji. He had been unnecessarily harsh to Liyun. He opened his fridge to get some beer. Vegetables, fruits, and other fresh ingredients occupied most of the shelves. There was also a box of milk and a carton of bottled juices with a 'Drink Me' note stuck on to them. Shouji ripped the label off and reached for a bottle of carrot juice. His kitchen staples normally consisted of only canned drinks and instant food. How had Liyun found the time to buy groceries, cook, and clean up in one day? She was like his mother, always able to put together a feast so quickly.

Stop that. He couldn't afford to get comfortable with Liyun. She couldn't stay with him for too long. He had to help her find a new place soon.

Returning to his room, Shouji passed the spare bedroom. The door was ajar, so he took a peek. The room was illuminated by the moonlight. Cardboard boxes filled up the space. Liyun had fallen asleep on top of one of them.

He went in and crouched next to her. She had a pen in her hand. A few stacks of magazines and a bunch of Post-it notes were scattered around her. What had she done? He took a magazine with some notes in it and flipped open the pages.

She had marked his articles.

Shouji kept over a thousand magazines in that room. It would take forever for her to go through them. He peered into the boxes. She had sorted them by publication title and date.

Liyun opened her eyes slightly. 'Sorry, I still haven't finished.' Her voice sounded half asleep.

'Stupid girl.' Shouji got up and offered his hand. 'Why did you sleep on the floor when there's a futon behind you? Do you want to catch a cold?'

A grin slid across Liyun's face. Instead of taking Shouji's hand, she climbed on to the futon. Her movements were graceful and lithe. She must have been a cat in her previous life. Shiny black fur, long, curling tail, pointed ears, striking eyes. Yes, he could picture it well.

Before he left the room, Shouji told Liyun, 'Thanks for the food. It's the best I've had recently.'

'I'm glad,' she whispered, and pulled her blanket up over her.

He paused. 'Also, about what happened earlier, it wasn't you I was angry with.' I was frustrated with myself, he wanted to say, but doing so would only confuse her. 'I'm sorry. I shouldn't have taken it out on you.'

'I know,' she said, her eyes closing. 'We're the same, Shouji.'

He wanted to ask her what she meant by that, but it looked like she was already falling asleep. He planned to bring up the topic the next day, but when the morning came the thought had slipped from his mind.

OKINAWA DAILY

Search Continues for Missing Divers in Kisejima

27 SEPTEMBER 1994

Okinawa, Japan. A group of four tourists have gone missing during a diving expedition off Kisejima with a local couple who acted as their guides. The tourists consisted of three Japanese and one Singaporean.

The group left early in the morning and did not return. The couple's son reported his parents' disappearance to the police that evening. Due to bad weather, the search and rescue mission was delayed.

The SAR team recovered the boat that had been used by the divers the following day. Personal belongings and diving equipment were found on board, but there was no sign of the divers or their guides. The police investigation is ongoing.

CHAPTER 17
IN THAT TINY RED PHONE BOOTH

Shouji packed up his briefcase and loosened his tie. 'I'm leaving,' he told Yoshioka, who was concentrating on a page proof.

'Thank you for your hard work,' his senior said. He paused, remembering something. 'Ah, I wanted to talk to you about the politician's wife you asked me to track down.'

Shouji stopped. 'Did you find anything?'

'Not yet, but I've made some calls,' Yoshioka said. 'I just want you to know that it might take a while. I'm sorry.'

Shouji lowered his head. 'I should be the one to apologise for troubling you.'

'Nah, it's no trouble at all.' Yoshioka glanced at the clock. 'You're leaving early.'

'Uh-huh,' Shouji mumbled awkwardly.

'Usually, you're the last to leave.' Yoshioka grinned. 'Are you seeing someone? Don't tell me it's the cat you picked up.'

'You have a good imagination.'

Shouji put on his coat and made his escape before Yoshioka could ask any more questions. He took the staircase to the ground floor and left the building. Strolling to the station, he breathed in the balmy summer night.

Nowadays, Shouji headed home early because Liyun prepared dinner. At her insistence, he'd started having a proper breakfast, even though he used to begin his day with just a cup of coffee. She'd even offered to pack him a boxed lunch to bring to work, but he had turned her down. His colleagues would ask who had made his bento, and it wouldn't be easy to explain that he was living with a woman, regardless of their platonic friendship.

While waiting for the traffic light's little man to change colour, Shouji stared at a stationary car on the other side of the road. The car — a red Mazda Miata — had stopped there despite the no-parking sign. A couple was seated inside. A long-haired woman sat in the driver's seat, her gloved fingers clutching the steering wheel. She brushed her hair behind her ear, revealing a familiar face.

'Youko!' he shouted.

The little man changed to green and Shouji dashed across the road. He ran over to the car. Youko — was that her? No … It wasn't her, though they had a similar facial structure and build. He cursed. What had he been thinking?

Shouji stopped for a moment, aware that people were staring at him. He slowed down his pace to match the rest of the pedestrians crossing.

The woman in the car laughed and leaned back, and the man next to her came into view. Shouji's heart skipped a beat. That cold, intimidating presence. Was that Kazuhiro Katou?

But before Shouji could get closer, the car drove away.

He felt his heart racing. What was wrong with him? First, he had mistaken that woman for Youko and then he'd convinced himself the man in the passenger seat was Mizuki's husband. But that couldn't be true. There was no way Kazuhiro Katou would turn up in Tokyo without his entourage of guards. He was delusional. Perhaps his earlier conversation with Yoshioka had affected him.

Youko was gone. He should have moved on by now, but why couldn't he?

He went to the station and took the train back. On his way out of the station, instead of heading straight home, he made his way into a red phone booth a ten-minute walk away.

The door felt heavy. He reached for the phone, inserted some coins, and punched a series of numbers on the worn-out panel. He hadn't called this number in a long time. It would probably be out of service now.

Shouji stared at the dust-coated glass panels, waiting for the ringing tone to end.

Hi, we're away right now. Leave us a message and we'll get back to you soon.

He froze. Youko's voice was still there.

Shouji closed his eyes, overwhelmed with emotion. His chest ached. Hearing Youko's voice brought back flashes of memories. She had recorded the message when they had just moved to Akakawa and bought that phone from the electronics shop in town.

'You don't need to bother,' Shouji had said. 'No one will call.'

'It's all right, I want to do it,' she'd replied, turning to face him. 'Hey, Shouji. Do you know that our voices sound different to us than to other people? In our heads, our vocals are deeper and more resonant. I have a friend who worked part-time as a voice actor, and he told me it took him a while to get comfortable with hearing his voice. Fascinating, isn't it?'

Shouji took the receiver from Youko and pressed the playback command.

Her recorded voice sang out:

Hi, we're away right now. Leave us a message and we'll get back to you soon.

'If you go through all the trouble to do the recording, you should at least include our names,' Shouji said.

Youko laughed. 'Anyone who calls us should know who we are.'

That was what she had said, but it wasn't true. Shouji was calling her now, but he wasn't sure if he did know her. He had no clue which city in Iwate prefecture she came from, or what kind of childhood she'd had, or who she had been close with. Even when they had been together, there were so many things she kept from him. For instance, those aquarium visits. He was certain she had been hiding something, yet he hadn't probed further.

Shouji clenched his fist and banged the phone booth.

'Youko …' His voice came out cracked. 'Where are you now?' There was so much more he wanted to learn about her, so many things he wanted to say to her, but those words would forever be stuck in his throat.

Crouching down inside the phone booth, Shouji wept quietly. He knew he should make his way back soon. Liyun would be waiting. He'd promised her he would be back for dinner. But at this moment he was such a wreck, and he wanted to be alone. He didn't have the energy to deal with anything or anyone. Shouji buried his head between his legs.

Gentle taps pattered on the glass panels. Drizzle quickly turned into a heavy downpour. Strange weather. The temperature had felt pleasantly warm an hour ago. Shouji stared at the drops of water falling on the black asphalt.

Resting his head against the glass panels, he closed his eyes. He sunk himself into the sound of rain. Slowly, he caught its rhythm, its music. A soft, lonely melody that felt so nostalgic. Or was it all in his head? He was exhausted. This life was wearing him out. Had he done enough? Was it time to give up?

Faintly, Shouji heard a woman's voice. He opened his eyes. He couldn't see clearly, but he was sure someone was out there, calling his name. He leaned on the glass panels, trying to see where the sound had come from, but the street was empty. The rain poured down with no hint of easing off.

And then he saw her, a woman standing not far from the phone booth. She was wearing a red trench coat and holding a translucent plastic umbrella.

'Youko?' Shouji shouted, pushing open the door.

Strong wind and splashes of rain buffeted him. He braced himself and was about to run towards her, but then he realised the woman was heading in his direction. She came closer. But she wasn't Youko.

Liyun joined Shouji inside the phone booth. She closed her umbrella, wringing it outside before resting it against the wooden frame. They faced each other. The phone booth was too cramped with the two of them inside. They had to stand uncomfortably close. She looked at him. Her fringe was wet from the rain. There were water droplets on her face, but she didn't bother to wipe them away.

'What are you doing here?' he asked.

'I saw on the news that a typhoon is coming, and I guessed correctly you were stuck somewhere,' she said, 'but I didn't expect to see you taking shelter in a phone booth.'

'You left the house in this weather to look for me?'

Liyun nodded.

'Isn't that a bit reckless? What if I were inside a department store or a restaurant? You would never be able to find me.'

She showed him her watch. 'A little late for shopping and dining, isn't it?'

'What about the pachinko parlour?'

'You don't play pachinko. Izakaya would be more likely, except there are no pubs around here.' She took her coat off. 'Anyway, stop asking me so many questions. I just got a hunch that you were stuck somewhere and I needed to rescue you.'

'Like a knight in shining armour.'

'Precisely,' she said, chuckling. 'And you're the damsel in distress.' She turned to the telephone. 'If you're going to take shelter inside a phone booth, the least you could do is to call me so I'm not worried.'

She was right. He should have done that. 'Sorry. That didn't cross my mind.'

'Stupid,' she said, laughing. But then, her smile disappeared. She bit her lip, seemingly trying to contain her emotions.

'What is it?' Shouji asked.

Liyun turned to Shouji, but she didn't say a word. The sound of rain and wind enveloped them. Yet, at that brief moment, Shouji thought he saw a spark in Liyun's eyes.

Eventually, she spoke. 'I told you I lost my brother, didn't I?'

'Uh-huh.'

'When he passed away, it was also raining. I remember looking out of the windows, barely seeing the trees that were just a few metres away.' She paused, lacing her fingers. 'Do you believe in women's intuition?' She looked down. 'I don't think I have it. At that time, I didn't feel anything. While my brother was fighting for his life, I was just thinking what terrible weather it was.'

Shouji mumbled, 'I'm sorry.'

'Ever since then, whenever it rains, I'll start mentally ticking off a list of the people I care about. My family, my friends ... I wonder whether they're all right, or if something terrible is happening to them.'

He didn't know what to say. She had been worrying about him.

She laughed awkwardly. 'Not that anything ever happens. Silly of me.'

'It's not silly,' he said. 'You've been through a lot. You've lost someone important. You've got this space inside you, a gaping hole you can't fill.'

'How do you know?'

He averted his eyes. 'Because I've lost someone too.'

'Your ex-girlfriend?'

An ex? They had never broken up.

Liyun stared off into the distance. 'The rain is not going to stop any time soon. Are we going to spend the entire night crammed in this tiny phone booth?'

Shouji shrugged. 'Probably.'

She rubbed her hands togetherr and breathed into them.

'Cold?' he asked.

Liyun shoved her hands into her pockets, keeping quiet. He turned away from her. The pouring rain blurred his view, as if a white veil had blanketed Tokyo. Or was it all of Japan? Shouji thought of Youko. Was she seeing the same thing as him now?

He imagined her in a tiny apartment somewhere, sitting by the window, gazing out over a park. Her oversized, brown woollen cardigan falling from her shoulders, revealing her protruding collarbone. She was holding a mug with two hands. He didn't need to check to know that she was drinking black coffee. No sugar, no milk.

She brought her mug to her lips. After a sip, she paused and whispered, 'It's cold.'

'Hey, Shouji.' Liyun's voice broke the silence. 'What are you thinking about?'

'Nothing,' he lied.

'You're always thinking too much. At times, when we're together, even when I'm talking to you, your mind is elsewhere. We live together but, somehow, I can't help but feel that you're keeping a distance between us.'

Was he? 'I'm sorry.'

'Don't be. You can't help it, can you?' Liyun gave a feeble smile. 'I feel lonely sometimes. What about you?'

'Well, kind of.'

'Somehow, I can relate to you. I heard the pain of losing someone brings you closer to each other. I guess it must be true.'

But their situations were different. Shouji didn't know whether Youko was dead or alive. Had she moved on and found someone new? He had no idea. He didn't have any closure, and that frustrated him.

'If you take the Namboku Line towards Kita, you'll pass by a particular stop,' Liyun said. 'It's one of those little stations in a small neighbourhood. I accidentally stumbled across it because I overslept once. After I got off the train, instead of going to the other platform, I walked out of the station and explored the place. I don't know why I had such a strong urge to do that.'

He listened in silence. Her clear, distinct voice resonated against the sound of the rain.

'I wandered around the peaceful residential area. I went along narrow roads behind old houses, listening to the clinking of pots and pans, and smelling the curries. I walked past stray cats, lazing under shady trees and meowing at each other. Somehow, I ended up in a field by the river.' She pressed her hands into the glass panel. 'It was quiet. The only thing I could hear was the rustle of grass and the water flowing. It dawned on me that I was alone in an unfamiliar neighbourhood, but I felt safe.

'On that day, I carried an unbearable weight inside me. There was a persistent pain I couldn't get rid of. I was suffocating. I couldn't hold myself in any longer. I opened my mouth and began to shout unintelligible words. I screamed my heart out, like a possessed person, until my voice became hoarse. Then I picked up the pebbles around me and threw them into the water. I only stopped after I collapsed from exhaustion. I lay on the grass patch and looked at the cloudless sky. Or perhaps, there were some clouds, but I couldn't see clearly ... because I was crying.

'I left when I noticed a group of teenagers coming with a soccer ball. But you know, for some strange reason, I skipped all the way back to the station. Somehow, I felt much lighter. The sadness lingered, but it no longer held me down. Is that what people refer to as letting go?'

She waited for him to answer. Instead, Shouji asked, 'Why are you telling me this?'

'I've no idea. I've never told anyone before,' Liyun said. 'Don't mind me. Sometimes I do weird things.' She turned to him. 'Do you want me to take you there? But you must promise to keep the place a secret.'

'Who do you think I'd want to share it with?'

'Who knows?' She shrugged and stared at him with her bright eyes. 'So, is that a yes?'

'All right.'

Her lips curved into a smile. 'It's a promise.' And then she looked at him gently. 'Shouji, I know you've been going through a lot. You don't need to always be strong. At least not in front of me. We're friends, aren't we? You can share your burden with me. You're not alone.'

Shouji averted his eyes. 'I don't know what you see in me. You probably think I'm a good guy, but I'm not. I've made many mistakes, and I've brought a lot of misfortune to the people around me. Whenever I care about someone, I always end up harming them. You should assume it's never going to be safe with me. You should lea—'

'Hey,' Liyun cut him off. 'It's all right. I'm not a good person either. And I might not look very dependable, but I'm strong. You don't need to protect me. I know how to take care of myself.'

'You wouldn't understand, Liyun.'

'Then explain it to me.'

'I can't,' he said. 'I don't know how.'

She took a deep breath. 'You're feeling frustrated, aren't you? I, too, have a lot of bitterness inside me. I'm trying to move on, but I'm struggling.' She extended her hand and patted his arm. 'But I think we'll be fine. I promise you, one day we'll be able to think about the past without all the anger and resentment, and all the tears and tightness in our chests.'

'That would be nice, but —'

'There is no but,' Liyun said. 'That day will come. All we need is a little time. So, until then, please hang on. The pain won't last forever.'

In the morning, Yoshioka came up to Shouji's desk. Must be an assignment, thought Shouji. But when he looked up, his senior's expression was solemn.

'Is there a problem?' Shouji asked.

Yoshioka nodded slowly. 'It's about that politician.'

'Did you manage to find any information?'

'Kind of.' He rubbed the nape of his neck. 'I hope you don't need anything from him, because he's dead.'

Shouji was stunned for a moment. 'When?'

'Last night.' Yoshioka tilted his head. 'During the typhoon. What fitting weather, eh?'

Could it be ... 'What happened? Was he in Tokyo?'

'No, of course not. The man passed away in Akakawa,' he said. 'The official cause of death was heart failure.'

'Is it confirmed?'

'Yes, it's in today's newspaper,' Yoshioka said.

'Uh-huh,' Shouji mumbled. 'What about his wife? Did you hear anything?'

'Not really. No one knows who she is. She never attended any public events and her maiden name was never mentioned in the press. I'm afraid I couldn't find out much about her at all, let alone her current whereabouts.'

Nevertheless, Mizuki was better off if her husband was no longer around. It wasn't right to rejoice at someone's death, but Shouji couldn't help but feel relieved that Kazuhiro Katou could no longer hurt her.

'Would it be possible for me to take some time off?' Shouji asked. 'I'd like to return to Akakawa, just to make sure my friend is safe.' He could probably enlist Uncle Hidetoshi's help to get in touch with her.

'Of course you can, but I wouldn't do that if I were you. Kazuhiro Katou may be dead, but the family influence is still strong. As we speak, his position is already being filled by his successor, a younger cousin. And right now, the situation in Akakawa is rather tense. You would be putting her in danger by going there.'

'I see.' He realised it wasn't going to be that simple.

'I know you're worried. I promise I'll ask around for more information,' Yoshioka said. 'Aside from that, is there anything I can do for you, Arai?'

'Ah. Actually, do you think you can help me ask around about another person?' He tore a piece of paper from a notepad and wrote Youko's name on it. 'She's someone very important to me, but we lost contact when I left Akakawa.'

'Youko Sasaki . . .' Yoshioka mumbled the name. 'Who is she?'

'She was a student at Waseda, but then she left to work for a shady company owned by Kazuhiro Katou. I'm not too sure what she's doing right now or where she is. Her former employer might be after her, so you'll need to be discreet.'

'I bet she's keeping a low profile.'

'Uh-huh. I believe so.'

'A civilian in hiding can be the toughest nut to crack, but I'll see what I can do. Anything else?'

'Nothing for now,' Shouji said. 'Thank you so much. I appreciate it. Can I treat you to a meal?'

'You don't need to.' He patted Shouji's back. 'I didn't do much.'

After Yoshioka left, Shouji called Uncle Hidetoshi's office, but the older man had been transferred somewhere else.

'He moved to the Osaka prefecture,' the officer said. 'I think he's in Ibaraki or Kishiwada. Or is it Matsubara?' A pause. 'I'm sorry, I can't recall.'

'It's all right,' Shouji said, cutting the conversation short. He didn't want to arouse suspicion.

Shouji thought of travelling to Akakawa in a few weeks, but with no name or address to go on, and with Mizuki's deceased husband's men possibly still after him, it would be a suicide mission.

He decided against it. He had learned from his mistake.

When he reached home, a small package was waiting for him on the table. Shouji picked it up, wondering what it could be. The sender's name was Jin Fujiwara.

CHAPTER 18
IT'S NOT SO BAD TO LIVE IN TOKYO

Shouji watched the foam on his beer subside. A group of salarymen seated nearby laughed. He checked his watch. An hour had passed, yet the person he was supposed to meet wasn't here. Perhaps she had been held up by work. He ate the last asparagus skewer on the ceramic plate, contemplating whether he should return to the office. He still had some unfinished work but, in the end, Shouji decided to call it a night and go home. It was a Friday, anyway.

He raised his hand to call over the izakaya's waiter, but a woman in a beige dress entered, stealing the young man's attention.

'Welcome,' the waiter said to her.

She gave him a polite bow. Her face was partially covered by long, wavy auburn hair.

'Eri?' Shouji asked.

The woman turned to him and paused. 'Shouji? You're early.' She took the seat next to him. Seeing the empty glass and dirty plates in front of him, she said, 'You should have told me you wanted to have dinner. When you suggested meeting at ten, I thought we were just going to have a drink.'

Shouji was pretty sure he had said nine, not ten, but then again, the office had been noisy when he had made the call. But he didn't want to make Eri feel bad. 'I was supposed to go for a company dinner, but it got rescheduled,' he lied.

'Ah, I see.' She looked him up and down. 'Wow, you've changed a lot. When you were working at my father's bookshop, you were so skinny. I was worried one day a strong wind would blow you away.'

He pretended to cough. 'Are you saying that I'm gaining weight?'

'Yes, and in a good way.' Eri smiled. 'It's nice to see you again after so many years. Though I must admit, I was surprised when I received your call. How did you get my office number?'

'Do you remember the poetry book you gave me on my last day?'

'Ah, of course.' Her face brightened. 'Have you read it?'

He stumbled to answer. 'Not really.'

Eri laughed, and Shouji laughed too.

'I was kind of half-expecting that,' she said, chuckling. 'Let me guess. I wrote down my number, but when you called me, I had already moved out. One way or another, the person who picked up the phone directed you to me.'

'Yes, someone named Watanabe.'

'Ah, that's Rie. I didn't know she had my office number.'

'She didn't, but she knew you were working at Sumitomo Mitsui so I called the main branch,' Shouji said. 'Anyway, let me buy you a drink. It's not every day I meet someone from my hometown. What would you like?'

'Now I can see that you're becoming a proper adult,' Eri teased him. 'I've got no preference. I'll leave it up to you.'

Shouji ordered a medium-sized bottle of chilled Junmai Ginjo sake to share.

'Cold sake is the best,' she said. 'The weather has been so hot recently.'

He gestured for a toast. 'What do you expect? It's summer now.'

'That's true. I've been so busy at work I haven't had the chance to check out this year's summer festivals schedule.' Eri shifted her eyes to Shouji. 'Hey, didn't you say you wanted to ask me something?'

Yes, he had. He had remembered that the mysterious man on the phone had made mention of his past and that he thought she might know something. 'Are you familiar with Kazuhiro Katou?'

'Wasn't that the politician who got murdered in Akakawa?'

Shouji paused. 'Where did you hear that?'

She furrowed her brow. 'Is anything wrong?'

'Well, you just told me something intriguing. The newspaper reported that he died of heart failure.'

'Really?' she asked, looking bewildered. 'To be honest, I'm not sure. I think I overheard someone talking about it in the office. You know, the usual bankers' chat. We tend to keep an eye on anything that might remotely affect the stock market. A lot of it is just rumours meant to fuel speculation. If I were you, I wouldn't read too much into it.'

'Uh-huh.'

Eri took a sip of her sake. 'But why do you ask about him?'

Shouji thought hard about what to say next. 'It's a long story I don't want to go into but, in short, I had a nasty brush with his family. An exchange I had with one of his men left me wondering if I'd known them previously, back in Fukuoka.'

She gave him a fleeting smile. 'If you're not sure, why would you think I'd know?'

'Fair question. I'm not in Fukuoka much these days, and I just wondered whether you know if the Katou family has any link to our hometown?'

'Not that I know of. I'm not home that much either.'

He paused. 'Do you think you can ask your old man?'

'Of course,' she said. 'I'll let you know if he knows anything.'

Eri brushed her hair behind her ear, and Shouji caught a glimpse of a vintage man's watch on her wrist. Silver-rimmed, paired with an aged, brown-leather strap, which emphasised her slim wrist.

'You've changed, Shouji,' she continued. 'You've become much more assertive now. You surprise me. The last time I saw you, you were just a kid.'

He didn't say it, but he thought that she too had changed.

Eri had always been attractive, the object of attention of the bookshop's customers, but she gave off an aura of belonging to a different world. But, seeing her here, he couldn't detect even a glimpse of that coldness. Perhaps it had been his youthful awkwardness.

Shouji had planned to ask Eri about Kazuhiro Katou and then have a short catch-up, but they ended up talking for a long time, reminiscing about their hometown and their memories of working at the bookshop together. That night, Shouji learned that he and Eri had had the same form teacher, but at different times. She was five years his senior.

'You look younger than your age,' he said. 'If you hadn't told me, I would've thought you were just a couple of years older than me.'

Eri's cheeks were red. Was she flustered, or was she getting drunk?

'You haven't told me what brought you to Tokyo,' she said. 'Are you wooing a Tokyo lady?'

She was probably half-drunk, but because of that he felt more comfortable talking. 'I used to date someone here. She and I met at Waseda, but she was originally from Iwate. Like you, I came to Tokyo to study.'

She nodded slowly. 'What happened after that?'

'Many things, and I ended up losing her.'

'Sometimes things don't work out the way we want them to.' Eri topped up Shouji's sake. 'Where is she now? Are you still in touch?'

'I heard she's in Tokyo. No idea where exactly. I'm not even sure if I will ever see her again.'

She looked at him wistfully. 'Tokyo is too big for a chance encounter.'

Eri proposed a toast and they finished their first bottle. After that, Shouji ordered another. This time, he chose a Junmai. Their conversation resumed. They spoke about his work, and then hers. Eri seemed to be doing well.

'Do you feel lonely living in Tokyo by yourself?' she asked.

He shook his head. 'I've got plenty of work. No time to be lonely.'

She stared at him. 'People who say they're not lonely are usually the loneliest.'

'I'm okay.' He glanced at the chef behind the counter. 'It's not so bad living in Tokyo, even all by yourself.'

The corners of her mouth curled up. 'That's true.'

Shouji hadn't noticed it at first, but he now realised what it was in Mizuki that reminded him of Eri. It wasn't just their disposition, but also the way they smiled so subtly.

'You're staring at me,' Eri said. 'What is it?'

He looked down. 'You remind me of someone.'

She gave him a playful look. 'The Iwate girl?'

'That would be a cliché,' he said, downing a glass of sake. 'No, a friend I regret not doing enough for, and now I have no idea what happened to her either.' He contemplated telling Eri about Mizuki, but eventually decided against it. The fewer people who knew about her, the better.

Eri poured more sake for Shouji. 'And what are you going to do about it?'

He leaned forward. 'I'm not sure. The last time I wanted to help, I ended up making a bigger mess.'

'Then do something,' she said. 'If you know you took the wrong step, then try something different. Fix it. Don't let that feeling of regret linger for ever.'

Shouji laughed. He was wrong. Eri wasn't like Mizuki.

'You're right,' he said. 'I should try harder.'

They finished their second bottle and left the izakaya. She told him it was already late so she would take a taxi back, and he walked her to the taxi stand. On their way there, their conversation shifted to where they currently lived. Eri had a studio apartment in Minato.

'What about you?' she asked. 'You're living on your own too, right?'

He shrugged. 'Mine is just an old apartment. I'm sharing it with a friend.'

'Is it nice to have a housemate? Do you get along with him?'

'Her, actually,' he said. 'I live with a girl, but she's just a friend. Nothing romantic.'

Eri narrowed her eyes. 'Are you sure?'

'Yeah,' he said, avoiding her stare. 'There's nothing between us.'

Her face brightened. 'Hey, why don't you come over to my place one of these weekends? Ask your housemate along. We can watch a movie and have popcorn, or play some board games. I'll order KFC. As a thank you for treating me tonight.'

He gave her a puzzled look. 'Why KFC?'

'Because it feels like Christmas.'

'We're still in summer.'

'Doesn't matter. Let's just pretend,' she insisted. 'I'll write down my address.'

After they parted ways, Shouji went to look for a place to smoke. As he lit up his cigarette, he thought of what Eri had said. Was there a way to help Mizuki? No, he had exhausted all his options. But it felt as if there might be something he hadn't noticed. What was that?

By the time he finished smoking, the last train had departed, so he spent the night at an internet café.

•

Shouji climbed the staircase to the third floor and walked through the corridor towards his apartment. Before he reached it, the door opened. Liyun craned her neck.

'Welcome home,' she greeted him.

He scratched his neck. 'How did you know I was coming?'

'I heard your footsteps on the staircase. Tap, tap, tap.' She used her fingers to illustrate her point. 'The rest of the occupants take the lift. You're such a health-conscious person.'

Shouji said nothing. He climbed the staircase out of habit. The apartment he'd lived in Akakawa with Youko had had no lift.

'Did you drink with Yoshioka until you missed the last train?' Liyun asked. 'You smell of alcohol.'

He took off his coat and shoes. 'I did, but not with Yoshioka. I was with an old friend from Fukuoka. We used to work together.'

'Don't tell me it's a woman,' she teased him. 'Is she cute? Did you spend the night with her?'

'Why do you need to know? It's none of your business.'

Liyun was quiet, then mumbled, 'Whatever.'

Something was off with her. He knew it, but he couldn't be bothered to find out what it was.

Shouji went into his apartment. The television was on, showing a children's cartoon. A blue cat robot took out a pink-coloured door from his magical pocket. 'The Anywhere Door!' the robot announced. The children around him cheered. They went through the door and came out on to a beautiful beach.

'You're watching *Doraemon*?' he asked.

'Not really,' she said. 'I just leave it on while I'm doing housework.'

'Uh-huh,' Shouji mumbled. He was about to enter his room when a thought came into his mind. It might be a far-fetched idea, but there was no harm in trying.

CHAPTER 19
THERE IS NO SMOKE WITHOUT FIRE

Shouji put his coat down on the sofa and reached for the phone. Liyun gave him a puzzled look as he dialled Yoshioka's home number.

Realising who it was calling, Yoshioka sounded alarmed. 'Is there anything wrong with the page proofs?'

'No. Don't worry. Nothing to do with work,' he said. 'I was hoping you could help me track down one more person.'

Yoshioka laughed. 'At this rate, I should open a detective agency. Anyway, go on. Tell me. Who is it this time? A newscaster? An actor? A sportsman?'

'A man named Takeshi Gouda,' he said. 'I believe he's a teacher in New York.'

'Did you just say New York? Is that the name of a cram school or something?'

'No,' Shouji said. 'The actual city in the United States.'

There was a long pause. 'Arai, I hate to say this, but this is a little …' His voice trailed off. 'Difficult?'

Shouji knew what that meant. 'I understand. My apologies for bothering you.'

'No, that's all right. I'll try to ask around,' Yoshioka said. 'Since you're calling, there's another thing I wanted to tell you. It's about Kazuhiro Katou.'

Shouji perked up. 'Did you find his wife?'

'Unfortunately, no,' he said. 'But a journalist I know told me there was a rumour circulating that the man didn't die of natural causes. He was murdered.'

Shouji's heart skipped a beat. 'Who did it?'

'No one knows, and this is just a rumour,' Yoshioka said. 'But you should know how this works. There is no smoke without fire. I've asked my journalist friend in Akakawa to look into the case.'

'Uh-huh.' Shouji paused. 'Did you find anything on Youko Sasaki?'

'I'm afraid not. She's not on the missing persons register in Akakawa or Tokyo. I'll continue to ask around, but don't expect too much.'

Shouji thanked his senior and put down the phone. He noticed Liyun staring at him, but she didn't say anything.

•

In the couple of weeks that followed, every few days Shouji would check with Yoshioka if his senior had heard anything new. But each time, he received the same reply: 'No, I couldn't find anything concrete. The politician's family is very tight-lipped. If you push too much, your luck might run out.'

'What about Youko Sasaki?'

'Also nothing.'

'I see.'

Eventually, in the last week of July, while they were walking to the station together, Yoshioka told Shouji of a rumour that the politician's widow had left Akakawa.

Shouji turned to his senior. 'Another rumour, huh?'

'Yeah, another rumour,' Yoshioka said, staring at the crowd. 'I'm sorry, none of this is conclusive.'

'It's all right,' Shouji said. 'I appreciate it.'

They waited for the traffic light to change colour. It was almost midnight, but Tokyo showed no sign of slowing down. Flashing billboards, traffic lights, and streetlamps made the city seem wide awake. An enthusiastic salesman spoke on a loudspeaker to advertise a closing-down sale.

'Excuse me.' A young girl in a bright haori greeted them energetically and offered two pocket tissues. 'Thank you.'

The traffic lights changed colour. Yoshioka and Shouji crossed the road, blending in with the crowd.

Shouji thought of Mizuki and her gentle smile. If she had left Akakawa, perhaps she was in a better place now. Wherever she was, he hoped she was happy and safe. But could he leave it like this?

•

Shouji blew out his cigarette smoke, watching it drift and vanish. All around him, the evening crowds never let up. Teenage girls in short skirts and platform boots, office ladies in perfectly coordinated uniforms, and salarymen in black suits toting similar-looking briefcases — all of them in a hurry.

He stared at the Mild Seven between his fingers. He should cut down, but smoking was a perfect excuse whenever he wished to get out of a situation. No one paid any attention to him, even if he lingered for a long time.

Shouji took another puff. A few days ago, he had been looking at the calendar when he realised that 7 August was circled.

'Do you want to go to Sendai Festival?' he asked Liyun.

She gave him a puzzled look. 'What's that?'

'You didn't know? It's probably the biggest Tanabata festival in Japan.' Ah, that was right. In Tokyo, people held the star festival on 7 July. 'Have you heard of it?'

She nodded. 'It celebrates the reunion of Orihime and Hikoboshi, doesn't it?'

'Yes, that's the one.' According to the legend, the lovers could only see each other once a year during the Tanabata. 'Isn't that the reason you circled the date?'

'No …' Her words faltered. 'It's my birthday.'

'Oh,' Shouji mumbled, not expecting that. 7 August was only two days from now. He was quiet for a moment. 'I know you probably have plans, but if you're free, perhaps we could go for dinner or something.'

'I'm free,' Liyun said, a little too quickly. 'Let's do it.'

'All right. Uhm. Is there anywhere you'd like to go? Or anything in particular you want to eat?'

'I'll leave it to you,' she said, smiling.

'Okay.' He hadn't taken any women for a proper dinner for years, except for business meetings. 'No preference at all?'

Liyun thought for a moment. 'Perhaps somewhere with a nice view? Doesn't have to be too fancy. Anywhere is fine. Surprise me.'

He'd suggested meeting after work near a station downtown. Shouji had arrived this evening at the agreed time, but Liyun was nowhere to be seen. His mind wandered as he smoked, then someone bumped into him. The cigarette between Shouji's fingers slipped. A bald man carrying a beaten-up leather briefcase bowed to him.

'I'm sorry,' he said. 'I wasn't paying attention.'

'It's all right,' Shouji said. The cigarette was almost finished anyway.

The man left after bowing a few more times. Shouji moved his fingers, feeling uneasy that his hand was empty. He shoved his hand into his pocket, intending to fish for his cigarette pack. But then he saw Liyun. She was in an elegant black dress with her hair up in a chignon.

'Sorry I'm late,' she said, her breathing uneven. 'Have you been waiting for long?'

'Not really, I just arrived,' he lied. 'Shall we go?'

She nodded. 'Where are you taking me? I realised this morning it wasn't a good idea to ask you to surprise me because I had no clue what kind of dress I should wear.'

He pretended to look her over. 'You must be a clairvoyant. I can't think of anything more fitting.'

Liyun laughed. She circled her hand around his arm. 'Now, will you do the honour of telling me what kind of place you're taking me to?'

CHAPTER 20
SMOKED BEEF BRISKET

The restaurant Shouji had in mind was ten minutes' walk from the station. The building had a modern design, painted in black and white, and bore a placard that read 'The Roast Yard'. He thought the chic eatery might appeal to a young woman like Liyun. Most importantly, the restaurant served great smoked meat. Shouji had only been there twice, once with Yoshioka and another time on his own after he received a bonus. The place was fancy, something to be saved for special occasions. A birthday celebration surely warranted that.

They arrived. A pleasant, smoky smell wafted in the air. There was a relaxing outdoor seating area on the ground floor, with contemporary chill-out music playing in the background. The restaurant was bustling with customers. Luckily, Shouji had made a reservation.

A lanky waiter in a white shirt and black apron welcomed them. The man's hair was coiffed to perfection. Shouji could imagine him combing it in front of a mirror, checking himself many times before letting out a satisfied sigh. Somehow, the waiter reminded him of Mr Satou and his white-gloved fingers.

'This is a great place,' Liyun whispered. 'I can't believe I've never heard of it.'

'It's quite new,' Shouji said.

The waiter led them to the staircase. So, they would be seated on the upper level, Shouji thought. While the ground-level floor had a casual, friendly vibe and was used mostly by small groups, the second floor was more for romantic dates. It was filled with square tables occupied by well-dressed couples.

While making the reservation, Shouji had mentioned that it was for a birthday celebration, so perhaps they would get one of the tables near the windows, facing the main street. But the waiter escorted them up even further. Shouji had had no idea there was another floor.

The narrow staircase led to a glass door. The waiter opened it and let Shouji and Liyun step out to the rooftop. What greeted them was a charming outdoor garden with fairy lights entwined around wooden pillars. A candlelit table for two was set in the middle. From where they stood, the nightscape was glittering.

Liyun shifted her eyes to Shouji and mouthed, 'Wow.'

He responded with a sheepish smile. The restaurant had promised him a nice table, but he hadn't expected this. Liyun and Shouji took their seats. The waiter placed the menus on the table and a waitress came to fill the glasses with water.

'It's beautiful,' Liyun said, easing her way into her seat. The candle gave a warm, flattering light which softened her features and made her look gorgeous. Flipping through the menu, she asked, 'What would you recommend?'

Shouji glanced at the list. 'You should try the smoked beef brisket. The meat is tender and flavourful, and it comes with a bowl of potato chips.'

'Hmm …' she mumbled, reading the menu. '"Our beef brisket is smoked for at least twenty-four hours with rambutan wood in a custom-built smoker."' She looked up. 'Sounds promising.'

'Ah, yes,' Shouji recalled. 'The smoker is located on the ground floor at the back of the building. You can see it later.'

'I'll have the brisket,' she told the waiter, before turning to Shouji. 'What about you?'

He thought of ordering the same thing, but it was on the pricier side. He decided on something more affordable. 'I'll have the roast beef and fries.'

'What about a drink?' the waiter asked.

Shouji turned to Liyun. 'What would you like?'

'Shall we get a glass of house wine?' she suggested.

'Sure,' he said. 'Two glasses of red, please.'

The waiter left them on their own. Shouji gazed at the scenery. The place was perfect for a date. Too perfect. It made him uneasy. He hoped Liyun wouldn't feel uncomfortable.

'What are you thinking about?' she asked.

'Nothing,' he said. 'Are you okay with this place?'

'Of course! I love it. This is the sort of place my brother ...' Her voice trailed off. She was quiet for a moment before continuing, 'In the past, my brother and I would go for dinner at fancy places like this. He was quite a food connoisseur, really, and a meticulous planner too. He would make the booking months in advance, insisting on the best table in the restaurant. If you ask me, I wouldn't bother. It's not like the meat is juicier when you get the prettiest table.'

Shouji forced an uncomfortable smile.

'But this is different.' Her tone turned serious. She seemed to notice his unease. 'This is a super-nice place. The food will taste better.'

He laughed. She tried too hard.

'How did you manage to snag this spot?' Liyun asked. 'Are you a regular?'

'Not really. I've only been here twice. The first was a celebratory treat from my senior after I got promoted to full-time. The second time I came alone.'

'This is the third time?'

'Uh-huh.'

The waiter came out with two glasses of wine. Liyun proposed a toast. Shouji swirled his glass, inhaling the aroma before taking the first sip. A medium-bodied red wine, it had a velvety texture and a nice backbone.

'Are you familiar with the rambutan wood they use to smoke the meat?' Liyun asked.

He tilted his head. 'Rambutan is a fruit, isn't it?'

She nodded. 'It's the name of the tropical tree, but also the fruit. Have you tried it?'

'Not yet.'

'I had one in Bali. The skin was red and leathery, and it was covered with short, pliable spines resembling hair. Once you peel the skin, you can see the white flesh. The fruit tastes sweet and juicy.' She bit her lip, seemingly thinking hard. 'Kind of similar to lychee.'

'Interesting.'

'The waiter who served me said he came from South Sulawesi. He said his parents live in a house on a street named Rambutan.' She turned to him. 'And guess what? In Singapore, there is another street called Rambutan.'

'Uh-huh. Do you travel overseas often?'

'Now and then. My brother was the traveller really,' she said. 'What about you?'

'I've never been out of Japan,' he said, and then he thought of Youko.

Before they got together, she'd travelled out of the country alone a lot. Armed with a worn-out backpack and little money, with not much planned ahead of time, she had plenty of guts. Whenever she talked about her overseas trips, Shouji used to think she seemed invincible, as if she could do anything she put her mind to.

The waiter returned with their food. Liyun's smoked beef brisket was presented on a wooden tray with a dip of special sauce, fresh green salad drizzled with lemon, and a bowl of thinly sliced potato chips. A crumbled biscuit mixed with a slice of orange completed the meal. Shouji's roast beef came with mushroom sauce and the same salad and dessert. Instead of potato chips, his was served with French fries, lightly flavoured with sea salt.

Liyun cut a small portion of the meat and brought it to her mouth, savouring it slowly. 'Hmmm,' she mumbled. 'This is wonderful. The meat is so tender and aromatic. It's slightly spicy, which gives it a nice punch.' She cut another piece and this time dipped the meat into the condiment. 'The sauce is nice too. Demi-glace?'

'Looks like it.' Shouji took a bite of his roasted meat. It didn't disappoint. The beef melted on his tongue, though it did not have the same spiciness as the smoked version.

'Can I try that?' she asked.

'Sure,' he said, cutting a generous portion for her. 'But I think the smoked beef is better.'

She put the meat into her mouth. 'Why didn't you order the same?'

'I wanted to try something new.' He didn't want to tell her he was trying not to spend too much. 'I like this too. Just that the flavour isn't as pronounced as yours.'

She paused for a moment. 'I prefer yours. Shall we swap?'

He didn't expect that. 'Are you sure?'

'Yeah,' she said, switching their trays. 'This is slightly too spicy for me.'

'Uh, okay.' He was more than happy to have his favourite dish.

Liyun talked about her early days in Tokyo. She'd had a hard time making friends until she joined the swimming club at Waseda.

'I was in the swimming club too,' Shouji said, 'but just for a short while.'

She cut her beef. 'Really? You don't seem like the sporty type.'

He tilted his head. 'Then what kind of person do you think I am?'

Liyun shrugged. 'Perhaps the book-club type?'

'Unlikely.' Shouji cut some meat. 'I do love reading, but I'm not sure if I'd like to discuss it with a group of people. I believe books are best indulged in alone. Reading is such a personal experience.' He took another bite of his favourite smoked beef. 'But you're close. I was also in the journalism club.'

'You've always wanted to be a journalist?'

'I wasn't completely sure when I had just started. I love reading and I like writing too. But the longer I've been in this position, the more I've realised this is my calling. Being a journalist, I get to meet lots of people I might not have encountered otherwise, and I have the opportunity to hear their stories. It allows me to gain a new perspective.'

Her lips curled up into a smile. 'That's nice.' She reached for her wine and took a sip. 'Hey, tell me about your time at the swimming club. I don't remember ever seeing you there.'

'Nothing much to say. I wasn't there for long. When I'd just started at university, I thought it would be a good idea to get involved in a few student activities. Swimming seemed to be an ideal choice as it's a sport that doesn't require much equipment.'

'True. And then what happened?'

'Just the usual,' he said. 'More and more work.'

She looked up. 'But do you like to swim?'

Shouji shrugged. 'I don't know. My mother was so adamant about me learning to swim, it kind of killed the joy. Back in Fukuoka, she would send me to swimming lessons twice a week. She wouldn't let me skip any unless I was sick. And she only let me off the hook after she was a hundred per cent assured I had become a strong swimmer.'

'Is she a big fan of swimming or something?'

'No, she's just paranoid about the possibility of me drowning. My mother is superstitious. When I was a kid, I dreamed of drowning.' Shouji reached for his wine. 'There was also a young cousin who died in a freak accident at my house. He fell into a bucket of water while he was playing.'

Liyun covered her mouth. 'That's awful. How did it happen? He was left unattended?'

'I'm not sure,' Shouji said, sipping the wine. 'I don't remember. I tried to bring it up twice, but each time my mother looked terrified and shushed me. I think she was traumatised.'

'And maybe she thinks you don't need to know.' She softened her voice. 'Ignorance is bliss.'

Shouji didn't tell Liyun, but there was something more to it. He felt uncomfortable talking about what had happened to Uncle Hidetoshi's son and was surprised he had brought it up. Prior to this, he had never told anyone, not even Youko.

At the end of the meal, Liyun proposed splitting the bill, but Shouji insisted on paying. 'It's your birthday,' he said. 'You can treat me next time, when you get a job.'

She was quiet for a moment. Eventually, she smiled and said, 'Thank you. I really appreciate it.'

He thought about asking how her job search was going, but in the end decided against it because he didn't want to make her feel uncomfortable.

After the satisfying meal, they walked together to the station. On her insistence, they took the longer route.

'I'm too full,' she said, clutching his arm. 'Let's stroll around the park.'

At night, the place was filled with couples occupying all the benches, but Liyun didn't seem to notice. She didn't let go of his arm either. She seemed to be in a jovial mood, so he decided to just let her be.

'Shouji.' Liyun pulled him a little. 'You know, I'm not a very good person. I have a lot of skeletons in my closet and I made a lot of bad decisions. Sometimes I worry that once you get to know me more, you'll grow to hate me.'

Hearing that made him think of Youko and his past. 'Everyone has their secrets. It would be strange if you didn't have any. I wouldn't worry if I were you.' He glanced at her. 'Also, maybe it is you who will dislike me if you learn more about me.'

She let go of his hand and gave him a playful, accusatory look. 'Really? What did you do? What kind of scandalous past do you have?'

'I'm not going to tell you,' he said in a whisper.

Liyun laughed, and Shouji laughed too. They continued to walk side by side.

'Do you think we can start again?' she asked. 'Is it too late to learn to be honest with each other?'

He shook his head. 'Of course not. It's never too late.'

'Okay.' She turned to him. 'In that case, shall we start now?'

'Uh-huh,' he said, shifting her eyes to her. 'And how do we do that?'

'Let me think.' She paused for a moment. 'Ah.' Her eyes lit up. 'Tell me one thing you've been hiding from me.'

That was direct. Shouji continued to walk a few steps forward as he thought of what to say next. 'All right. What about this? The truth is I wanted to order the smoked beef instead of the roast one, but the roast is cheaper.' He softened his voice. 'I'm kind of broke.'

Liyun sneered. 'That's so uncool.'

'Hey, Tokyo is expensive, and I don't earn much.'

She chuckled. Crossing her arms, she smiled at him. 'Now, it's my turn, huh?' She hummed a little before saying, 'To tell you the truth, I liked the smoked beef better. I love spicy food. But I asked to swap because I knew you liked mine better.'

This time, it was Shouji who sneered. 'You're trying to be cool, huh?'

'I *am* cool,' she said with a laugh.

She spread out her arms and looked up at the sky. He wanted

to ask what was she doing. People were staring. But then she closed her eyes and grinned widely. Looking at her, he couldn't help but be amused.

Liyun opened her eyes and turned to Shouji. 'Hey, you're smiling.'

He was stunned for a moment. Was he? Yes, he was.

'I like you better with that kind of expression,' she continued. 'You should keep it that way. Stop scowling all the time. Try to take things easy.'

He didn't say anything, but some questions ran through his mind. Was it all right for him to be happy? Could he afford to feel this way, after all the mistakes he had made?

'Hey, why are you standing there?' Liyun gestured towards the station. 'Let's go. If you don't move, we'll never get anywhere.'

Yeah, that was right. He had to learn to let go.

CHAPTER 21
SOMETHING LIKE CHRISTMAS

Eri was the one who spotted Shouji first, waving at him as he exited the station on a Saturday night. She looked fresh in a chequered short-sleeved top paired with black capri pants. Her hair was tied up into a small bun.

'Where is your friend?' Eri asked.

'She couldn't come,' Shouji said. In truth, he hadn't asked Liyun. He was worried about what Eri would say.

She looked genuinely disappointed. 'That's too bad. We should arrange it for another time.'

He averted his eyes. 'Yeah.'

Eri's place was five minutes' walk from Shibakoen Station. They passed by a KFC, where they ordered takeaway. Unlike Shouji's old-fashioned apartment, Eri's was a luxurious high-rise complete with a security guard. The middle-aged man in dark uniform greeted them as they entered, and Eri exchanged a few words with him. Once they were in the lift, she inserted her access card and pressed number thirteen.

'The rent must be expensive,' Shouji said, 'especially in such a prime location.'

'It is,' she said, 'but I hardly spend on anything else.'

The lift pinged and the door opened.

She walked out. 'I like it here. It's near my office, and the view is great. Wait until you see it for yourself. I'm sure you'll love it.'

'Uh-huh.'

The carpeted floor silenced their steps. A waft of lavender scented the air. The atmosphere was that of a hotel, not an apartment.

Eri stopped and inserted her card into a slot in the front door. A tiny red light turned green and she pushed the door open. Once she put her card into a slot on the wall, light flooded in.

'Here it is,' she said, glancing at Shouji. 'Welcome to my place.'

He followed her and put the KFC bucket on the white coffee table. Eri lived in a studio apartment, tastefully furnished with modern furniture. A Bordeaux-coloured sofa perched in the middle of the room, contrasting with the monochrome wallpaper and steel fittings. With a press of a button, she opened the thick brocade curtain, revealing a floor-to-ceiling glass window overlooking Tokyo Bay. Thousands of lights glittered like precious gems against the dark water.

'What do you want to drink?' Eri asked.

He turned to her. 'Do you have beer?'

'Only Sochu and Coke.'

'Coke then.'

Shouji sat down on the sofa facing the view. He narrowed his eyes, blurring the lights into each other. In the distance, he heard Eri opening the fridge and cracking some ice cubes. The ice clanked against the glass, followed by a gassy sound of soda and a low thud when the fridge was closed.

Eri returned with two glasses of Coke and sat next to him. 'Tell me which beer you prefer. I'll stock up next time.'

'Asahi Super Dry.' Shouji took a gulp to ease his thirst, but the bubbles irritated his throat and made him cough.

She passed him a box of tissues. 'You should let the fizz settle first.'

He glanced around the room, clearing his throat. A framed photograph was displayed on top of a cabinet. A man, a woman, and a little girl holding a red balloon. But on a closer inspection, it wasn't a balloon but a circular traffic sign. The man was Eri's father when he was young. The woman had the same dimpled smile as Eri. She had to be her mother. He remembered what her father had told him about the accident.

Shouji stared at Eri, who was still holding the tissue box. She had come a long way since then, comfortably settled in a well-paid job that allowed her to rent such a nice apartment. But he wondered if the scar from that incident had healed.

He looked at the photograph again. Eri's old man was a serious-looking guy, but in this picture, he was laughing heartily. He wore a straw hat and held a fishing rod.

'Are you an only child?' Shouji asked.

Eri nodded. 'Just like you.'

'How did you know?'

She crossed her legs. 'Everyone in our hometown knows your parents. Your father was a military general, wasn't he? And your mother came from a distinguished koto-playing family.'

Her words transported him back to Fukuoka. He remembered growing up listening to the sound of his mother's koto. The notes she played were tender and calming, just like her. Always kind, always patient, always understanding.

But his mother had stopped playing koto a long time ago and he could no longer picture her with the instrument. When he thought of his mother, he saw a perfect model of a dutiful housewife, cooking delicious meals in the kitchen, tidying up the house, and tending to the garden. She was the mistress of the Arai household, no longer the prodigy koto player she had once been. All that was left was a faint recollection of those beautiful notes, vibrating softly inside him on quiet nights.

'My father has long retired,' Shouji said, 'and my mother stopped playing koto years ago.'

'That's a shame,' Eri said. 'Why?'

'I'm not sure. It feels like something I shouldn't ask. Probably hurt her finger or something.'

'Oh, no. That's unfortunate.' She paused. 'But at least it's better than an old-fashioned excuse, like women shouldn't work. My mother used to be an academic, but after she got married, my grandparents pressured her to quit.'

'What was her field?'

'Mathematics. I guess I take after her. I love working with numerical problems. I remember my mother used to tell me this.' She lowered her voice into a whisper, 'Numbers are magical.'

'Really?'

'You don't believe me?' She laughed and took a sip of her drink. 'You're a writer. Do you feel the same way about language?'

'I'm more of a journalist,' he said. 'Anyway, what I'm trying to say is our family is just an ordinary, middle-class household, nothing special.'

Eri raised her brow. 'Doesn't sound that ordinary to me.'

He shrugged, but then he noticed her dark, prominent eye bags. 'Have you been sleeping well? You look tired.'

'Yeah, a lot of work recently.' She took a deep sigh. 'Ah. Before I forget, my father called yesterday, and I asked about Kazuhiro Katou.'

Shouji straightened up. 'What did he say?'

'He doesn't believe the family influence stretches to Fukuoka. Of course, there are crime syndicates there too, but he doesn't think they're related to the group in Akakawa.' She paused to finish her drink. 'I'm not sure, Shouji. They might be affiliated somehow, or maybe they're rivals. I kind of feel that politics and the underworld are just one tangled mess.'

'Uh-huh.' Perhaps he had been overthinking it. 'I take it that your old man is still healthy, running his bookshop seven days a week?'

'You know him. Retirement doesn't exist in his vocabulary.'

Their conversation topic moved to Eri's family bookshop, which had been passed down from her grandfather, great-grandfather, and great-great-grandfather. The family had been booksellers for generations.

'Business used to be better,' Eri said. 'Nowadays it's in decline. Younger people prefer chain bookshops. Bigger variety, more promotions. Not to mention, these days, everyone has a shorter attention span. Many people prefer to watch television rather than read books. I've told my father to diversify the business. I'm not saying we should start selling buns. I was thinking of stuff like stationery and craft materials, but that old man is stubborn. "We're a bookshop, not a stationery shop," he says. So strongheaded.' She chuckled. 'But that's what I love most about him.'

Shouji imagined a bookshop selling freshly baked bread and cakes. 'Don't you think it might be nice? To have a place where you can sit down and relax, enjoy a cup of coffee and a slice of cake while browsing for books.'

She thought it through. 'Ah, true. It could be a good idea. I should tell him the next time I call, though he'd probably say it's another silly suggestion.'

'Hey, don't jinx it.'

She dismissed him with a laugh.

Shouji gestured towards the kitchen. 'Shall we have our dinner?'

'Of course,' Eri said, getting up. 'I'll check if the food needs heating up.'

Shouji brought their glasses to the dining table while Eri returned with the bucket of chicken and two packets of fries. She also topped up their drinks and brought in two cold hand towels.

He opened the bucket. 'You bought a dozen? Isn't it too much?'

'My mother used to say, when it comes to food, better too much than too little.' She passed the towel to Shouji.

He wiped his hands. 'My mother says the same thing all the time.'

'Maybe that is the motto of all mothers in Fukuoka,' she said. 'Let's dig in.'

There was plenty of meat, all coated nicely and evenly with well-seasoned batter.

In Fukuoka, Shouji hadn't celebrated Christmas. It was only after moving to Tokyo that he started following the KFC Christmas tradition, mostly courtesy of the various girls Jin was seeing. They would usually ask him to join in.

And then Youko had come. He remembered how she'd remarked that Japan was the only country to celebrate Christmas with fried chicken. She had chuckled in amusement. Years had gone by, yet he still missed that laughter.

'Hey, Shouji,' Eri said, tearing the meat with her manicured fingers. 'You didn't ask your friend to come along, did you?'

He was taken aback for a moment. 'How did you know?'

'Just a feeling,' she said. 'You looked stiff when you told me she couldn't come.'

'Sorry, I forgot to ask her, and this afternoon she went out before I got the chance.'

Eri stared into his eyes. 'Did you forget, or did you try to forget?'

'Why would I do that?'

'I don't know,' she said, shrugging. 'Perhaps you don't want me to meet her.'

'Why not?'

'Maybe you don't think I would approve of this arrangement?'

He laughed. 'So now you're my mother?'

'I prefer to think of myself as a smart and beautiful older sister,' she said. 'You're an adult now. You don't need anyone's approval. But if I see something that's not right, I'm going to call you out on it.'

'Like every self-respecting older sister should.'

'That's right,' she said, pausing. 'Are you sure you're not stringing her along?'

The suggestion made him uneasy. He shifted his eyes. 'You're overthinking this. There's really nothing between us. She's just a friend who's short on cash. I'm helping her until she can find a permanent place to stay. That's it.' But even as he said those words aloud, he began to question his feelings.

'Then that's fine. Sorry for assuming.' Eri took a bite of a chicken thigh. 'But don't give her false hope, okay? A clear rejection is way kinder.'

He felt increasingly uncomfortable. 'I know. I never promised her anything.'

'That doesn't mean she isn't expecting something. And try not to lie or hide things. You don't want it to become a habit, or to have to keep on lying to cover up the previous lies.'

'Uh-huh,' he mumbled in agreement, but he wasn't sure if he could ever be fully truthful with anyone. It wasn't that he tried to be deceitful, but there were things he'd rather not talk about.

'It's nice to have dinner together,' Eri said.'When I'm on my own, I usually just make instant noodles.'

'Why don't you come over to my place next Friday? My housemate is a great cook,' Shouji said. But as soon as he said those words, he wondered if it was a good idea. He should have checked with Liyun first.

Eri's eyes lit up. 'I'd love to.'

Too late to retract now. He just hoped it wouldn't be disastrous.

FUKUOKA NEWS

Toddler Drowns in Tragic Accident

26 AUGUST 1980

Fukuoka, Japan. A 23-month-old boy, identified as Ichirou Oda, died when he accidentally fell into a bucket of water at a relatives' house in Minami ward.

According to a source close to the family, Oda was the only child of a widowed Japan Self-Defense Forces officer. The toddler's mother passed away during childbirth. The father and son were visiting a relative who lived nearby when the boy was left unsupervised in the backyard for a short moment. He fell headfirst into the bucket. By the time his relatives found him, it was already too late.

The family performed CPR on the child, but they couldn't revive him. He was subsequently brought to Fukuoka General Hospital and pronounced dead on arrival. The boy's father refused to comment. His son was only one week short of turning two when the incident took place.

Police have ruled out foul play and are treating the case as an accident. They urge parents to be vigilant and not to leave their children unattended.

CHAPTER 22
THE PERSISTENT ONES

Shouji reached home, drenched from the rain. He shook his translucent umbrella and rested it against the wall to dry. Taking his shoes off, he mopped droplets of water off the floor with his socks. Usually, Liyun would greet him before he could reach the door handle, but that night, she didn't. Could it be that she was still cooking? And Eri. He had invited her over but, glancing at his watch, he realised he was more than two hours late.

A fragrant smell greeted Shouji when he opened the door.

'I'm home,' he said aloud.

The apartment was quiet, except for the sound of the television — one of Liyun's bad habits was leaving the television on even though no one was watching. On the screen, a busty young girl tried to convince him that eating a special vanilla pudding would help him to lose weight. *Yeah, right.* He reached for the remote control and turned the television off.

The door to Liyun's room opened.

Eri emerged first. She wore a classic white shirt paired with a sensible grey pencil skirt.

'Finally!' she exclaimed. 'I thought you'd been abducted by aliens.'

'I got caught in the rain.'

'He's always late, rain or shine,' Liyun said, coming out behind Eri. 'We're starving. Why don't you get changed and, after that, we can have dinner together?'

'Ah, yeah,' Shouji mumbled. He looked at Eri. 'I'm sorry you waited so long.'

'Don't worry. I had a nice time talking to Liyun and helping her prepare dinner. She's a great cook.'

'Yes, she's wonderful,' he agreed.

Liyun blushed. 'Tonight is just a simple affair. I whipped it up quickly.'

'Don't be too modest. It's amazing.' Eri turned to Shouji. 'Wait until you see it yourself.'

He laughed. 'Now I'm excited.'

'You're lucky we're not neighbours, otherwise I would come over every night.'

'And we'd pretend to be away,' he said, making his way to his bedroom. 'Back soon.'

When Shouji returned, the table had been set beautifully. Liyun was hovering around, putting down the last pieces of cutlery while Eri poured white wine into three glasses. On the table was a gorgeously plated fish on top of a bed of quinoa shaped like a leaf, garnished with sliced fruit and herbs.

Shouji took one of the seats. 'Anyone care to explain what this is?'

'Eri brought white wine,' Liyun said, 'so I thought we should have fish to complement it.'

Wow, they were already on a first-name basis, Shouji thought.

Liyun gestured to the fish. 'This is pan-fried kinmedai served with herbed quinoa and golden kiwi. I've just used what we had in the fridge.'

He had known that she was excellent at cooking Asian cuisine, but he hadn't expected her to be adept at creating fusion dishes too. 'What's the herb?'

'It's thyme,' Eri chimed in, taking the seat opposite him.

Liyun sat next to her. 'Give it a try.'

'Uh-huh.' Shouji took a cut of the fish and put it in his mouth. The flesh was perfectly tender. And that distinct aroma, could it be … 'Did you use my sake?'

Eri clapped her hands. 'Correct.'

Shouji chuckled, digging his spoon into the quinoa. He took a spoonful. The herbs gave the grains a refreshing sour taste, and the sweet kiwi balanced the flavour so well. 'Liyun, you should open a restaurant.'

'That's what I told her too,' Eri said. 'Such a waste of talent to cook just for you.'

They all laughed.

'Try the wine,' Eri said, leading them in a toast. 'Cheers.'

They clinked their wine glasses. Shouji held the stem, admiring the bright, golden colour. He swirled his wine and took a sniff. The aroma was rich and intense. On the first sip, he tasted honey and preserved fruits. A truly great pairing with the food.

Shouji reached for the bottle to read the label: 1990 Bâtard-Montrachet Grand Cru.

'Don't ask me about it,' Eri said. 'I know nothing about wine.'

He put it back. 'Why did you get this? A recommendation from someone?'

'A date that didn't work out gave it to me. Rather than leaving it in the fridge, I thought I should bring it over so we can enjoy it together. It's not like I can finish the entire bottle by myself.'

'Why not?' Liyun took a sip. 'You could drink it slowly.'

'True,' Eri said, 'but I think wine is better enjoyed together.'

'What happened to your date? Why didn't it work out?' Liyun asked.

Shouji frowned. Wasn't she being a bit too upfront?

Eri shrugged, taking a bite of the fish. 'Perhaps he's too fancy for me. Wine and all that. I'm just an average office worker.' She glanced at Liyun. 'It's good to be young. As you get older, it's more and more challenging to find a decent man to date. Maybe it's time for me to give up.'

'Don't be hard on yourself,' Shouji said. 'You're an amazing woman, Eri. You're smart, independent, and hard-working, even though sometimes you can be harsh and stubborn.'

Eri laughed. 'Hey, are you insulting me?' She averted her eyes, probably out of embarrassment.

Her words reminded him of Youko. She had responded in the same way when he told her he loved everything about her.

After they had finished dinner, Liyun suggested Eri and Shouji finish up the wine while she cleared away. Eri volunteered to help, but Liyun turned her down, saying, 'You're our guest.' While Liyun was in the kitchen, Eri and Shouji settled on the sofa, cradling their glasses.

'Thanks for inviting me over,' she said, drinking her wine. 'Also, for making me feel better just now.'

'Hey, those are my honest thoughts,' he said. 'Any man would be lucky to have you.'

She leaned back on the sofa. 'I usually don't mind being on my own but, from time to time, I long for a companion.'

He poured her the remaining wine, though there wasn't much left.

'My father said I'm too much like him. Too stubborn. Men don't like it,' she continued. 'He said if I were more like my mother, I would have been married with kids. But then, if I were anything like her, I probably wouldn't be working right now.'

'Uh-huh.'

Eri gazed off into the distance. 'I don't want to change for a man. If I were to change, it would have to be for myself.' She finished off her wine and put the empty glass on the table. 'I want to live by my own rules. And if that means I'll be single forever, so be it.'

Shouji gave her arm a gentle pat. 'That sounds like my sister.'

She responded with a chuckle, and then she said, 'Hey, Shouji. Are you avoiding Fukuoka?'

His heart skipped a beat. 'Why do you ask that?'

'My father told me you haven't been back in years, ever since you left to study in Tokyo. I phone him every Thursday and I told him we were meeting. He said your mother came to the bookshop and they chatted, and he was surprised to learn that you've never returned to your hometown.'

Shouji stared at his glass. 'Did he say how she was?'

'Kind of. He said she was all right.' Eri gave a forced smile. 'Just a little lonely and missing her son.'

He downed the rest of his wine.

'I know it's not my place to say this, but your parents are no longer young,' she said. 'Maybe you should visit them sometime.'

'I know,' he mumbled.

Eri stood, about to pick up the empty wine glasses, but Shouji stopped her. 'Let me handle that. You should relax. You're the guest, remember?'

'Wow.' She gave him a playful smile. 'You two are spoiling me.'

'Do you want anything? Coke, water, more alcohol?'

She shook her head. 'I'm good.'

'All right,' he said, carrying the empty bottle with one hand and the wine glasses with another.

When Shouji reached the kitchen, he was surprised to see Liyun standing by the door. She gestured at him to keep quiet as she took the dirty glasses.

'How much did you hear?' Shouji asked in a small voice.

'Let's just pretend I didn't hear anything.' She turned on the tap and rinsed the glasses. 'You said the two of you worked together? You seem close.'

He nodded. 'She took care of me when I was working at her father's bookshop. She's like a big sister, though, back then, she used to be a little cold to everyone. She also introduced me to some books that started my interest in journalism.'

'That's great,' Liyun said. 'She mentioned earlier that you only got in touch recently, but I'm glad you managed to see her before she left.'

Wait. 'What do you mean by "left"?'

Liyun's eyes widened. 'You didn't know? Eri is going to leave Japan.'

CHAPTER 23
THE CAT'S PARADISE

'I told you I can get to the station alone,' Eri protested, clutching her black workbag. 'Didn't I manage to find my way to your apartment?'

'I didn't say you'd get lost,' Shouji said. 'I just thought it would be nice to take a walk after dinner, enjoy the night breeze.'

They strolled through a small, sloping alley, passing low-rise apartments packed close to each other. Now and then, tree branches peeked out above the walls. In the distance, tall buildings stood, surrounded by a dizzying array of city lights.

Eventually, they passed a small playground, partially blocked by a big tree and surrounded by a two-storey house and two apartment blocks. It had a play area with a slide and two climbing frames. On one side, there were four wooden benches. On the other, there was a row of five single-person seats made out of stone. A clock perched atop a lamppost showed that it was quarter past eleven.

'Shall we stop for a while?' Shouji asked.

Eri nodded. 'Sure.'

He led her to one of the benches. They sat side by side, she with her workbag on her lap. Shouji looked up. The moon was full and round but, covered by the cloud, it appeared blurry. He contemplated asking Eri about her impending move, but wondered if it was better if he didn't say anything. She would have told him if she thought it was necessary. Or perhaps she had assumed that he would hear it from Liyun.

Shouji fished out a box of cigarettes from his pocket. 'Do you mind?'

'Erm …' She pressed her lips together. 'I'm allergic to the smoke.'

'Ah, sorry,' he said, putting it back.

'I didn't know you smoked,' she said. 'When did you start? You weren't smoking when you were working in the bookshop, were you?'

'I was, but only if a friend offered me a cigarette. I wouldn't buy them myself.'

'And now?'

'I should cut down, but I've been saying that for a few years.'

They both laughed. The wind blew, stirring the tree branches.

Eri straightened her legs. They were quiet for a moment.

'I heard that you're going to leave Tokyo,' he said eventually.

'Liyun told you?' She glanced at him. 'I kind of expected that to happen. I'm going to New York.'

He turned to her. 'That's far.'

'I know.' She crossed her legs. 'My superiors offered me a good position there. It's a two-year assignment, with a possibility of an extension. I wanted to take it, but I wasn't sure because of my father. I didn't even tell him.' She gazed into the distance. 'But I can't hide things from him. Somehow, he just sensed it. And when I told him what was bothering me, he chided me for being stupid. "Of course you should take it. What are you hesitating for? Don't be silly." I wasn't sure what to say, so I just laughed and cried.'

He looked at her gently. 'Your old man is a good man.'

'I know,' she said. 'I couldn't ask for any better.'

Shouji took a deep breath. 'Well. If this is what you've decided, I wish you all the best in New York.'

'Thank you.' She leaned towards him. 'I'm going to miss my little brother.'

'It's not as if we'll never see each other. As long as we're both alive, we're bound to meet again.'

The corners of her mouth curled up a little. 'That's true.'

'Let me know when you're back in town.'

'I will,' she promised. 'And please contact me if you're coming to New York.'

'Unlikely, but if that happens, you'll be the first to know.' And then a thought came into his mind. 'By any chance, if you ever came across someone named Takeshi Gouda, could you let me know?'

'Takeshi Gouda?' She paused. 'Is he another politician?'

'No, I think he's a teacher. Not a public figure or anything. But please contact me if you happen to hear anything about him.'

'Uh-huh.'

'When are you going to leave?'

Eri shrugged. 'As soon as possible. Maybe in a few weeks.'

'Let me know when you have the date,' he said. 'I'd like to see you off.'

'Please don't. If you do that, I might cry.' She crossed her ankles. 'I'd prefer to go alone.'

'I understand.' He glanced at the clock. It was almost midnight. 'Shall we walk to the station?'

Eri stood, slinging her bag over her shoulder. 'Thanks for accompanying me.'

'I'm glad I insisted,' Shouji said, leading her out of the park. 'I still can't believe you almost left Japan without telling me. A nice older sister you are.'

She laughed at his teasing. 'Come on, don't you think it sounds romantic? To suddenly disappear into thin air, as if everything had been a dream.'

Shouji thought of Youko. 'Not to me.'

They returned to the alley and walked towards the station. The street was empty and quiet.

'Also, about Liyun,' Eri said. 'She's a sweet girl, but she has feelings for you. I don't think you should let her stay unless you plan to develop a romantic relationship with her.'

Ah, finally she had brought it up. 'Did you hear that from her?'

'No,' she said. 'I did ask, and she denied it.'

'Because there's really nothing romantic between us.'

Eri glanced at Shouji. 'Are you sure?'

He shifted. 'We're just friends.' Were they just friends, though? It had started to feel like something more, although not exactly a romantic relationship. 'I'm helping her because she's having a rough time finding a job. I can't just leave her on her own. She's all alone in Japan with no family.'

She sighed. 'Tokyo is a huge city. If you're not picky, you can find a job. She's young and likeable, and she's a good cook. She probably has her reasons.'

'What kind of reasons?' he asked.

'I don't know,' Eri said. 'It could be anything. We can't speculate.'

That was true, but ... 'What do you think I should do?'

'You'll have to decide that yourself.'

She stopped walking. They were about to reach the main street.

'Romantic feelings, unresolved trauma, plain laziness, or whatever it is — we won't know for sure,' Eri said. 'But this arrangement isn't good for either of you, and you know it.'

He said nothing, but his silence could only be interpreted as an admission.

'Talk to her, ask her if there's anything you can do for her.' Her tone was firm. 'As a good friend, you shouldn't encourage this dependency.'

A black cat came out from the shadows, startling them both. It wound between Shouji and Eri. The cat curled up around his feet, and he crouched down to pet it. He rubbed its shiny fur as the cat purred.

'Liyun is like a wandering cat,' Shouji said, 'turning up in front of your door on a rainy day. Seeing it so small, alone and shivering, you can't help but look after it.'

'Fair enough,' Eri said. 'But the rain stopped long ago and you're still feeding her every day. Unless you plan to take care of her foever, you should let her go. The longer the cat stays at your place, the more difficult it will be for her to return to her previous life. Trust me, she has been doing well fending for herself for years, but now you're stripping her of her ability to live as a stray.'

Shouji couldn't say a word. What she had said made sense, but it wasn't that simple.

'Or is there something more to this?' she asked.

He looked at her. 'What do you mean?'

'Is it about the woman you dated before?' She patted his shoulder. 'Shouji, don't use other people to heal yourself. You need to be able to love yourself and thrive on your own first before extending that to others.'

'You're reading too much into it,' he said.

'Then my apologies for being presumptuous.' Eri lowered herself next to Shouji. 'Hey, have you heard of the cats' paradise?'

'No,' he said. 'What's that?'

'My mother told me about it when the stray cat we used to feed disappeared.' Her voice was soothing, and she had a gentle expression on her face. 'According to her, the cats' paradise exists in a completely different dimension from our world. Cats all over the world are drawn to it by an inexplicable force. They'll enter an abandoned house, a hole in a stone wall, or the shadow under a bridge, and then they'll end up in cats' paradise.'

Shouji rubbed the cat's belly.

'My mother said it's a huge, comfortable house,' Eri continued. 'It's warm inside, and the weather outside is always nice. Cats laze and nap all over, in the corridors and in the rooms. There are plenty of cushions on the floor, and even a big kotatsu in the biggest room.'

'A kotatsu?'

'Yes, a heated table covered with a thick, patchwork blanket.' Eri rested her head on her arms, cradling her bag. 'It's so cosy there.'

'Who takes care of them?' he asked. 'Let me guess, a kind old lady?'

Eri shook her head. 'No one. Humans can't enter that space, because it's the cats' paradise.'

'Don't they die of hunger?'

Again, she shook her head. 'They don't get hungry and thirsty, and they don't fight with each other. The cats are always sleepy, napping and lazing around. It's so peaceful.'

'Such bliss,' he murmured.

'And there's no night. It's forever daytime.' She paused, seemingly trying to remember something. 'Or rather, time works differently in that space. These cats spend their days sleeping, losing track of time. It's so comfortable that they don't feel like moving at all.'

'Uh-huh.'

Eri stood. 'That's why, sometimes, cats go missing, only to return after a long time. Perhaps a little scruffy from the journey but, all things considered, they're fine.'

Shouji patted the cat before waving goodbye. 'If this place is so great, why do they still leave? Isn't it better to just stay there forever?'

'It doesn't happen often, but sometimes one of the cats remembers its owners and decides to return. There's no goodbye, no parting words. The cat will walk quietly through one of the doors and make the journey home.' She gestured to the main road. 'Shall we go?'

'Ah, yeah. It's getting late.'

Shouji looked at the stray cat one last time. In turn, it stared at him with its round, blue eyes. A moment later, the cat turned around and disappeared into the shadows.

CHAPTER 24
WHITE CURTAINS, TINY ROSES

When Shouji returned home, Liyun seemed to be asleep in her room, yet she'd left the television in the living room on, as usual. The channel was showing a Hollywood spy thriller. Normally, Shouji would enjoy an action-packed, fast-paced movie, but it was too near the end. Settling on the sofa, he reached for the remote control and turned it off.

The front door opened and Liyun came in, carrying two huge plastic bags from the supermarket.

Shouji raised his eyebrow. 'You went food shopping?'

Liyun nodded, putting down the bags and taking off her shoes. 'This shop discounts the price just before midnight.' She looked at him. 'Is everything okay? Did you get to say a proper farewell to Eri?'

Shouji nodded, getting up to help her. 'Thanks for letting me know.'

'I can handle this on my own.' She gestured at him to stay put.

He returned to the sofa. 'Let me know if you need any help.'

'I'm okay,' she insisted. 'Did Eri tell you where is she going? She only mentioned overseas.'

'She's going to take a job in New York.'

Her eyes widened. 'That's far away. When is she leaving? Are you going to see her off at the airport?'

'She's keen to move soon,' he said, 'but she told me not to see her off.'

186

'I see,' she mumbled. 'Anyway, let me put these away.'

Liyun disappeared into the kitchen. There came sounds of plastic wrappers being torn, the refrigerator opening and closing, and finally, she returned.

'I'm going to sleep,' she said. 'Don't stay up too late.'

She was about to go into her bedroom when he called after her.

'Wait,' he said. He cleared his throat. 'Can we talk for a while?'

She looked at him. 'What about?'

He averted his eyes, feeling increasingly uncomfortable. But he knew he couldn't delay the conversation perpetually. 'How long do you plan to stay here?'

Liyun was silent for a moment then asked, 'Why did you suddenly bring that up? Did Eri tell you to kick me out?' She crossed her arms. 'You haven't brought up the topic for a while, it feels strange to talk about it now.'

'It's not her,' he said quickly, but then he thought of what Eri had told him, about not lying. 'I mean, she did ask me some questions, which got me thinking.' He paused and took a deep breath. 'This is not a permanent solution. We both know that.'

'Are you kicking me out?'

He sighed. 'Liyun, we're friends. I'm not sure what your real reason for staying here is but, as your friend, I want to help you. I want you to be independent. If you need me to help you find work, let me know. If money is an issue, I can lend you some. You can pay it back once you have a stable job.'

She lowered her head. 'I like living here. That's the real reason.'

Hearing that, Shouji was at a loss for words. Both of them were silent.

Eventually, Liyun looked up and said, 'But I understand where you're coming from. I'll pack up tomorrow.'

'Hey, I'm not asking you to move out immediately. Perhaps —'

'It's okay. You've done enough,' she said, cutting him off. 'Good night.'

She went into her room and shut the door.

•

That Saturday, Liyun packed all her belongings. By the time she had almost finished, it was past lunchtime. She had prepared something, but Shouji didn't bother to look to see what it was. He didn't have any appetite. He felt miserable, and the summer heat made it worse. The fan whirled at full speed, blowing nothing but hot air. The buzzing sound resonated in Liyun's half-empty room.

'Where are you going to stay?' Shouji asked.

Liyun shrugged, folding the last few of her clothes. 'Who knows?'

He took all the notes from his wallet and gave them to her.

She chuckled. 'What is this? A parting gift?'

'For the groceries,' he said, well knowing it covered way more than that. 'I'm sorry. I did ask you to find your own place, but you don't need to move out so soon. If you've got nowhere to go yet, you don't need to leave today.'

Liyun shook her head. 'It's all right. I was imposing myself on you. Anyway, it wasn't sudden. You've been asking me for some time.' She looked at him and smiled. 'Keep your money. I don't want it, and I don't need it.'

Feeling uneasy, Shouji put the folded bills back in his wallet. 'Can I see you to the —'

'I'm okay,' she said, her tone firm. 'Don't worry about me. I'll be fine.'

He nodded. She had also turned down his offer to help her pack.

In the end, Shouji could only stand in the corner of the room, watching Liyun pack her belongings into two big suitcases. One was maroon and the other dark grey. They were the same ones she had used when she had come to his apartment eight months ago.

She opened the curtains. The afternoon sun flooded in, washing the tiny room in warm golden hues. A flock of black birds passed by, making loud screeching sounds. She turned to him and their eyes met.

Liyun kept quiet, but Shouji could tell from her unwavering eyes that she wanted him to tell her something. He couldn't find the right words. Eventually, she closed the curtains and dragged her suitcases out. He followed her towards the door.

They stood in front of each other in silence. After a while, Liyun looked up and said, 'You know, I wish we could have been more honest with each other.'

'What do you mean?' he asked.

'I don't know,' she said. 'Somehow, I always feel that you've built an invisible wall around you that no one can get through. Such a pity. I wanted to get to know you.'

He shifted his eyes. 'There's no such thing. You're just imagining it.'

Liyun gave a fleeting smile. She returned the apartment key. 'Take care, Shouji.'

He nodded. 'You too. Call me after you've settled down.'

With those words, they parted ways.

A couple of hours later, Shouji dragged himself to the kitchen and checked what Liyun had left for him. Inside the pot was Japanese curry. Slow-braised beef ribs in herb-infused tomato sauce with carrot, daikon, and potato. The rice cooker was on, keeping the rice warm. He took a plate and scooped a portion. Sitting at the table alone, he thought the kitchen was unbearably silent. He didn't finish his meal, leaving the dirty dishes in the sink for another day.

After that day, Liyun never called Shouji. The only things she left were the white curtains patterned with tiny roses she had bought after she'd moved in with him.

•

For the next couple of weekends, Shouji made it a mission to find the secret spot Liyun had told him about. It took him some time to find the river — five weekends, to be exact.

During his search, Shouji had taken the Namboku Line towards Kita. Whenever he passed a station around a residential area, he would get off and wander around for a couple of hours. He could have found the place sooner if he had checked the map, but he wanted to stumble across it by himself, even if doing so would take him weeks, even months.

Shouji wiped the sweat from his forehead. A black and white cat meowed and ran towards a grass field. Another grey cat followed. Both of them vanished near a crack on the low wall that separated the grass field and a stream. For a moment, he wondered if the crack was one of the portals that led to the cats' paradise.

Looking at the flowing river, Shouji was certain he'd finally found the secret place Liyun had told him about. The setting sun gave off an orange glow and made the water glisten. The wind blew into his face as he walked through the field. When he finally reached the crumbling wall, he stopped and took a deep breath.

He climbed the barrier and sat on the wall, gazing at the stream. The water wasn't deep, but it flowed steadily. He sat still in silence as the night swallowed the sun and its rays disappeared over the horizon. The place became dark, illuminated only by the light that came from the rows of warehouses a distance away. Occasionally, the wind would rustle the wild grass.

As the night went on, the breeze became stronger. Soon, rumbles of thunder sounded. Shouji knew he should make his way back to the station — there was no shelter around — but somehow, he wanted to stay there longer.

He recalled the night he'd spent with Liyun inside the telephone booth. If he ever saw her again, he would tell her how he'd managed to finally find this spot. He missed her cooking and her laughter. He even missed the way she would leave the television on, no matter what he told her. His cheap apartment had been so much warmer with her around. He had no idea where she was, but he hoped she would be fine. She was a smart and talented woman. She should do well wherever she was.

He thought of Mizuki. How was she? Would things be better for her now that her husband was no longer around? He hoped that she could restart her life, that she would have the courage to leave the cage she was trapped in. Someone so kind and compassionate deserved much better.

And then, he thought of Youko, and the run-down apartment in Akakawa they used to share. They didn't have much money, and the building was aged and falling apart, but those days had been the happiest of his life. Many things had not been perfect, but that hadn't mattered. When he was with her, he had felt like he was finally home. If only he could return to that time.

The cold wind continued to caress Shouji as he started to sob under the darkness of the night. It was oddly satisfying to show his weakness, to admit defeat. Yet, at that moment he thought of what he had told Eri. As long as we're both alive, I'm sure we're bound to meet again. He wanted so badly to believe it. For all of them.

Shouji stayed by the river the whole night, listening to the rustling wind, the flowing stream, and occasional rumbles of thunder that never materialised into rain. Eventually, the dawn came, along with the glaring morning sun.

He got up, feeling sore and slightly dizzy. Despite having been awake the whole night, Shouji wasn't sleepy. He walked to the station, realising that his head had started to hurt. Yet he didn't feel like boarding the subway. He walked home, a good four-hour stroll. On his way, he stopped by a convenience store to get a bottle of water and a cup of coffee, which only made his headache worse.

But his steps were lighter, as if he had grown tiny springs in his soles.

ASIA BUSINESS AND FINANCE
MARKET INSIGHTS

Researchers Discover a Mathematical Model to Manage the Risks of Future Financial Crisis in Japan

14 SEPTEMBER 2000

Tokyo, Japan. As new internet technologies show promising returns, the world seems to be heading towards strong economic growth. Yet many economists warn that this bubble could burst, echoing what happened in Japan's real estate and stock markets in early 1992. A team of mathematicians at the University of Tokyo led by Professor Takeshi Gouda has developed a mathematical model of market design that they claim will secure Japan's economic growth and sustainability.

Continued on p. 7

CHAPTER 25
HUNTING THE GIANT

The middle-aged man in the photograph had greying hair. There were wrinkle lines around his eyes and mouth. People probably said he was the fatherly type — a little old-fashioned, but in a good way. How would someone like him sound on the phone?

'His voice was low,' Mizuki had told Shouji. 'I like men with deep voices.'

Mizuki had also said that she had never seen him, yet she had confidently confessed she was in love. She was probably infatuated with her imagined version of him. She'd been lonely in New York. She must have constructed her perfect man and fitted it to him. If Mr Gouda were horrendous looking, would that change anything?

'He's the head of the maths department at the University of Tokyo,' Yoshioka said, leaning against the partition next to Shouji's desk. 'He often travels overseas for seminars.'

Shouji continued to look at the photograph. 'A big shot?'

'In his field, yes.' Yoshioka crossed his arms. 'He used to be based in New York, but he returned to Japan ten years ago, in 1990.'

Shouji's attention shifted to the business card. 'How did you manage to get this?'

'A friend of mine works in academic journals. It was helpful that you told me he could be a mathematics professor. Once I had that information, everything became easier.'

'I'm lucky my friend in New York came across an article about him,' Shouji said, making a mental note to thank Eri. She had called him after coming across his name in a finance magazine. 'But I'm impressed you managed to obtain his business card too.'

'I told you, this job is all about making contacts. It would help you, Arai,' Yoshioka said. 'But if I'd known he was a professor, I could have found this information so much faster.'

'I didn't know either. I thought he was just a teacher.' Shouji turned to Yoshioka. 'Thank you for this. I appreciate it.'

'Don't mention it,' his senior replied, returning to his new desk. Yoshioka had been promoted to Chief Editor the week before.

Shouji stared at the business card in his hand.

Takeshi Gouda

University of Tokyo

Head of Mathematics

Now that he thought about it properly, he had no idea why he'd tracked down the professor. Even Mizuki herself did not know his whereabouts. What was Shouji expecting? But Takeshi Gouda was his last hope. At this point, the professor was the only link he had with Mizuki. Shouji picked up his office phone and dialled the number on the card. After two rings, someone answered.

'Good morning. Professor Gouda's office,' a woman said. 'This is Harada. How may I assist you?'

The minute Shouji heard the voice, he recognised it. He slammed the receiver down without thinking, surprising Yoshioka who sat nearby.

'Is everything okay, Arai?' his senior asked.

'Yes, yes,' he said, straightening up. Calm down. Don't be hasty, but ... Shouji turned to Yoshioka. 'Hey, Chief, can you do me one more small favour?'

'Of course. What do you need?' He grinned. 'But there is no need to call me Chief. Yoshioka is fine. We've known each other for so long.'

At Shouji's request, Yoshioka called Takeshi Gouda's office, pretending to be a reporter hoping to interview the professor on his latest research.

'Professor Gouda is currently in Washington for a conference,' Yoshioka told Shouji after he got off the phone with the professor's secretary, Miss Harada. 'He won't be back until next week. Right now, only his secretary is in his office. I told her we need a high-res-olution photograph of Professor Gouda for our interview, but our office email restricts large attachments. She gave me his office address and invited me to come over anytime during office hours to get the file. She'll save it onto a disk.' Yoshioka passed a piece of paper to Shouji. 'I guess a junior of mine could pick it up on my behalf?'

'Smooth.' Shouji took the paper from him and read the first line. *Mizuki Harada.*

•

Mizuki Harada was as impeccable as she had always been. Her hair was tied into a low bun, not a single strand out of place. The indigo chiffon dress she wore fluttered.

Now that Shouji was so close to the woman he'd thought he would never see again, he had no idea what to say. Where should he begin? 'So, your name is Mizuki.' Yes, he could start with that, but he wasn't ready yet. His heart pounded.

'Harada!'

A woman's sharp voice startled Shouji. A young lady waved, less than a metre away from where he stood. He turned to Mizuki. She was looking in his direction too. If he were to walk away now, would she think that she had mistaken a stranger for him? Unlikely. Anyway, he hadn't come here to observe her from afar.

The young lady walked over to Mizuki and passed her a stack of documents. 'For Professor Gouda. He needs to be able to check through them by the end of the month.'

'Thank you,' Mizuki said. 'I'll make sure he has them in time.'

After the woman left, Mizuki walked over to Shouji. She greeted him with a composed smile and an air of confidence he hadn't seen in her before. 'You should've told me you were coming.'

'I thought you'd like a surprise.'

'That depends on what kind of surprise.' She gestured for him to follow her. 'What brings you here?'

For a moment, he stumbled to find the right words. 'I'm here to collect Professor Gouda's high-resolution photograph.'

'The junior reporter?' She laughed, leading him into a small reception office. 'You can do better than that.'

The room was furnished with two long, white-leather sofas facing each other. A wooden coffee table — complete with mathematics journals and economics magazines stylishly arranged on top — was sandwiched between them.

'Please take a seat,' Mizuki said. 'Can I get you something to drink? Coffee or tea?'

'Just water,' Shouji said. 'You serve water here, don't you?'

Hearing that, Mizuki chuckled. She went into another room and returned shortly with two glasses of water. Shouji reached for one and took a big gulp.

'Let's cut to the chase, shall we?' She took a seat across from him. 'Are you going to tell me why you're here? It's been five years.'

'I've always wanted to see you again,' he said.

She looked into his eyes.

'But it wasn't easy after what happened,' he continued, clenching his fists. 'Everything was my fault. I owe you an apology.'

'For talking about my late husband to that bogus freelance reporter?'

Shouji lowered his head. 'I'm sorry. I was so naïve. I wasn't thinking properly.'

Mizuki shook her head. 'Please, don't be.'

He raised his head. She had a serene expression on her face.

'You did the right thing,' she said. 'The result might not have been what you intended, but you had my best interests at heart.'

'Can you forgive me?'

She smiled. 'There is nothing to forgive. I'm in a much better place right now.'

Hearing that, he felt so relieved, as if a heavy burden he had been carrying had finally been lifted. 'I'm glad to hear that, and I'm so happy for you, Mizuki.' He thought for a while. 'About your late husband ...'

She bit her lip. 'You probably heard. He passed away not long after you left Akakawa. Murdered in a karaoke joint he used to frequent, inside the VIP bathroom.'

Even though Yoshioka had mentioned the suspicion surrounding his death, hearing it directly from Mizuki still shocked him.

'It was gruesome, like a scene from a budget horror movie. His bodyguards were shot, but he was drowned. His head forcefully submerged in a toilet bowl.' She paused, lacing her fingers together. 'They could've shot him like the rest, but they didn't. They wanted him to die slowly and in agony. They took pleasure in watching him struggle in vain.' She lowered her head. 'I heard that he soiled himself.'

An image of Mr Katou flashed into Shouji's mind. His eyes bulged out and his mouth gaped as if he were still screaming for help. His body had turned cold and stiff, his complexion had lost its vitality. Bodily fluids wetted his trousers.

'The police never caught the murderers,' Mizuki said. 'We more or less knew it was the work of one of his business rivals. The problem is, there are so many of them, it's hard to pinpoint who did it.' She bit her lip. 'For the first time in my life, I pitied him.'

'It must have been difficult for you.'

She stared off into the distance. 'Even though we didn't love each other.'

'Then why were you with him?'

'Fate, perhaps?' Her voice was small. 'I suppose he was fond of me. Otherwise, he wouldn't have agreed to the marriage. But it was a business transaction. My family are well respected in the community.'

'You should've left him a long time ago. You've suffered too much.'

Mizuki went quiet and stared at her fingers. The silence made Shouji uneasy. Through the glass behind her, he saw a group of students walk past, chattering with each other and bursting into laughter.

'Everything is fine now,' she eventually said, 'I don't dwell on the past.'

Shouji nodded, realising too late he had reopened an old wound. 'I'm glad you finally found your Giant.'

Her face lit up. 'You know about that too.'

'He's the reason I managed to find you.'

'What are you?' she said, laughing. 'A private detective?'

Her remark flustered him. 'No, nothing like that.' He paused. 'I'm a journalist now.' Though it would be nice if he could afford to hire a private detective.

'That's great,' Mizuki said, nodding a few times. 'That was what you wanted to do?'

'Yeah. Kind of,' Shouji said. 'So, you're his secretary, and the professor's wife?'

'The professor's wife?' Mizuki chuckled. 'No, you're mistaken. I'm not married to Professor Gouda. I'm just his secretary.'

'Ah, I see,' Shouji murmured, unsure of what to say. 'But that can't be a coincidence.'

She reached for her glass and took a sip of water. 'It's a long story.'

'Why don't you tell me?' he said.

'Just like old times?' Mizuki returned his gaze. 'Well, if you insist.'

CHAPTER 26
MIZUKI HARADA

After her husband died, Mizuki Harada returned to her parents' house in Akakawa. She spent most of her time at home, avoiding social functions, which was expected of a grieving widow. But when a year had passed and Mizuki was still confining herself at home, her parents started to question her.

'What are you planning to do?' her mother asked.

Mizuki averted her eyes. She didn't know how to answer.

'What about remarrying? I'll ask your father to arrange an introduction.'

She forced a smile. 'I appreciate that but, at my age, it will be hard to find a good match.'

The older woman sighed.

Mizuki reached for her mother's hands. 'I've been thinking of going back to study, perhaps in Tokyo. I'd like to take some secretarial courses.'

Her mother looked at her. 'Is that what you really want?'

Mizuki nodded. She wasn't sure if that was what she wanted, but she didn't want her parents to be worried, and she couldn't stay in the family home indefinitely. Leaving Akakawa would be a good decision.

•

'And that was how you found your Giant?' Shouji asked.

'That's right, but not until I'd been in Tokyo for a couple of years,' Mizuki said. 'After I completed my course, I worked as an administrative officer for a small printing firm, which happened to print scientific and mathematical journals.'

He glanced at the magazines on top of the table. 'And you saw an article by Professor Gouda?'

'Close.' She indicated a small gap between her thumb and fore-finger. 'It was an advertisement for a conference. He was listed as one of the speakers. Just one line, and there was no photograph of him either. I only glimpsed it by pure luck.'

'Even if there had been a photograph, you wouldn't have been able to tell whether it was him.'

She nodded. 'Good point.'

'But I doubt anyone else would have the same name.'

'Which was why I was sure it was him.'

•

Mizuki had gone to the conference, hoping she would finally find the man she'd spoken with so many times in New York. The seminar was held in a packed auditorium at the University of Tokyo. Most of the audience looked like they were undergraduates. Among the sea of people, Mizuki waited nervously while the moderator introduced the speakers one by one.

Professor Gouda looked like an ordinary middle-aged man. He wore a tailored dark suit over a crisp, white shirt. When the moder-ator called his name, the professor bowed. The man seemed kind, and Mizuki felt a sense of familiarity. Her optimism increased. She was almost sure he was the one she'd been looking for.

Her heart raced as the speakers took turns presenting their papers. She held her breath when Professor Gouda took the central podium. He inched closer to the microphone. He opened his mouth to speak, and then, everything became clear.

•

The face of the woman in front of Shouji lit up.

'I knew for sure he was the one,' she said. 'His voice ... there was no way I would get it wrong. It was slightly different from on the phone, but it was him. I knew it was him.'

•

After the seminar, Mizuki had gathered her courage to speak to Professor Gouda, but she had not been the only one. Others had wanted to talk to him too: academics looking for intellectual debate, students with questions. Some of them bought his books and asked for an autograph.

•

'He wrote books too?' Shouji asked Mizuki.

'Quite a number,' she said. 'They're mainly reference texts, not widely available in bookshops.'

'Uh-huh.' What an accomplished man.

•

Mizuki had waited for the others to finish their business with Professor Gouda, but everyone had been so enthusiastic. Time dragged. She started to worry he would brush everyone off and leave.

Or, what if he had forgotten all about her? Twenty years had passed. No matter how she looked at it, she was only a telemarketer who'd happened to canvass him when he'd been working in New York. They didn't exactly know each other. Perhaps she should leave.

After more or less everyone was gone, Professor Gouda came over to Mizuki.

'Miss, is there something I can do for you?' he asked. 'You seem to be waiting for me, but my apologies if I've made the wrong assumption.'

Mizuki was struck by his sincerity. She'd had a lot of things she wanted to tell him, but now, face to face with the man himself, she was at a loss for words. After a long silence, she asked him, 'Do you know who I am?'

He looked at her with a warm smile. 'You're the girl who kept asking me to sign up for a credit card.'

Hearing that, all her worries vanished.

'It's been a long time,' he continued. 'What are you doing in Tokyo?' Before she could answer, he glanced at his watch. 'I've got some time before my next engagement. Say, would you like to go for a cup of coffee?'

•

'I told him my parents asked me to return to Japan to get married,' Mizuki said. 'After my husband passed away, I moved to Tokyo to take a secretarial course and find a job here. The rest is what I've told you already, about how I saw his name in the journal.'

Shouji nodded. 'Don't you think it was amazing how you managed to find him?'

'Yes,' she said. 'It was unbelievable.'

•

Professor Gouda led Mizuki to a café a ten-minute walk from the university. Decorated with fresh flowers and fairy lights, the place was cosy and inviting, yet not too crowded. Apart from them, there were only two small groups of students.

'What would you like?' Professor Gouda passed Mizuki the menu.

She glanced at the list. Most of the items were coffee-based, but she wasn't a coffee drinker.

'I'm going to order hot chocolate,' he said, seemingly reading her mind. 'Would you like the same?'

She nodded, and he went to the counter.

Professor Gouda was exactly how she had imagined him — friendly and considerate. He might not have been particularly good-looking, but he was warm. He returned to their table, balancing two mugs of hot chocolate in one hand, and a platter of mini sandwiches in another.

'Small bites for sharing.' He put everything on the table. 'Let me know if there's anything else you'd like.'

She shook her head. 'This is fine.'

He took a seat in front of her.

'You finally returned to Japan,' she said.

He nodded. 'Yes, my son and I.'

Mizuki tried not to flinch. For someone his age with a respectable job, it was only natural he was a family man.

'I like it here,' he continued. 'I don't need to wake up early to prepare breakfast. Around my house, there are lots of supermarkets and convenience stores I can buy cooked food from. In the past, I always did the cooking. I never got used to American food. I guess I'm a Japanese man through and through.'

'What about your wife?' Mizuki asked in a small voice. 'Doesn't she cook?'

'Ah, my wife ...' He paused. 'She's no longer around.'

Mizuki averted her eyes. 'I'm sorry to hear that.'

'I mean, she's still alive. We got divorced and she remarried.' Professor Gouda reached for his drink and took a sip. 'The hot chocolate in this café is good. They use real chocolate. Drink it before it gets cold.'

Mizuki did as he said.

'Did you find a job in Tokyo?' he asked.

'Yes.' She decided to push her luck. 'But I've been thinking of quitting. The hours are too long.' That was only partly true. Even though Mizuki worked until late every day, it was never an issue. She didn't have anything to do at home and liked the extra income.

•

'And the gamble paid off,' Shouji commented.

'His secretary was expecting, so he needed maternity cover,' Mizuki said. 'He warned me it wouldn't be a permanent position, but I agreed to take it. As luck would have it, once the baby was born, my predecessor decided she no longer wanted to work. I took over her position.'

'Everything worked out in your favour.'

'You could say that.' She sipped her drink. 'But if you think that we're together, then you're mistaken. I support him professionally as his secretary, and personally as his friend. There is no romantic relationship between us.'

He found it hard to believe. 'Aren't you in love with him?'

'Yes, but there is only one woman in his life — his ex-wife,' she said with a rueful smile. 'What about you, Shouji?'

He thought of Youko. Memories he had tried so hard to bury started to resurface. 'You know my girlfriend disappeared, don't you? Your late husband hunted us down.' His happiness at finding Mizuki began to dissipate as he remembered how he had failed Youko.

'Her name is Sasaki, isn't it?' Mizuki's voice was gentle.

'That's right.' He didn't think he had ever told her Youko's name.

'I heard what happened, but I couldn't do anything. I blamed myself for it, especially since everything you did was to help me. I'm sorry for dragging you and her into my mess.'

He hadn't expected her to say that. 'Please don't. It wasn't your fault. I should be the one apologising. What I did was my decision, so the blame is all mine.'

Mizuki bit her lip. 'You make me feel worse, saying that.'

'That wasn't my intention.'

'But when it comes to Miss Sasaki, I might have an idea of what happened.'

Shouji tensed. How could that be possible? As far as he knew, the two of them were strangers.

Mizuki looked into his eyes. 'You're still in love with her, aren't you?'

He returned her stare. 'Do you know where she is?'

'Not exactly, but what I found might be of interest,' she said. 'Unfortunately, I don't have it here. Will you be able to come again tomorrow? Say, ten in the morning?'

•

That night, Shouji couldn't sleep. He kept thinking about what Mizuki had told him. She knew something about Youko. Could it be that Youko was unwell? The image of her motionless body lying in a white hospital bed sent shivers down his spine. Or what if she had been left somewhere to die?

These thoughts continued to run wild in his mind until the sunlight seeped through the white curtains. When had it become morning? Shouji hadn't had any sleep. He got up and went to shower.

Mizuki probably noticed the dark rings under his eyes, but she didn't say anything. Perhaps she was being polite. Escorting Shouji into the same office, she asked, 'What do you want to drink?'

'Coffee, please.' He needed his caffeine fix.

She went into another room. He heard the sound of a coffee grinder. The office was fancy for an academic. Resting his back on the sofa, Shouji closed his eyes in an attempt to catch some rest. A rich, nutty aroma wafted into the room, awakening his senses. It reminded him of something, but he couldn't remember what.

In the distance, the chatter of passers-by grew louder. Sunlight shone into the room, warming him up.

'Sorry to keep you waiting.' Mizuki put a cup of coffee and a glass of water on the table. 'Is the sun too bright? Should I close the blinds?'

'I'm fine.'

Mizuki sat in front of Shouji and adjusted her hair. This time, she had it down, held back from her face by a blue flower pin. Wearing a white blouse paired with a beige wool skirt, she looked more down to earth than he'd remembered.

'Excuse me for being direct,' Shouji began. 'You told me you knew something about Youko.'

'Yes, the file is in front of you.'

She gestured to a blue folder on the table, on top of a pile of mathematical journals. A yellow Post-it note with 'for Shouji Arai' in neat handwriting was stuck on it. How could he have missed it? He was so tired and disorientated.

'May I?' Shouji asked.

'Please do,' Mizuki said, reaching for her glass of water. 'It's a report done by a private detective I hired after my husband passed away.'

'Why would you do that?'

She paused. 'I wanted to do something for you.'

'Your husband's family let you investigate?'

'Nobody knows. I commissioned the detective myself,' she said. 'My husband and I had no children, so after he died his family took care of his affairs. I got a decent settlement and was left on my own. No one pays attention to what I do, as long as I keep quiet.'

Shouji opened the file and saw an enlarged close-up photograph of Youko, alongside her name, age, height, and weight. Underneath the page were various pixellated printouts taken from security cameras. Youko wore a white sweater and jeans. She carried a huge rucksack as if she were going on a long backpacking trip. He examined the pictures closely. The place looked familiar.

'Is this Narita airport?' Shouji asked.

'That's right,' Mizuki said. 'We're lucky the airport kept their footage for so long. Security reasons, I suppose.'

'Uh-huh. Where did she go?'

Mizuki pursed her lips. 'I've no idea.'

'When were these photographs taken?'

'The same week my late husband found out what had happened,' Mizuki said. 'Four days after the fire.'

Shouji paused. 'She knew something was going to happen.'

'She must have got wind of it somehow and hastily packed up.'

'I don't understand …' He stared at the printouts again. No doubt about it, the woman in the picture was Youko. 'Who told her?' Could it be the mysterious man he spoke with on the phone? 'Why did she leave without telling me? If I hadn't been out, I could have been burned alive in that building.'

Mizuki bit her lip. 'I'm not trying to justify the fire, but it wasn't meant to take any lives. It was a warning. Were you aware that there were zero casualties?'

Shouji nodded, remembering what Uncle Hidetoshi had told him. 'Kind of.'

'That's good. I thought you didn't know, since you disappeared on the same day. Wise choice. Youko must have had her reasons to do the same.'

Shouji thought for a moment. 'But if you could track Youko down, wouldn't it have been easy for you to find me? I wasn't exactly hiding.'

'That's true, but …' Mizuki appeared to be hesitating. 'According to the report I received, it seemed like you were trying to rebuild your life with a new girlfriend, and I didn't want to interfere.'

'I see.' The detective must have seen him with Liyun and mistaken the nature of their relationship. Anyway, that was irrelevant now. Pointing out otherwise would only make Mizuki felt bad.

Shouji turned his attention back to the printouts. Behind the photographs, there was a photocopy of Youko's passport. She had short, cropped hair and gave off a slightly different vibe to what he remembered, but the woman in the photograph was unmistakably her.

'Youko Sasaki,' he mumbled her name. But something wasn't right.

'We don't know if she went overseas, but we can't discount the possibility,' Mizuki said.

Shouji continued to stare at Youko's passport. Should he tell Mizuki? No, he would only confuse her further. 'Is there anything else I need to know?'

She shook her head. 'That's about it.'

He closed the folder. There were so many questions in his mind. 'Are you okay?'

Shouji nodded. 'Yeah,' he said, trying to dissipate the tension that had been building between them. 'I'm glad you trusted me with your real name. Mizuki is your real name, isn't it?'

'It is. I didn't expect you to suggest it.' Mizuki gave him a feeble smile. 'I guess I can't run away from who I am, no matter how much I detest it.'

'Why don't you like your name?'

Instead of answering, Mizuki went quiet. She looked into the distance.

'I used to have a twin sister,' she eventually said. 'Her name was Umi. She was named after the character for sea, and I was named after the character for water. Our mother chose them because she loves swimming. My sister was one minute younger than me.'

Why was she talking about her sister? But Shouji decided to play along. 'Where is she now?'

'She's dead, drowned in a pool,' Mizuki said. 'And I was the one who killed her.'

CHAPTER 27
THE WATER AND THE SEA

Mizuki and Umi had been inseparable since they were small. Their parents were busy running the family businesses, so they spent all their time in each other's company.

'Even after we entered high school, we were close,' Mizuki said. 'Our boyfriends were good friends. The four of us always hung out after school.'

Shouji reached for his coffee and took his first sip.

'As you know, there's not much to do in Akakawa. But back then, it was even worse. We only had a cinema, a small shopping mall, a public library, and a few karaoke joints. Bars were strict about not allowing high school students in, especially when we were in school uniform.'

'Uh-huh.'

'My family ran a public swimming pool. Once a week, it was closed for maintenance, but my sister and I had secretly made a duplicate key. By the time school was over, the cleaner would've left the premises. My sister and I, and our boyfriends, would discreetly slip in and have the entire pool to ourselves.'

Mizuki closed her eyes, remembering. Shouji pictured her with three other high school students, laughing and shoving each other.

•

The young Mizuki in her school uniform inserted an oversized key into a big lock. The door opened with a creak. Four teenagers entered. The swimming pool building was empty. The air was tepid, and the smell of chlorine lingered. White tiles gleamed in the warm afternoon sun that filtered in through the glass windows. The pool water glistened, translucent and still.

The four of them wasted no time. They dropped their school bags and took their shoes and socks off. The boys rolled up their trousers and the girls tied up their hair. Sitting by the edge of the pool, they dipped their bare feet into the cold water.

●

'We loved spending time there,' Mizuki continued. 'Umi, especially, loved the pool. Sometimes she would get into the water, even in her uniform. She'd jump in and sink to the bottom, curling herself in and wrapping her arms around her knees, like a foetus. She could stay in that position for a long time.'

'What about you?'

Mizuki shook her head. 'I couldn't swim that well.'

●

One afternoon, the four of them had gone to the swimming pool as usual. But on that day, Umi wasn't her usual self. Her head hung low and she was quiet.

'What's happened?' Umi's boyfriend whispered to Mizuki.

Mizuki shook her head. 'I don't know. She's been like that since class was over.' She remembered that, earlier, they'd received their mock exam results. 'Maybe she failed the test.'

'Really?'

She shrugged. She wasn't sure either, but it was unusual for Umi to look gloomy. She wondered what she could do to cheer up her sister.

Mizuki signalled to the rest to keep quiet. She tiptoed towards Umi, who was sitting on the ledge of the pool. The two boys understood her intention. They slowly inched over to Umi from behind and, together, they pushed her into the water.

The water splashed as Umi plunged into the pool. The three of them laughed.

Umi kept on trying to raise her head, but they pushed her down into the water. They knew she was a good swimmer. She could hold her breath for a long time. They had counted a couple of times, and she could stay underwater for almost four minutes. All of them remembered that, so they laughed and dunked her head.

One of the boys — Mizuki couldn't remember which — started singing a Happy Birthday song. The rest of them joined in. Umi continued to struggle in the pool as they merrily sang the song.

> *Today is a happy day,*
> *Today is a pleasant day.*
> *Happy birthday to you,*
> *Let's sing a song.*

> *Today is a happy day,*
> *Today is a pleasant day.*
> *Happy birthday to you,*
> *Let's sing a song.*

'One more time!' someone shouted. 'Let's make today her birthday.' They laughed, and then they sang again, from start to finish. On that balmy afternoon, the three high school students in their navy school uniforms sang the Happy Birthday song three times at the top of their lungs.

•

Mizuki laced her fingers together. She stared at them for a long time, biting her lower lip. The silence filled Professor Gouda's stylish office. Shouji hesitated. Should he tell her not to force herself if she didn't want to talk about the incident? But she'd probably waited for a long time to have someone listen to her story, to share the burden she'd been keeping deep inside her all this time.

'What happened after that?' Shouji eventually asked.

Mizuki lifted her face. Her eyes were watery. 'That day, my sister wasn't feeling well. We caught her by surprise. She didn't have time to take a deep breath before we pushed her in. Not knowing she was struggling for her life, we continued to hold her down until ...'

No, this was too hard for her ... Shouji looked into Mizuki's eyes. 'Are you all right?'

She nodded and mouthed, 'I'm fine.'

'It was an accident,' he said. 'Nobody wanted it to happen.'

'The three of us killed her, and it was me who started it. The prank was my idea. I was the one who wanted to push her into the swimming pool. We only stopped when she was no longer moving.'

Shouji thought Mizuki was going to break down and cry, but she didn't. She managed to keep her composure, but he could see from her stiff posture that she was hurting inside.

•

Realising what had happened, the teenagers stared at each other, frozen. No one said a word until one of the boys pulled Umi from the water. She was motionless. He laid Umi on the ground and brought his finger near her nose. A moment later, he turned to Mizuki. His face was pale.

'She's dead,' he said in a small voice.

Mizuki felt a jab in her stomach. She stared blankly at Umi, who lay on top of the glazed tiles. Her white underwear showed through her drenched uniform. A tiny pink ribbon was sewn on the bridge of her bra.

The three teenagers were still, looking at the motionless body in front of them. Time seemed to stop as the pool surface glistened. A trail of water gleamed on the freshly scrubbed floor and a ragged mop was propped against the wall.

•

Mizuki stood up. Looking out of the window, she brushed her hair behind her ear, even though there was not a single strand out of place.

•

Everyone was silent until someone asked, 'Is that blood?'

The water around Umi's legs had started to turn red. They turned to each other. No one knew what to do. And then, all of a sudden, one of the boys — Umi's boyfriend — lunged forward and tore her shirt.

'What are you doing?' Mizuki shouted.

He glared at her. 'Can't you tell? I'm trying to make this look like a robbery.'

She went quiet, dumbfounded.

'Stop giving me that look. Do you want to be tried for murder?' He turned to the other boy. 'Get Umi's bag and take out her wallet.'

The other boy did as instructed.

'Mizuki, you keep a look-out in case anyone comes.'

But she was unable to move. She just stood and watched the scene unfolding in front of her. To make the robbery scenario more convincing, the boys slammed Umi's head on the pool edge a couple of times. All the while, Mizuki remained rooted to the ground. The noises around her grew faint and distant.

For a moment, she felt as if she had been removed to another dimension. She was on her sofa in her living room, watching the gruesome scene on the television. Next to her, Umi was munching a pack of seaweed-flavoured Calbee Potato Chips.

'What are they doing?' Umi sneered. 'Those kids are crazy, aren't they?'

Mizuki didn't respond. She was too fixated on the screen.

Umi reached for the remote control. 'I don't like this show. Let's watch something else.'

•

Mizuki turned to Shouji.

'I was in a daze. They had to pull me out of the building. All of us went to a nearby river. The boys dropped the duplicate key and Umi's wallet into a black plastic bag. They filled the bag with rocks and threw it into the water.' She stood and looked out of the window. 'I don't remember how I got home. Everything was hazy.'

Shouji kept quiet.

'Do you know how long it takes to lose consciousness under water?'

He didn't answer.

'As little as two minutes,' Mizuki said. 'In four to six minutes of drowning, a person can sustain permanent brain damage.' Her fingers grazed the window frame. 'By contrast, a human can hold their breath for more than five minutes. Interesting, isn't it? The key is preparation. Breathe slowly for several minutes and, before you dive in, take a deep breath.'

'Mizuki ...'

'Don't you think it's strange? It didn't occur to us to try to revive her,' she said. 'I kept thinking about that afternoon, even months after. Umi could have fainted. I tried singing Happy Birthday three times and timed it. Even adding in the time between the songs, it should only take about two to three minutes. She wasn't dead when we pulled her out of the pool. My sister might still be around if we had called the paramedics instead of trying to cover up our foolish act.'

'You were in a panic. She wasn't breathing, was she? Anyone would've thought she was dead, and then the survival instinct kicked in.'

Mizuki shook her head. 'No matter what, we killed her. That's a fact. Let's not gloss over it.' She returned to her seat. 'We could've saved my sister if we hadn't tried desperately to save ourselves first. We decided to sacrifice Umi. We chose to live in denial, but her death continued to echo in our lives.'

Shouji felt a lump in his throat. None of them had wanted the accident to happen, but the reality was that a life had been lost.

But something about the story was strange. 'You said your sister was bleeding, didn't you? That shouldn't happen if she had drowned and fainted.'

'About that ...' Mizuki paused. 'It's a woman's thing, you know.'

He hesitated. 'Was she menstruating?'

'Yes, she got her first period ahead of me. That was probably what had made her upset. Umi hated growing up. She had always been slightly bigger than me. She was taller and her breasts were more developed. I used to be jealous of her.' Mizuki turned to Shouji. 'It's silly. We're always dissatisfied with ourselves.'

'Uh-huh. What happened to the other two?'

'We never spoke to each other after the accident,' she said, 'but I still saw them around, since we were schoolmates. My sister's boyfriend was the star of the basketball club. After Umi's death, he quit the team and became a delinquent. Less than a year later he died in a freak accident. He got drunk and fell from a high-rise building. But who knows?'

'You might be overthinking it.'

'Possibly,' Mizuki said. 'The other boy was an average guy. He disappeared. He'd never been remarkable, other than the fact that he was Umi's boyfriend's best friend.'

'There are people like that in every school.' Shouji had been one of them. In university, everyone had known him because he was Jin's flatmate. But most of them, especially the girls, had never learned his name. He had always been 'the guy who shares a place with Jin'.

'Umi's death changed everything,' Mizuki said. 'It was hard to live with the thought of killing my sister and never paying the price for it. We successfully fabricated the whole incident. The police concluded it was a robbery gone wrong.'

'I see.'

'After my sister's death, my parents closed the swimming pool. Nobody wanted to go there, knowing what had happened. The news was all over the local papers.'

'A lot of people are superstitious.'

'Uh-huh. Especially in a small town like Akakawa.'

•

A few months later, Mizuki learned that her former boyfriend had relocated to another city because of his father's work. No one knew where. Mizuki never heard from him again.

Being the only one left in Akakawa, she decided to confess to her parents what had happened. But when she told them she'd like to give herself up to the police, they were against it.

'We've already lost Umi,' her mother said, sobbing. 'We can't lose you too.'

•

'My parents were adamant no one should learn the truth. They decided to send me to study in Tokyo,' Mizuki said. 'But even after I left Akakawa, I continued to be haunted by my sister's death. I wasn't interested in studying. I was on my own all the time. I kept losing weight and falling ill. Thinking a more drastic change of scenery might do me good, my parents pulled me out of college and sent me to my aunt in New York.'

'And that's how you met Professor Gouda,' Shouji said.

'That's right. Talking to him encouraged me. I started to look forward to life like I used to.' She looked into his eyes. 'Are you surprised? Now you know, I'm not the innocent victim you pictured me to be.'

'All of us make wrong decisions at some point,' he said. Could this be the reason she had tolerated her husband's violence? Had she taken his abuse as her punishment for letting her sister die? He felt a beat of understanding. 'What's important is not to let those decisions ruin our lives. No matter what, everyone has the right to try their best to be happy, as long as it doesn't hurt others.'

Mizuki straightened her legs. 'What about you, Shouji? Are you happy now?'

Her question caught him off guard. Happy? Was he happy? He wasn't sure, but ... 'I guess I'm satisfied.'

'Satisfied ...' she repeated after him softly, before falling into silence.

He stared at the glass of water on the table. 'Now I understand why you said you hated your name.'

She nodded. 'Ironic, isn't it?'

'A lot of things in life are ironic,' Shouji said, recalling that he'd moved to Akakawa to be with Youko, only to end up losing her. 'Why did you return to Akakawa?'

'I couldn't stay in New York indefinitely. It was supposed to be temporary. I needed to carry on the family traditions.'

'Marrying for business.'

'You could say that, but it's a duty that women in a lot of families like mine have been fulfilling for generations. It's not a bad idea. If not for my parents' intervention, I would've remained unmarried my entire life.'

Shouji shook his head. 'There is nothing wrong with being single. Having an abusive partner is much worse.'

'My parents didn't know that. As far as they were concerned, they married off their only daughter to a successful man from an established family. My wellbeing was guaranteed for life.'

'Your misery was guaranteed for life,' he corrected.

'Then what do you suggest? Marrying for love?' She shook her head. 'Not everyone has that option.'

Shouji sighed. 'I don't know, Mizuki. I've never been married. But if I do marry, I hope it's to someone I love.'

'Do you even know what love is?'

'I can't say a hundred per cent for now, but I intend to find out.'

'Good for you.' She looked at him. 'You're always so earnest, aren't you?'

Shouji took another sip of his coffee. Mizuki always saw the best in him, but who was he kidding? He'd tried to reassure her, but his own life was a mess. He glanced at the clock on the wall. An hour and a half had passed. He'd asked for some urgent time off, but he should probably return to the office soon.

'I have to go now,' he said. 'Thank you for the information. I appreciate it.'

She stood. 'Don't mention it. I should be the one thanking you for making your way down here. You have no idea how glad I am to see you well.'

'Me too. It's good to see you again.'

Mizuki offered to escort Shouji off campus, but he told her not to bother. She did, however, follow him out of the office building. While she walked him down the staircase, she pointed out a shrub near the entrance.

'Do you know what kind of plant that is?' she asked.

Shouji looked at the green leaves. 'I don't think so. Tell me.'

'They're hydrangeas,' she said. 'They change colour depending on the soil they grow in.'

He nodded, remembering that his mother had told him that.

'My friend once said that hydrangeas reminded her of how people can change, depending on the situation,' she continued. 'But I think hydrangeas also speak of grit and perseverance. Something that constantly learns and adjusts, and can survive challenges and the test of time.' She paused and looked at Shouji with a gentle smile. 'An enduring love, perhaps.'

They bade each other farewell. For a moment, he remembered those days in Akakawa when he would see her off after their listening sessions. Looking at Mizuki, Shouji felt so proud of her now.

Clutching the folder, he walked back towards the main gate. The stream of students never seemed to cease. Amid lush greenery, the sunlight felt a little brighter and warmer than usual.

This place seemed like a good environment for Mizuki Harada to rebuild her life. What had happened to her twin sister was an unfortunate accident. But hopefully, one day, she would stop blaming herself and find her inner peace.

Now that he was away from Mizuki's sight, Shouji opened the folder and looked at the copy of Youko's passport. Her name was Youko Sasaki, as she had told him, but it was *you* for ocean, and *ko* for child.

The ocean's child.

His mind wandered to the second time he had met her, at the campus cafeteria. On that day, she'd worn a chic faded denim dress. And she'd told him her name, Youko, after the characters for sunshine and child. Why would she lie?

CHAPTER 28
LIKE A MILD TOKYO EARTHQUAKE

Shouji rummaged in his pocket and retrieved his key. The door made a screeching sound as he pushed it open. One of these days, he ought to oil the hinges.

Dropping his bag on the floor, he threw himself onto the sofa. He fished out a cigarette, lit it, and took a deep puff. The white smoke danced around the room. He felt a little more relaxed looking at it. After meeting Mizuki, he'd been so busy at the office he hadn't had the chance to go for a cigarette break all day.

Shouji put his legs up on the sofa and rested his head on its arm. The dark patches on the ceiling from the leaking roof had grown. This place was getting old. He, too, was getting old.

One of the main reasons Shouji had rented this apartment was because the place was dirt cheap, probably because the building was located next to the railway tracks. When he had first moved in, he had been nervous about the lack of a smoke alarm. But after a while, he welcomed the convenience of being able to smoke inside his apartment. It was the first and only place he'd lived in after leaving Akakawa.

Five years later, he still lived here. The flowered curtains Liyun had bought still hung at the windows, discoloured from years of exposure to the sun.

Shouji stubbed his cigarette out and went to the fridge. He

reached for a carton of milk. When he unscrewed the cap, a rancid smell escaped. The rubbish bin in the kitchen was full to the brim. He poured the milk down the sink and used the carton to prod the piled-up junk until there was a little room and it would fit.

On his way to bed, he glanced at the living room. Books and magazines were strewn all over the floor. A pot with a withered plant full of cigarette butts stood alone on the balcony. Opening his bedroom door, he saw a mountain of crumpled clothes waiting to be ironed covering his bed. Had he always been this messy? Well, he had no incentive to keep the house tidy. He hardly had any visitors.

Shouji dropped onto the bed. He ought to tidy this place up.

Before long, he fell asleep and dreamed of Youko.

In his dream, they were back in their bedroom in Akakawa. He was lying on their bed, and she was getting dressed next to him. She tied her hair up in a high ponytail and put on a white Adidas baseball cap.

'Where are you going?' Shouji asked.

'Shinagawa Aquarium.' Youko grabbed a black canvas rucksack. 'I won't be joining you for dinner.'

'What about work?'

She leaned closer and kissed him. 'Today is my day off.'

He frowned. 'Isn't it a pain to travel to Tokyo just to visit an aquarium?'

'Not really. I also need to run some errands. Do you want anything?'

Shouji shook his head. 'Nothing. I'm fine.'

'All right then,' she said, walking out. 'I might be late back. If you're tired, go to sleep. Don't wait for me.'

He stared at Youko. From this angle, her back looked small and fragile and, somehow, he felt a strong urge to stop her going.

'Youko!' he called.

She turned around. 'Yes?'

He went quiet. He had no idea why he'd called her. He wanted her to stay, but why?

Youko stared at him. 'What's wrong, Shouji?'

'Ah, nothing …' He paused, thinking of something to say. 'I was wondering if I could come with you next time.'

'To Tokyo? You can, but not today. You'll take a while to get ready, and I need to leave now.'

'That's not what I meant.' She was never going to agree. She always went alone. 'Can I come with you to the aquarium?'

She tilted her head. 'Why? You've never been interested before.'

He shrugged. 'I don't know. Curious, maybe? What could be so interesting that you go there so often? Also, I've never been to the Shinagawa aquarium.'

'But you lived in Tokyo for so long.'

Shouji laughed. 'As a poor student, yes. I never had any spare cash to play around with.'

'All right, we'll go together next time,' Youko said, flashing him a smile before leaving the room.

The door opened and closed with a creak. Shouji lay still on the bed. He wanted to smoke, but he couldn't bring himself to get up and grab the cigarettes from the dressing table. A sense of unease crawled up his spine to the back of his neck. He'd forgotten something important, but what was it?

A gust of wind blew, and he turned to the window. The sky was clear, devoid of any clouds. The weather was pleasant, but Shouji felt unbearably lost and lonely.

•

Even after he woke, the emptiness lingered.

When Shouji had first moved back to Tokyo, he used to dream about Youko a lot. But after a few weeks, it happened less and less, until the dreams finally stopped. Well, almost. Sometimes, out of the blue, he would still dream of Youko. Like a mild Tokyo earthquake, the dreams were unexpected yet non-intrusive.

A few years had passed without him dreaming about her. Yet now it had happened again. He buried his face in his palms. Why was he still unable to move on? Shouldn't he let her go now that he knew she was probably safe?

Getting up, he washed his face and brushed his teeth. His head hurt a little, probably from the lack of sleep. Good thing it was a Saturday so he could afford to take things easy. He changed into an old T-shirt and shorts. He wanted to drink some milk, but then recalled it had gone rancid. Luckily, he found a pack of Oreos and ate them for breakfast.

Shouji looked around his room. This place was such a mess. He rolled up his sleeves and decided to clean it up. He started by emptying the rubbish bin. Then he checked the fridge and removed everything that had gone bad, which was pretty much all the perishable items. He made a mental note to make a trip to the supermarket to stock up on essentials. Next, he dumped all the clothes into a huge laundry basket. They needed ironing. But before that, he ought to pick up those books and magazines. They were all over the place.

Yoshioka would laugh if he learned that Shouji had ended up spending his weekend tidying up his apartment. Then again, he probably couldn't imagine an apartment that was as messy as this.

Shouji divided the books and magazines into two piles: throw away or keep. In the past, he had saved all his articles, but he started to wonder if there was any point, especially now that the pages had turned yellow. He couldn't think of any use for them.

Picking through the items, he came across a white, hardcover book. '100th Anniversary' was embossed on the cover in silver foil. He had brought the album back from Fukuoka when he visited a year ago.

CHAPTER 29
WATER WOMEN

The family house in Fukuoka hadn't changed much. Glazed tiles with ornate ends, aged wooden walls, thin sliding doors — features he was too familiar with. The garden, though, was slightly different. Some bonsai and a few potted plants he didn't remember now lined the pond. Carefully tended by his mother, as always, he thought.

Another new addition welcomed Shouji when he entered the house — an air-conditioning unit. *Finally*. He'd been asking his mother to get one for a long time, but she'd always said no, telling him it was unnatural.

'The fan is good enough,' she said. 'Air-conditioning makes your bones weak.'

He'd explained to her countless times that this was just a superstition, but she wouldn't listen. She was stubborn, which made him wonder what had changed her mind.

'I'm home,' Shouji said aloud, taking his shoes off at the door.

'Shouji, you're already here? I didn't expect you to take the first train.'

His mother's warm voice and hurried footsteps greeted him. She appeared in a beige kimono embroidered with tiny leaves, looking as elegant as ever. The fabric paired nicely with her gold obi and matching pastel-yellow obijime and obiage, though the combination looked too fancy for everyday wear.

'Are you going out?' he asked.

Her face lit up. 'Since you're back, we should head out and eat something special to celebrate. What do you think?'

Shouji chuckled. His mother was still the same as she'd always been. He stepped into the house, carrying his bag. 'Can I use my old room?'

'Of course. Don't be silly. That room is always yours.' She looked at the duffel bag and frowned slightly. 'Is that your only luggage? How long are you planning to stay?'

'Just for the weekend.' He could see her smile fade. 'I've got plenty of work waiting for me in the office.'

She sighed. 'Can't they give you a little more time off? I haven't seen my only child in years.'

'It's the quality of time that matters, not the quantity,' he teased her. Looking around, Shouji realised the housekeeper was unusually absent. 'Where is Mrs Sakamoto?'

'She wasn't feeling well, so I asked her to rest.'

He nodded, and they walked to his room.

'Mrs Sakamoto is getting old. I told her to return to her family, but she said she'd been away from them for too long, she feels more at home here. When she put it like that, I couldn't ask her to leave.'

Shouji's mother opened the sliding door to his room. He went in and put his bag down. The room was clean and fresh. Each time he came here, he marvelled at how the place always looked as if he'd never left Fukuoka. Nothing had changed, except ...

'You finally installed an air-conditioning unit,' he said.

His mother laughed and reached for the remote control. 'I was tired of hearing you say it's too hot in the summer and too cold in the winter. You always complained about living in such an old-fashioned house. I thought if we modernised it a bit, you might come home more often. At least for the Obon and the new year.'

Shouji avoided her eyes.

'Why don't you take a bath?' She clasped her hands. 'But before that, tell me where you want to eat. I'll make a reservation.'

'Actually, it's your cooking that I miss the most.'

'Really?'

He nodded. 'But if it's too much trouble, we can eat out.'

She shook her head. 'It's not a problem at all.'

'I'm sorry, especially after you've dressed up in such a gorgeous kimono. You look beautiful.'

His mother burst out laughing. 'You're getting cheeky.'

She left the room and he lay on his mattress, running his fingers along the surface. He could easily imagine his mother airing it a day before he'd arrived. She was right. He ought to come home more often. Then again, he didn't want to see that man.

Shouji took a deep breath and smelled the fresh tatami matt. It seemed like his mother had replaced the flooring too. She took good care of the house, as if the family home were a precious heirloom. He supposed it was, though Shouji still didn't like the place. He always felt uneasy here. He had the feeling that everyone was holding their breath, and one escaped, tiny sigh would topple everything.

He glanced around his room. The furniture was the same as before he had left — an old wooden cupboard, a toy cabinet full of cheap plastic toys, and a western-style desk, which stood out oddly in this traditional house.

But what was that on top of the desk? Shouji got up to take a closer look. A white paper bag. Had his mother left it there accidentally? He grabbed the bag and went to look for her.

On the way to the kitchen, Shouji saw his father emerging from a room. He tensed up. Dressed in a hakama, his father was stocky and expressionless. He gave Shouji a cold stare. Shouji clenched his fists and bowed.

'It's been a while,' he greeted him. 'I hope you've been well.'

His father was quiet for a moment before asking, 'How long are you planning to stay?'

'Just over the weekend.'

His father didn't respond. He walked to the other side of the house, most likely to his workshop.

After Shouji's father had retired from the army, he had taken an interest in pottery, probably because of his fascination with Nobunaga Oda. A large painting of the famed warlord hung in his workshop. According to legend, Nobunaga had been a collector of pottery. Then again, his father could have taken it up for any other reason. Perhaps he was bored. Who knew? The strange thing was, he only ever made teacups.

Shouji wondered what would happen to his father's large collection when he passed away. His father never sold or gave his teacups to anyone. Shouji knew nothing about pottery, so he couldn't tell whether they were good. Regardless, his father was calmer when he was inside that room with his cups.

Shouji went into the kitchen. His mother's murmuring voice blended with the fragrance of miso. She had a habit of talking to herself when she was cooking.

'Excuse me,' he said in a soft voice, not wanting to startle her.

She turned around, holding a ladle. Looking at the huge pot in front of her, Shouji had no doubt she was planning a feast. Even though he always told her not to cook too much, she always did. Perhaps he shouldn't bother saying anything this time.

Shouji lifted the paper bag. 'I found this in my room.'

Her face beamed. 'Ah, I forgot to tell you. A few weeks ago, a girl called from Waseda. She said she was from the swimming club.'

He vaguely recalled the brief period he'd been a member.

'The club is celebrating its anniversary,' his mother continued. 'They printed commemorative books and gave them out to those featured. She said you represented the university in a competition. Why didn't you tell me?'

'It was a small competition.' Shouji had won a bronze medal in an inter-university men's relay race, but his interest had soon dwindled as college work started piling up.

'Did you get a medal?' she asked.

'Yes.' Though he'd accidentally left it in the old apartment he'd shared with Jin. 'But really, it wasn't a big deal.'

His mother sighed. 'I wonder what other things I have missed. I don't even know your girlfriend.'

Shouji waved her off. 'That's because I haven't got one.'

'At your age?' She made a serious face. 'Do you think your mother will believe that?'

'That's the truth,' he said, forcing a laugh. 'I won't disturb you. Try not to cook too much. There are only a few of us here.'

Shouji's mother turned to face the stove. 'When you told me you were coming after so long, I thought you were going to bring a woman.'

'I'm sorry to disappoint you.' The truth was, he'd felt guilty after Eri had chided him for never visiting.

'All my friends' children are married. I only have one son, and he's well into his thirties, but he refuses to settle down. What should I do? I don't know any single ladies to introduce you to.' She glanced at him. 'But perhaps Tokyo women are different. Do they get married much later?'

There it came, the obligatory marriage conversation. 'Some of them do.'

'I'm not a grateful person, am I? You've got a good job, and you're healthy. I should be content.'

He shouldn't let her prolong this conversation. 'I'm going to take a bath.'

She turned down the heat. 'Don't open the commemorative book yet. Let's take a look at it together later.'

'All right,' he said and left.

•

Shouji put down his chopsticks and clasped his hands together. 'Thank you for the meal. It was delicious.'

'Have you finished?' His mother looked disappointed. 'There's still so much left.'

He stood. 'I can't eat any more. It's too much. Let me help you clear the table.'

'Don't bother. It's faster if I do it alone,' his mother said, stacking the dirty plates. Despite wearing a kimono, her movements were swift. 'Why don't you go to your room? But wait for a while before you lie down, or else you'll turn into a cow. I'll join you shortly. I want to see the photograph of my son on the podium.'

'Don't expect too much,' he said. 'I'm not sure if there will be any photographs of me. For all we know, it might just be my name appearing on one small line somewhere.'

Shouji's mother gestured for him to leave. He went to his room and lay down on the mattress, ignoring her superstitious warning, but only for a short while. She wouldn't take long. True enough, in less than five minutes, there was a knock at the door.

'Please come in,' Shouji said.

His mother entered with a tray. She brought a glass of fresh milk and a red bean dessert. That was so like her.

'I'm too full,' he protested. 'I can't eat anything else.'

She put down the tray. 'Just wait for a while. You'll get hungry soon.'

He doubted that.

'I still remember the day you told me you got accepted into a university in Tokyo,' his mother said. 'At first, I thought you were going to be away for your studies and return here after graduation, but instead you moved to Akakawa.'

Shouji gave her a dry laugh.

'When you said you'd left Akakawa, my hopes went up again. This time, I thought, my son would surely return home. But instead, you went back to Tokyo.' She sighed. 'I'm already old. I won't be around for long. You should return to my side. Don't tell me there are no jobs in Fukuoka.'

'You know there's no way I would return here. At least, not to this house.'

Shouji's mother glanced at him. 'Do you still think about the past? You should learn to forgive and forget.'

He didn't respond. She wouldn't like what he had to say.

'I met Uncle Hidetoshi when I was in Akakawa,' Shouji said. 'He asked me to send his regards to you. I'm sorry I forgot to tell you until now.'

She shifted her eyes. 'How was he?'

'He seemed well. Still in the police force. He has been redeployed to another city now.'

'I see.'

Shouji looked at his mother. 'The reason he left his job was because of Father, wasn't it?'

She averted her eyes. 'I don't know what you're talking about.'

'It's not something I can easily forget.'

'Shouji, it happened so many years ago.'

'I still remember it,' he said. 'And I still remember being beaten and locked up in the shed.'

His mother gave him a pleading look. 'Can we not talk about it?'

Hearing that, Shouji's anger rose. 'You did nothing to stop him. You told me to lie about my injuries. You didn't even say a word when my teacher came to visit us.'

She shook her head. 'You don't understand. It's not like that.'

He stared into her eyes. 'You're my mother. All I wanted was for you to protect me.'

'Shouji, your father did what he thought was right for you.' She reached for his hand. 'He might not be perfect, but he loves you. As a family, we should be understanding.'

He couldn't believe what she was saying. 'I've no idea why you stood by him, but let me make this clear. What he did was despicable.'

His mother went quiet. Shouji felt a pinch in his chest. It pained him to see her looking like that. He regretted bringing up the past, yet ...

'I'm sorry, but I've had enough of us pretending nothing happened,' he said.

His mother looked at him with a pained expression.

What was he doing? He hadn't come here for this. He took a deep breath. 'Shall we take a look at the commemorative book?'

She said nothing, and he took it as agreement.

He reached for the paper bag and sat next to his mother. The hardcover book was thick and heavy. His mother ran her fingers over the cover. The chapters were organised by year. Shouji was in the club around 1991, so he flipped to the 1990–94 section.

He recognised some of the people in the photographs. The seniors in his club and the captain.

His mother pointed out a photograph. 'That's you.'

Indeed, there he was, standing awkwardly with the rest of his teammates. They wore the university sports jacket, medals hanging around their necks. He was on the far left with one arm around the person next to him. He couldn't remember the guy's name. It'd been a long time.

'You look great,' his mother said, seemingly forgetting their earlier disagreement. 'How I wish I'd been there to see you.'

He was relieved she hadn't taken the argument too hard. 'No parents come for such a small event.'

'I need to photocopy the page and frame it,' she said, clasping her hands. 'Or do you think you can call up your club and ask for the negative?'

His mother's enthusiasm made Shouji embarrassed. 'Let's not

bother them. You can have the book and cut out the page.'

'No, you should keep it. These are precious memories.' She flipped the page and looked at the female members' photographs. 'Did you date any of these girls? You had a girlfriend back in university, didn't you?'

He paused, feeling a familiar ache. 'She was never in any clubs.'

'What happened to that girl? You seemed serious about her.'

He shrugged. 'Sometimes things don't work out.'

His mother mumbled in agreement. She didn't press any further.

Shouji crossed his legs and leaned against the wall. From this low angle, the white hair near his mother's neck was visible. She had a pot of black dye in her bathroom and touched up her roots twice a week, but that section was hard for her to see. It wasn't obvious, but it made him realise his mother was getting old.

'Hey, Shouji.' She turned to him. 'Isn't this girl a beauty?'

He peered at the book. His mother was pointing to a young woman at the centre of a photograph. Despite being in a group picture, she stole the limelight. There were a few medals around her neck, and she was carrying a huge bouquet. Her sharp face and delicate features were familiar.

He searched for her name. There it was. Sachiko Hayami. *Ah, one of Jin's girls.* He'd seen her twice, coming into their apartment. 'She was my university flatmate's girlfriend. Do you remember, the son of the confectionery businessman?'

'Ah, yes. You did tell me about him. Are they married now?'

Jin? Married? Shouji resisted the urge to laugh. 'I doubt it. He's a commitment-phobe.'

'Sachiko Hayami … Sachiko Hayami … Is she an actress, or a model? I think I've heard her name before.'

'I wouldn't be surprised, but I rarely watch television.'

Shouji looked at the rest of the girls around Sachiko Hayami. One of them was Liyun. Standing a little behind Sachiko, she wasn't smiling. She wasn't even looking at the camera. It was as if she had been caught in a bad moment.

'Who are you looking at?' Shouji's mother teased him. 'Another old flame?'

'No, just a friend.' He pointed to her photograph. 'We used to be close. I forgot she was even in the swimming club.'

What had Liyun won? Shouji looked at the chart, searching for her name, and noticed his mother was staring intently at the page.

'Anything wrong?' he asked.

'Nothing,' she answered quickly. A little too quickly. She always did that whenever she was trying to hide something.

'There is something, isn't there?' Shouji said. 'What is it?'

'Ah, why don't you eat the dessert? You should have space for it now.'

He knew she was changing the subject.

•

Looking at the page again back in his apartment in Tokyo, Shouji realised what had flustered his mother so much. One of the Chinese characters in Liyun's name stood for cloud. Another woman with a water element.

He turned to the telephone in his room and dialled his family home in Fukuoka. It was his mother who picked up the call.

'Shouji, it's been so long since you called,' she said in delight. 'How have you been?'

'I'm sorry, but there's something I need to check urgently,' he said, skipping the pleasantries. 'Remember the time you took me to see a fortune-teller when I was young?'

There was a pause. 'What about it?'

'Is she still around?'

'Hmmm. I don't think so. When we went there, she was in her late eighties.'

'I see,' he mumbled. 'Do you remember what she told us?'

'How could I not? She was always so accurate.'

'Are you sure?'

'Shouji, people came from other prefectures to see that for-tune-teller. I'd personally asked her for advice many times. On each occasion, she was always spot on,' his mother said. 'But why are you suddenly interested in this? You told me you didn't believe in fortune-telling.'

He ignored her question. 'From what I remember, she said that I would meet three women with the water element in their names, and I would marry one of them.' Shouji glanced at the page. 'Is that why you were looking at Liyun's name in the commemorative book?'

Her mother took a deep breath. 'The fortune-teller didn't say anything about marriage.'

'Then what did she say?'

'She said ...' His mother paused, gathering her thoughts. 'In your life, you would encounter three women with a water element in their names, and one of them could be your soulmate. There was also another part ...'

'Just tell me.'

His mother sighed. 'It might be nothing.'

'If it's nothing, then tell me,' he insisted.

'She warned about death.'

'Whose death?'

'It could be your death, or the death of someone close to you,' she said, then paused a moment before adding: 'by drowning.'

Shouji felt his stomach twist.

The first woman was Youko. Child of the sea. He had no idea of her whereabouts or wellbeing.

Then there was Mizuki, whose name meant water. She was alive, but her sister had died in that bizarre swimming pool accident. Her husband had drowned too.

The third one must be Liyun.

'Don't worry, Shouji,' his mother said. 'You're a strong swimmer, aren't you?'

He swallowed hard. If only she knew what had happened to Mizuki's late husband. 'Is that why you were so persistent about me learning to swim?'

'I only have one child. I did all I could to protect you.'

Shouji ran her words through his mind. One of the women with the water element in their names might be the person he was destined to be with, but getting close to them could end in death.

'What are you planning to do now?' his mother asked.

'I'm not sure yet,' he said. 'Probably meet an old friend.'

'You're not trying to track down that girl, are you?'

He didn't want to lie, but he didn't want her to be worried.

'Shouji, I don't want anything bad to happen to you. Please stay away from her,' his mother pleaded.

'Nothing bad will happen to me,' he reassured her. 'I'm a strong swimmer, remember?'

CHAPTER 30
WELCOME TO SINGAPORE

Dragging a rolling suitcase, Shouji went to the Changi airport immigration counter and handed over his passport. The officer stamped the travel document and returned it to him. When their fingers touched, her hand felt warm. Or was it his fingers that were freezing? It had been colder on the aeroplane than he would've liked.

A few days ago, Shouji had gone to Yoshioka's desk and asked his senior if he could take a one-week holiday.

'Finally! I started to think you might be a robot.' Yoshioka gave him a big grin. 'Where are you going?'

'Singapore,' Shouji said.

Yoshioka's eyes widened. 'You have a passport, Arai?'

'Yeah,' he said. 'Just got it today.'

'Why so sudden?'

'I'm planning to visit an old friend.'

Trying to get information about Youko from the university had been extremely challenging but, thankfully, getting in touch with the swimming club alumni group had proved a lot easier, especially since Jin had Sachiko's number. His mother had been right. She was kind of a celebrity, though she hadn't become an actress or a model. She had built a name for herself as a fashion designer. Sachiko helpfully gave him the name of the student currently in charge of all alumni correspondence. Name-dropping went a long way and the girl eagerly gave Shouji everything he needed. Apparently, Liyun had returned to Singapore a while ago.

Yoshioka raised an eyebrow. 'It seems strange. You've always avoided overseas assignments.'

Shouji shrugged. 'Maybe I'm having a mid-life crisis.'

'Well, whatever it is, you should go. You've worked hard.' He glanced at the calendar. 'But this is a bad time. We have the yearly editorial meeting coming up, don't we? And you need to be there.'

'I'll take whatever I can get,' Shouji said. 'This is important to me.'

Yoshioka gave him a long look. 'I understand. I'll talk to the management.'

In the end, they only gave him three days. Yoshioka was apologetic about it. 'As you know, we're short on staff, and the meeting is important.'

'That can't be helped,' Shouji said, and thanked his senior.

•

After immigration, Shouji passed by the airport's duty-free store. He'd forgotten to pack a gift, but he ought to bring something. A bottle of wine? Or what about perfume?

Shouji stood in the fragrance aisle, feeling overwhelmed by the huge selection. Rows of dainty bottles fought for his attention. He often reviewed fragrances for magazines, but the companies sent them in. He'd never had to pick one himself. He merely allocated them scores based on set parameters.

'Can I help you?' a shop assistant asked.

He looked at the eager-looking young woman. She would know more than him. 'I'm looking for a gift for a lady.'

'Do you have any particular brand or scent in mind?'

'Not really.'

She nodded a few times, seemingly digesting what he'd told her. 'In that case, what about a fresh fragrance?' She went closer to the shelves and fetched a bottle, spraying the perfume on to a white paper strip, which she gave to him. 'This is one of our bestsellers with women, and a personal favourite of mine.'

Shouji sniffed it. The floral perfume has a hint of citrus. He glanced at the bottle. *Happy*.

'I'll take this,' he said.

'Certainly,' the shop assistant replied. 'Please follow me to the cashier.'

As he made his way through the various aisles, Shouji remembered a conversation he'd once had with Youko about being happy. They were relaxing in their small apartment after a long day at work. Youko was painting her toenails. Shouji was lying on the couch when the question drifted into his mind.

'What do you think happiness and success are?' he asked her.

She narrowed her eyes. 'Why do you ask?'

He shrugged. 'Just thought of it.'

'Oh.' She dipped the tiny brush into the nail polish bottle. 'I think happiness depends on your priorities, and success depends on your goals.'

'Then what are your priorities and goals?'

'My priorities ... survival, I guess?' She made careful strokes. 'I want to have enough to eat and a place to rest without compromising my dignity. My goal right now is also to survive. That sounds too generic, but I don't have high aims. I'm not planning to be a millionaire.'

'What will you do if you win a lottery?'

Youko laughed. 'That's not going to happen. I would never buy a lottery ticket. It's a waste of money. The probability of winning is too low.'

'What if you saw a ticket lying on the street and picked it up, and it happened to be the winning numbers?'

She shook her head. 'I wouldn't pick it up.'

'Let's say that you did buy one, or you did pick it up. What would you spend it on? A round-the-world trip? Early retirement?'

Youko put on the last stroke on her little toenail. 'I'd do the same thing as I've been doing.'

'Donate the money to charity?'

'Yes.' She closed the cap, took a newspaper, and used it to fan her nails. 'I'm content with the way things are right now. I don't think it's necessary to make any drastic changes. The balance is nice, and introducing a new element would only upset the ratio and topple everything.'

'Are you happy now?'

Youko paused for a few seconds. 'Yes, I'm happy. I'm happy now.'

But had she been lying back then? Had that been the reason for her slight hesitation?

·

'Over here, sir,' the shop assistant said, cutting short his thoughts.

Shouji followed her and made the payment. The cashier put the perfume inside a black plastic carrier bag and handed it to him. He went down to the arrivals hall, joining the queue for a taxi. Through the clear glass ceiling, Shouji saw dark clouds forming. Rumbles of thunder could be heard in the distance. When it was his turn to get into the taxi, the rain started to pour.

'Where would you like to go, sir?' the driver asked.

Shouji gave the name of his hotel as he buckled his seat belt.

The taxi left the airport and headed to the expressway. Purple bougainvillea bloomed by the roadside. The bright colour popped, blurred by rainwater. Shouji pressed his head against the cold glass window. He gazed at streams of cars and the endless number of overhead bridges.

Half an hour later, he arrived at his hotel. It was a business hotel recommended by Yoshioka. After Shouji checked in, a staff member helped him with his luggage and escorted him to his room.

'Enjoy your stay, sir,' the young man said.

Thanking him, Shouji slipped him some notes as a tip.

The room had a warm, earth-tone interior. A king-sized bed perched in the middle, plush and welcoming. Shouji went over to the window and opened the thick curtains. The rain had stopped. A stunning view of the sea and the city greeted him. It was the perfect time of day, just when the night was about to arrive. In the distance, white and grey buildings contrasted against colourful cargo ships in the water. The sea glistened and the shadows grew long.

When the afternoon sun had completely gone, Shouji sat on the bed and took off his shoes. The journey had left him exhausted, but he didn't feel sleepy. He ordered room service for dinner.

While waiting for the food to be delivered, he debated whether to call Liyun's house from the in-room phone. But what should he say when she answered the call?

'Hi, Liyun. This is Shouji. I happen to be in Singapore. Can we meet up and have a little chat? For old times' sake.'

As if that were the case … He was the man who had chosen to take a seven-hour flight from Tokyo to Singapore to discuss a matter that could have been resolved by a single international phone call.

He was still considering his options when the doorbell rang. A hotel waiter delivered his dinner, setting it up on the table.

Cajun-marinated chicken breast and rosti potatoes, finished with a warm chocolate tart. The food was delicious, though the tart was a little too sweet for his liking. Shouji wiped his mouth with the white napkin. It was now quarter past nine.

He showered and changed into a dark-blue shirt and black trousers. Then he went to the hotel bar on the highest floor of the building. It was a picture of opulence. A dizzying array of curved, golden decorations adorned the ceiling.

A lanky bartender in a black uniform greeted him from the circular counter.

'What would you like, sir?' he asked.

Shouji leaned closer. 'Is there a cocktail you'd recommend?'

'What about our signature cocktail? Tropical Daydreamer. It's a blend of pink champagne, umeshu, ginger, and lime.'

'I'll have that,' said Shouji.

The bartender promptly mixed his drink, while Shouji scanned the bar. It was full of young professionals. Not surprising, since the hotel was located in the business district. Unlike in Tokyo, the women here wore outfits with bold designs. In Japan, the more money a woman had, the more she'd wear an understated garment and blend in with the crowd.

'Enjoy your drink,' the bartender said.

Shouji thanked him and took the cocktail, moving to stand at a circular table next to a glass partition.

Thanks to the guidebook project he was working on, he was getting sick of hotel bars. They were the same everywhere. They provided impeccable service — albeit often impersonal — an extensive menu and a precise standard. When he told them he was from the press, the staff would usually be friendlier. But somehow, he still preferred those tiny bars in Ginza. The bartenders knew him and remembered the drink he had ordered on his last visit.

Still, as he stood at the edge of the bar sipping a tropical cocktail, the magnificent night view of the Central Business District didn't fail to stir him. The plum liquor in his drink brought an odd sense of familiarity to this foreign place.

●

Shouji woke up with the sun shining into his eyes. He sat up, squinting. Slowly, he adjusted to the brightness. He was in his bedroom in Tokyo. And next to him was Liyun. Her long locks were down, and she was wearing Shouji's old T-shirt.

'Good morning,' she whispered.

'Good morning,' he repeated after her. What was happening? He wasn't sure, but somehow the scene felt familiar.

She tilted her head. 'I'm hungry. What about you? Shall I make breakfast?'

'Ah, I'm …'

'You drank a lot last night.' She inched closer. 'You reek of alcohol.' She pursed her lips and folded her legs in front of her chest. 'Don't tell me you forgot what happened.'

Shouji's stomach churned and, finally, he realised what was going on. 'I'm sorry.' He lowered his head. 'I shouldn't have got drunk. I know my apologies can't change anything, but … I'm sorry.'

Liyun bit her lip. Her expression hardened. Had he offended her? 'Is there anything I can do to make it up to you?' he asked.

He hadn't fully grasped the situation when her manner changed again. She smiled cheerfully. 'I can ask you for anything? That's helpful. I'm broke, and I've got no job. Can I stay here for a while?'

'I don't think it's appropriate. You're a woman, and I'm a man.'

'We've slept together, haven't we? What are you worried about?'

Her words made him feel guiltier. He had to make it up to her. 'If that's what you want, but only for a short while. I'll help you look for a new place.' He paused. 'I'm sorry. It won't happen again.'

She leaned closer. 'Is that so?'

He looked away, feeling flushed.

Liyun got down from the bed. 'I'm all sweaty, I'm going to shower,' she said. She pulled her hair up into a messy bun. The morning sun shone on her tanned skin. She turned to face him and asked, 'Can I borrow a towel?'

'There's one in the cabinet,' he said. 'In the first drawer.'

Not wanting to continue looking at Liyun, Shouji lay on the bed and turned his back to her. He could hear her humming and closing the bathroom door. Soon her voice was masked by the sound of the gushing water.

Had he made a mistake? Yes, no doubt about it, he shouldn't have let her stay at his place. This situation would end up becoming problematic.

'Then why didn't you tell her to leave?'

Without him noticing, Youko had slipped into his room and sat next to him — at the exact spot where Liyun had just been.

Shouji got up in a hurry. 'When did you arrive?'

'Just now,' she said, gesturing to the door. 'I did knock, but you didn't answer.'

'I didn't hear anything.'

'You were too busy thinking.'

He stared at her, dumbfounded. 'What are you doing here? Didn't you disappear after the fire? I was looking for you, but I couldn't find you. Where did you go?'

She lay down next to him, not saying a word. The sound of water stopped and Liyun's hums returned. Youko kept quiet as she stared at the window. He couldn't tell what was on her mind. The door opened and Liyun came out, wearing a white bath towel.

'Shouji, were you talking to someone?' she asked.

'Yes, I was talking to …' His words trailed off. Youko wasn't there. Where had she gone? He quickly got down from the bed. Putting on a shirt, he ran out to chase after Youko, but the living room was empty.

'Where are you going?' Liyun shouted, but Shouji didn't answer.

He grabbed the door handle and opened it. To his surprise, he was back in his living room. That old sofa with a cigarette burn, that low table with chipped edges — it was definitely his apartment in Tokyo.

Undeterred, Shouji opened the door again and tried to get out. But the same thing happened. He was back where he'd started.

'Liyun, something weird is going on,' he said, returning to the bedroom.

But she, too, was no longer there.

He looked into the bathroom. The shower was empty. The glass panels still had water droplets on them. He could feel the hot steam. The heat was choking him. He couldn't breathe. Feeling dizzy, he fell on to the hard tiles.

Strange. He didn't feel any pain. His mind hazy, he smelled a familiar floral fragrance. A hint of citrus. Where was the scent coming from? A woman, that much he knew.

•

Shouji woke up from his dream, gasping. He was drenched in sweat, despite the blasting air-conditioning unit. It took him a while to calm down. That was the first time he'd ever dreamed of Liyun. He shook his head, trying to clear his mind. It must be because he was in Singapore.

He glanced at the clock. Six in the morning. The pool should be open, and there wouldn't be that many people there yet. Shouji grabbed his swimming trunks and a pair of goggles before making his way down.

The wooden platform was illuminated by warm lighting. The chilly morning wind brushed his bare skin. Only a couple of hotel guests were there. Shouji walked to the end of the platform before settling in a corner. Slowly, he lowered his legs into the water. He shivered. It was icy. Bracing himself for the cold, he put on his goggles and leaped into the pool.

After a few laps, he grew used to the low temperature. More and more people streamed in and the sky gradually became brighter. The sun rose and warmed the water, giving it a gorgeous sparkle. He rested at the side of the pool, watching people come and go.

A couple locked in a close embrace, honeymooners maybe. A group of middle-aged men doing their laps. They were probably business travellers. A realisation came to him. It might be rude to turn up unannounced at Liyun's house, especially considering how they had parted ways. Or she might no longer live there.

Shouji got up, took a towel, and dried himself.

No point in worrying now.

CHAPTER 31
I HOPE YOU'RE HAPPY

Shouji got out of the taxi carrying the shopping bag from the airport. Holding a piece of paper with Liyun's address scribbled on it, he went to the lift lobby. Another man was also waiting. He glanced at Shouji before averting his eyes. The lift opened and both of them got in.

Getting off on the sixth floor, Shouji looked for unit twenty-one. He finally found the door between two potted yellow palms. The arching feather-shaped fronds partially covered the door number.

Shouji pressed the doorbell and waited. An elderly woman in a loose floral dress came out, opening the wooden door but leaving the metal grille in front of it remained locked.

He bowed and greeted her in English. 'I'm Shouji Arai, Liyun's friend. Is this her house?'

The woman frowned. 'She asked you to come here?'

Not exactly. Shouji cleared his throat. 'I've travelled from Japan, and I thought I'd drop by to see her, if she still lives here.'

'Ah, no wonder.' She unlocked the grille. 'Please come in. You must be a university friend. I'm Liyun's mother.'

He nodded obligingly and took his shoes off.

'Liyun has her own place now, but she still visits me at weekends. You came at the right time. She should be here soon.'

Shouji looked around. The apartment seemed worn but clean and comfortable. An aged leather sofa stood against the wall, taking up half the living room. Facing it was a TV in the middle of a cabinet full of books and decorative statues. The television was turned on, despite the old lady seemingly not watching. Seeing it made Shouji feel nostalgic.

In the corner of the room, he spotted an altar on top of a wooden cabinet. There was a framed photograph of a bespectacled young man, who must be Liyun's deceased brother.

'Take a seat,' the woman said. 'What would you like to drink? It's a hot day, isn't it? What about an iced drink? Honey water, or barley?'

'Please don't trouble yourself.'

Their exchange was cut short by a clanking noise. Shouji turned around to see Liyun opening the door, carrying two red plastic bags. She didn't look any different from the last time he'd seen her a year ago. Perhaps a little more tanned, but that was it.

Liyun's mother rushed to the door. 'Where's James?'

'He needed to leave after dropping me here. He has a few appointments today,' she said. 'Have you had breakfast? I bought bee hoon.'

'I ate, but we can have that for lunch. I'll make chicken curry to go with it.' The older woman took the plastic bags from Liyun. She glanced at Shouji. 'We have a guest. I didn't know you had a handsome friend in Japan. James would be jealous if he found out.'

Liyun's eyes widened as she saw him. 'Shouji, what are you doing here?'

He hadn't had a chance to answer when Liyun's mother said, 'Why don't you bring your friend to your room? Turn on the air-con. It's a hot day.'

The suggestion embarrassed Shouji. 'I'm all right here.'

'Come with me,' Liyun said, making her way into one of the rooms.

'You'll join us for lunch, won't you?' Liyun's mother asked him. 'I insist.'

Would that be a good idea? 'Ah, I—'

'That settles it then,' the old woman said, disappearing into the kitchen.

Shouji followed Liyun into the room. It wasn't that different from his room in Tokyo in terms of size and layout — a single bed on one side, a desk and chair on another, and a wardrobe on the wall in between.

'Mum is always like that,' Liyun said, closing the door behind him and turning on the air-conditioning. 'Don't worry about her. She loves cooking for others. Trust me, you're doing her a favour.'

'Now I see where your talent comes from. Your mother taught you well.'

'But she always told me cooking is learned, not taught.'

'What does that mean?'

Liyun shrugged. 'Beats me.'

There was an awkward pause.

'I'm sorry for troubling you, coming unannounced,' Shouji eventually said.

Liyun stared at him, and their eyes met. For a long time, neither said a word. Shouji cracked his knuckles, trying to suppress his unease. Finally, he waved at her, and she burst out laughing.

'What's so funny?' He rubbed the nape of his neck. 'Stop that.'

'What are you doing in Singapore?' she asked after catching her breath. 'You've appeared out of nowhere.'

He didn't answer. Instead, he looked around the room. The wall was decorated with colourful Japanese animation posters. 'I didn't know you liked anime.'

Liyun sat on the bed. 'You don't know a lot of things about me.'

Shouji pulled out a chair for himself and gave the shopping bag from the airport to Liyun.

'What's this?' she asked.

He leaned closer. 'A small present.'

'Wow, I'm excited.' She opened the bag and took the perfume out. 'Did you pick it out yourself? Or did your pretty secretary choose it for you?'

'What are you talking about? I don't have a secretary,' Shouji said. 'I bought it because the shop assistant said it was popular, and I like the name of the perfume. I hope you're happy.'

Liyun bit her lip. Her expression mellowed. 'Are you talking about James?'

James … Her mother had mentioned that name, hadn't she? The one who had driven her here, since she no longer lived with her parents.

Shouji caught a glimpse of a ring on Liyun's finger. A classic four-claw setting in white gold. The slim silhouette gave it a timeless elegance. Why hadn't he seen it earlier? He gave her a clumsy smile. 'Congratulations on your wedding.'

'Not yet. We're just engaged,' Liyun said, breaking into a grin.

Ah. She wasn't married. He wasn't sure how he should respond. In the end, he simply mumbled, 'Uh-huh.'

'Anyway, thank you,' she continued. 'But you haven't told me why you're here.'

'I had an assignment in Singapore, so I thought of visiting you,' he lied. 'It's good to see you, healthy and happy. I'm glad you found someone.'

She nodded, but didn't say anything.

'Who is this lucky guy?' Shouji asked. 'Do I know him?'

Liyun shook her head. 'Doubt it. He's my junior college friend. We used to date before I went to Japan to study. I ran into him after I returned to Singapore.' She touched the nape of her neck. The ring on her finger glinted. 'I decided to come back after I left your place.'

So, she had left Japan after that. No wonder they'd never crossed paths.

'He asked if I was willing to give our relationship another try.'

Liyun crossed her legs. 'Since I wasn't seeing anyone, I agreed. He's a kind person, and he's smart too. We'd broken up because I'd decided to study in Japan. We both felt a long-distance relationship wouldn't work.' She tilted her head as if she was thinking hard about what to say next. 'I've always liked him. There is nothing fundamentally wrong with him.'

'You haven't changed, have you?' Shouji said. '"There is nothing fundamentally wrong with him." Only Liyun would come out with a statement like that.'

'Not really, I think I've changed a lot.' She shifted her position, leaning closer. 'What about you? Has anything changed?'

He shook his head. 'Not really.'

Both of them were quiet for a moment.

Eventually, she asked, 'When are you going to return to Japan?'

'Tomorrow,' he said.

Liyun stared at Shouji but, again, said nothing. He took a good look at her. Liyun still had eyes that spoke her mind.

'You're hiding something, aren't you?' she said. 'Even if you're here for business, there must be a reason you looked me up. How did you even know I was in Singapore? Who gave you my parents' address? You must have gone to significant trouble to get it.'

He avoided her gaze. Women are sharp. That thing called women's intuition — he'd started to believe in it. It was probably best to get straight to the point. He glanced at the blonde-haired schoolgirl figurine on top of the desk. But he wasn't sure what to say.

Liyun leaned in. 'You did it.'

'Did what?' Shouji asked.

'Your "I'm thinking deeply about something" sigh. Do you know that each time you do that, half of your happiness evaporates?' Liyun grabbed a pillow and hugged it. 'Shouji Arai, what's on your mind?'

CHAPTER 32
AN EMPTY TIN OF MINTS

Shouji swallowed hard. It was now or never. 'Your name has a water element in it.'

'Ah, so you know,' Liyun said, not looking surprised. 'How did you find out?'

'I saw it in the swimming club commemorative album.'

She put her pillow down. 'What are you going to do? Are you relieved that you've found your second water woman, so the third one should be coming along anytime now?'

His heart skipped a beat. 'Wait, how did you know?'

'I can read your mind.'

'Liyun, I'm asking seriously.'

She rolled her eyes. 'Because you told me. Otherwise, how would I know?'

'I don't remember telling you.'

'You don't remember a lot of things.' She looked into his eyes. 'What are you going to do now? Search for your destined third woman?'

Shouji paused. 'You're the third one.' Mizuki's image flashed into his mind. 'An old acquaintance has a name which also contains a water element.'

Liyun raised her brow. 'In that case, the reading wasn't accurate.'

'Probably,' he said. 'I don't recall ever telling you this. Why would I do that?'

She shrugged. 'You were drunk.'

251

He paused. 'Was it …?'

'Yup, it was that night,' she said.

Liyun looked away. Outside the window, the sky was clear. An extremely pale shade of blue.

If he'd told her about the reading that night when he'd been drunk, then she would have heard the incomplete version. But he couldn't tell her the truth now, that their relationship could result in death.

Shouji turned to Liyun's desk. She'd hung a pinboard on the wall and filled it with Polaroid prints of what looked like still-life photos taken in Japan. She'd also pinned up some handwritten quotes, mainly about love or life. He read them one by one.

'We accept the love we think we deserve.' – Stephen Chbosky

'We fall in love by chance, we stay in love by choice.' – Anon.

One was handwritten: 'I write your name over and over to get it off my mind but, instead, it sinks to my bones.'

'Why would anyone write a person's name to forget about that person?' Shouji asked. 'Don't you think it would have the opposite effect?'

Getting up, Liyun took the quote off the wall and crumpled it into a ball.

He hadn't expected that reaction. 'Why did you take it down?'

She threw the balled-up paper into the bin. 'It's embarrassing. I made that up when I was drunk.'

Then why did you put it up in the first place, he wanted to ask, but didn't. Liyun looked flustered. Was he being too personal? He looked away from her and glanced at her stationery box. Next to it, he saw a tin of his favourite mints.

'They sell these in Singapore?'

Shouji reached for the tin and opened it, but there were no mints left. He was about to throw it into the rubbish bin when Liyun took it from his hand.

'I know it's empty,' she said.

'Then why ...?'

She held the tin as if it were something precious. 'This was yours,' she eventually said. 'The day I left, I fished it out of the kitchen bin when you weren't looking.'

He stared at her.

'I wanted a souvenir. Something to remind me of the brief time we were together.'

He was taken aback by her honesty. 'I didn't know.'

Liyun chuckled. 'Of course you didn't know. That's why I took it. Who would've noticed if an empty tin went missing from their bin?'

'I ...'

She leaned forward. 'Are you worried I'm still in love with you?'

He froze.

She waited for his answer, but when it became obvious he wasn't going to respond, she laughed. 'Aren't you full of yourself?'

Shouji couldn't utter a single word.

Liyun stretched her arms. 'Honestly, I did love you, until the day I left your apartment. I knew you were hurt. You were afraid of people leaving you. You were not in a position to start a relationship. I was aware of all that.'

He felt a lump in his throat.

'But if you wanted me, I would've stayed. I would never, ever have left you, as Youko did.'

'I'm sorry,' he finally said. 'I didn't know how you felt.' Or rather, he'd preferred not to find out.

'You didn't understand a thing about me.' She took a deep breath. 'That's fine, Shouji. You want to chase after a shadow from your past. I can't say I liked it, but I accepted my defeat.'

He tried to think of something to say to her. But it seemed that whatever he said wouldn't be something she wanted to hear. 'I'm sorry,' he said, again. 'I was clueless.'

'Stop saying that you're sorry. There's nothing to be sorry about.'

Liyun stood and walked to the window, staring at the sky. When she didn't seem to be moving from her spot, he got up and joined her. He stood behind her, peering over her shoulder. High-rise apartments stood in close proximity, not unlike in Tokyo.

'What are you looking at?' Shouji asked.

'The train,' Liyun said. 'Can you see the tracks over there?'

He narrowed his eyes and traced her gaze into the distance. It wasn't obvious at first, but he finally spotted an overhead track peeking through a tiny gap between two apartment buildings. A few seconds later, a train passed by.

'The train reminds me of your apartment,' she said. 'Or rather, your apartment reminds me of my family home.'

'Uh-huh.'

Liyun turned to Shouji. 'You lived in another apartment before, didn't you? With Jin.'

He nodded.

'Why did you share an apartment with him, out of so many people?'

'Why not? He's easy-going, a friend of a friend.' He recalled his first meeting with Liyun at the reunion, and what she had said at that time. 'The sex parties, those were rumours. Jin brought girls back from time to time, but it wasn't any different from other guys who bring their girlfriends to their apartments.'

She laughed. 'Even if the rumours are true, I know you had nothing to do with it. You're the kind of guy who gets flustered when you find out you've slept with someone while drunk.'

He looked away.

'Sometimes, I think about that night. What if I'd never approached you? What if we hadn't had a few drinks together, or if I had asked someone else to take you home instead? How different things would've been for us. I probably would never have fallen for you.'

'Do you regret it?'

She shook her head. 'You gave me some good memories.'

They were quiet for a moment before Shouji said, 'I miss your cooking.'

'Yeah. It's been so long since I last cooked for you.' Liyun rested her head on the wall. 'Do you remember the day Eri came? You were late, so I spent some time with her. We talked. About you, mostly. At first, I thought she might be someone who was interested in you romantically, but once I got to know her, I realised I was so wrong. We barely knew each other, but somehow I felt like I could trust her.'

'Uh-huh.'

'Eri told me I should give up on you,' she continued. 'She told me I deserved someone better, someone who could love me whole-heartedly and not be stuck in the past. She said I should move out as soon as possible, for my own good.'

That sounded like Eri.

'At first, I told her I didn't know what she was talking about. I told her we were friends, even though I knew I wanted so badly for us to be more than that. But I kept thinking about what she had told me long after she left. She was right. I couldn't deny it. I knew I couldn't stay at your place indefinitely.'

'I had no clue.' At least, not until Eri had told him, though, at that time, he hadn't wanted to know the truth.

She straightened up and turned to him. She looked into his eyes. After a long time, she finally said. 'There is something you need to know.'

'Uh-huh?'

'It's about the night we went home together after the reunion,' she said, lowering her eyes. 'I wasn't being exactly truthful. The thing is, nothing happened.'

Shouji's heart skipped a beat. 'What do you mean?'

Liyun bit her lip. 'You misread the situation, and I didn't make any attempts to correct it. I wanted to make you feel guilty, so you would try to make it up to me one way or another.' She glanced at him, seemingly waiting for him to react. 'And I was right. You let me stay in your apartment.'

He swallowed hard. 'Go on.'

'I wasn't running out of money. I wanted to get closer to you, and what better way to do it than to move into your place?' She paused. 'But I was wrong. Being physically close to each other didn't make you fall for me.'

Shouji didn't know how to respond.

'Are you angry?' she asked, shifting her eyes.

'Yes,' he said. 'What you did was …'

'Outrageous,' she said.

'Yes, outrageous,' Shouji said. 'So, what exactly happened that night?'

'Nothing much. You were drunk. I volunteered to drag you back to your apartment. It was hard to walk with you leaning on my shoulders, so we stopped at a small playground near your place. You told me about that fortune-teller story from your childhood. After that, we talked about random things. We talked about love. We talked about Youko, and … You told me how you couldn't move on from her.'

He waited for her to continue, but when she didn't, he asked. 'Was that all?'

She nodded.

'Why are you telling me this now?' he asked.

'You need to know the truth,' Liyun said. 'I owe you that much.'

Shouji took a deep breath to calm himself.

'Are you angry?' she asked for the second time.

'It's in the past,' he said. 'It's not relevant anymore.'

Liyun bit her lip. 'Are we okay?'

'If you insist.'

She broke into a smile. 'Then I insist.'

'Don't do that again,' he said. 'Don't play mind games.'

'All right,' she said, nodding. Then she paused and bit her lip. 'But there's another thing.'

He tensed up. What else could there be?

Liyun walked to the bed and sat there. 'I knew Youko.'

'That's hardly surprising,' he said, feeling relieved it was only that. He sat down in the chair in front of her. 'The three of us used to study at the same university. You're also around the same age as her. It's only natural that you knew her.'

'That's not it,' Liyun said. 'I knew Youko from way, way back.'

'What do you mean?'

'She used to date my brother.'

Something wasn't right. 'But your brother, didn't he …?'

'Yes, he passed away,' she said, 'drowned during a diving trip.'

Shouji stared at Liyun.

'In the beginning, I approached you because I was curious what kind of man Youko was dating,' she said. 'After my brother's death, she acted as if nothing had happened. She even got herself a new boyfriend. You wouldn't know this, but he went on that diving trip because he wanted to make a video proposal for Youko. Something that would suit her, he said.'

Her name … No wonder she hated it.

'My brother loved Youko. She was everything to him. I didn't expect her to mourn him forever, but she was way too nonchalant about his death. She cut her hair short, wrote her name differently, and got into a new relationship. Not even a month had passed when she started to go out with you. Didn't my brother mean anything to her?'

Liyun's breathing was rapid.

'I hated how you and my brother had both been so foolishly in love with her. The second time we met, I learned that you were still waiting for her, even after she'd been gone for so long. Someone like Youko, who could simply move on from one man to another, didn't deserve you, or my brother. I wanted to punish her, to take you away from her.'

Shouji sighed. *It all makes sense now.* He waited until she calmed down before speaking.

'Youko didn't forget about your brother,' he said. 'She kept on blaming herself. I bet that's why she changed her name. Why did she go out with me? Who knows? Perhaps she was trying to get over him. But trust me, he was always on her mind.'

Liyun looked up. Her eyes glistened. 'What makes you so sure?'

'Back when I was with Youko, she always made it a point to visit the aquarium often. I used to wonder why, but now everything is clear. She missed him, and she blamed herself for his death. Even after we had moved to Akakawa, she still made frequent day trips to Tokyo just to go to the aquarium.'

Liyun had said nothing. Was she listening?

'What happened to your brother was an accident,' Shouji said. 'You can't blame Youko for that.'

Liyun looked down and crossed her fingers.

He reached for her hands, patting them. 'Your brother wouldn't be happy if he knew you were holding a grudge.'

'I know,' she muttered. She paused and took a deep breath. 'I know you're right, but at the time I was angry.'

'So, you pretended to be interested in me?'

Liyun raised her head. 'That was only in the beginning.'

'Hmmm?'

'After I moved in, I got to know you more as a person, and I found you interesting.' She chuckled. 'And your reaction after that night too, so innocent and trusting.'

'Hey,' he protested.

She looked at him. 'I liked your work, especially your opinion pieces. They were sensitive and well thought out. I told myself that the man who wrote them must be a sincere person.'

He averted his eyes. 'You thought too highly of me.'

'No, I really love your writing.' Her tone was firm. 'When I first read your articles, I felt like I wanted to know you better. But you didn't know that, did you?'

Shouji thought carefully about what to say. 'Let's not dwell on the past. It's not a good idea.'

'It's not good idea for me, or for you?'

'For either of us.'

Liyun opened the window. A gust of warm air entered. The curtain waved gently, taking him back to the time he'd spent with her in Tokyo.

The apartment they had shared was cheap, the best he could find based on his meagre salary. After Youko had disappeared, Shouji had lived day to day, frustrated with his life, but he couldn't say there had been no happy moments. Even now, he missed those days when he and Liyun ate together in the tiny living room. She made the best pickled vegetables. And he would never forget those weekend afternoons they used to spend together, sitting across from each other. He, smoking while drinking coffee, and she, talking and laughing. The coffee she made was good, even though she wasn't a coffee drinker. Behind her, the white curtains with tiny floral patterns flapped around in the wind.

'I still have those curtains you gave me,' Shouji said. 'They've got two tiny holes. I wasn't careful when I hung them out to dry after washing, and the fabric caught in the pegs.'

Liyun turned to face him. 'How long has it been? You should've replaced them with new ones.'

'There's something comforting about sticking to the old stuff.'

'Stop being sentimental.'

Liyun smiled. Shouji was glad her mood had improved.

She shifted her eyes. 'Since we're friends again, what if I told you something interesting?'

He grinned. 'You still have something to tell me?'

'Never underestimate women. We're full of secrets,' Liyun said. 'Especially that woman of yours.'

Shouji's throat felt dry. 'Youko?'

Liyun nodded and then stared off into the distance. 'What if I told you I know where she is?'

YOUKO
洋子

CHAPTER 33
TRACING WATER

Kisejima, 2000. Located south-west of Kyushu, Kisejima — also known as Kise Island — is part of the Ryukyu Islands. Famous for its pristine beaches, beautiful coral reefs, and the diversity of its aquatic life, it is a popular destination with beginner and experienced divers. Because of its location, the weather is warm most of the year.

After checking in to the Ocean View Kise Hotel, Shouji called Yoshioka using the in-room phone. Waiting for his senior to pick up, he stared out of the window. It was raining. The sparkling sea could be seen from the villa, even though the beach was a long walk away.

'What do you mean, you're not returning tomorrow?' Yoshioka said. 'Didn't I make it clear you could only take three days off? We have the editorial meeting.'

'My apologies,' Shouji said, lowering his head. 'Think of it as a once-in-a-lifetime favour.'

Yoshioka groaned. 'Do you need me to personally come and get you from Singapore?'

'I'm in Japan.'

'Good. I'll see you tomorrow morning then.'

'But, right now, I'm somewhere near Okinawa.'

There was a brief pause. 'Arai, is this a joke?'

'I'm serious.'

To reach the island from Singapore, Shouji had taken three different flights. One from Singapore to Narita, and then another from Narita to Naha, and finally, a domestic flight to Kisejima.

Yoshioka took a deep breath. 'Arai, I thought you were serious about your job. That was why I recommended you for promotion. You're showing yourself in a bad light. How am I going to explain this to the management?'

Shouji tightened his grip. 'I need to be here even if I lose my job.'

Yoshioka went quiet. It was a bold move for Shouji to say this. It would be difficult for him to find other employment if he were to leave the company. But he had to do what he had to do, whatever the cost.

After a long silence, Yoshioka asked, 'Can you be back in a week?'

'That should be fine.' Shouji breathed a sigh of relief.

'I'll get a doctor friend of mine to write a medical certificate saying you're unwell or something ... But only this once. And please keep it to yourself.'

'I appreciate it.'

After the phone call, Shouji took a taxi to Kisejima Ocean Science Museum in the pouring rain. Water droplets pelting on the window made it hard to see outside. Bright billboards blurred into each other. People scurried under colourful umbrellas while some took cover under shelters.

'The weather has been like this since this morning,' the taxi driver said. 'It gets heavier whenever you think it's going to stop.'

Shouji said nothing. The white sedan he was in crept along in the congested traffic.

'Strange,' the driver murmured, 'we don't usually have traffic jams.'

Still silent, Shouji closed his eyes and tried to rest. The flight had left him exhausted. He hadn't managed to get any sleep. Too many things were weighing him down. He felt like he was sinking in a bottomless sea.

'Youko is alive and well,' Liyun had told him. 'At least she was, up until two weeks ago.'

Shouji stared. 'What do you mean?'

'She came to Singapore on the anniversary of my brother's death.'

'Do you know where she is now?'

'Not the exact address, but she told me she's working for a conservation organisation. Their headquarters are in Okinawa.'

•

The taxi came to a halt.

'We're trapped,' the driver said. 'It's going to take a while before we reach the next turn.'

'Uh-huh.'

The driver turned on the radio, and the sound of an orchestra filled the car. Shouji closed his eyes. Exquisite and haunting, the melody sounded familiar. Ah, the song was one of the pieces he used to listen to when he'd been working in the tearoom. The beautiful notes had given the place a sophisticated ambiance.

'It's Chopin,' Youko had once told him. 'I overheard Madam telling Mr Satou the music has to be Chopin.'

'Why Chopin? There are many other famous composers — Bach, or Beethoven, or Mozart.'

'Maybe because his music sounds good?' She thought about it again before reframing what she'd said. 'His music makes the piano sound good.'

'I didn't know you were a classical music aficionado.'

'You don't need to be an expert to appreciate Chopin. I'm sure you get the same feeling too? There is a dark undertone beneath the beautiful melody. It appeals to our humanity.'

'What do you mean?'

Youko pursed her lips. 'Well, everyone has a secret they don't want anyone to ever find out.'

He thought for a while before saying, 'Maybe.'

Back then, Shouji had thought only of himself. He hadn't wanted Youko to learn about his strained relationship with his father. Why hadn't he realised she had been referring to her own secret? The more Shouji learned about Youko, the more he thought he'd never really known her.

'There's been an accident,' the taxi driver said.

Shouji looked out of the window. He could make out a mangled motorbike lying on the ground. A truck with a badly dented bumper had stopped nearby. Not far from the vehicles, a body was covered with a blue tarpaulin. Two policemen were busy at the scene, and a third was desperately trying to direct the traffic onwards. Yellow and black police tape circled the area.

On the other side of the road, onlookers had gathered under shop awnings. An ambulance was parked nearby, but the paramedics were standing idly by the vehicle. The victim had probably died instantly. One moment riding the motorbike, then suddenly flung off, landing on the asphalt. He could've had no idea that morning he would get into a fatal accident. He might have had plans to go somewhere or to meet someone. If he could've chosen, he probably wouldn't have wanted to die that day, or in that way.

Once the taxi had passed the scene of the accident, the traffic flow returned to normal. The stereo played a cheerful tune — a Mozart sonata. The rain, too, had finally subsided. Sun shone through the window on to Shouji's right hand. There was a tiny scratch on his forefinger. The blood had dried. He had probably cut himself while packing in a hurry. How many other things had he not realised until they were staring him in the face?

•

The Kisejima Ocean Science Museum was housed in a two-storey building with a large parking area. The building's brick walls gave it a warm and cosy look. The rack in front was filled with bicycles of various colours and models. Judging from the outside, the museum wasn't huge. A wooden standee was placed at the entrance. On it, was a cartoon illustration of a diver surrounded by fish. There was a hole where the diver's face should be, offering a photo opportunity.

Shouji walked towards the entrance and pushed open the glass doors. The reception area was wide and spacious, with more wooden standees scattered around the place.

The woman manning the information counter greeted him. 'Good afternoon. What can I do for you?'

'I'm looking for a staff member,' he said. 'Her name is Youko Sasaki.'

Her eyes lit up. 'Ah, Manager Sasaki? My apologies, you are ...'

'Shouji Arai.'

She nodded and reached for her phone.

So Youko was the manager. She was probably in charge of overseeing the whole place. After all these years, it felt so surreal that he would see her again.

The receptionist put the phone down. 'Manager Sasaki will be here shortly. Why don't you take a seat?'

There were a few wooden benches in the reception area but, instead of sitting down, Shouji went over to read the information posters displayed on a board.

Kisejima Ocean Science Museum was dedicated to marine life and its biodiversity. The museum was owned and managed by a non-profit organisation focusing on ocean conservation and education. The first floor showcased Okinawa's sea geology, ecosystems, and abundant marine wildlife. The second floor was dedicated to historical developments in the marine industry and various efforts to protect the sea environment. The museum was also equipped with an auditorium that periodically screened documentaries on ocean conservation. To visit the various exhibits, there was a fee of 500 yen for adults and 300 yen for children. The documentary was an additional payment of 100 yen.

He was still reading the information, though nothing seemed to register, when he heard footsteps coming closer.

CHAPTER 34
WHAT YOU DIDN'T KNOW

She walked towards him, her movements lithe and swift. Wearing a white top paired with camel-coloured trousers, Youko was as slender and beautiful as ever. Her hair was permed and cascaded over her shoulders. She had dyed it a lovely shade of ash brown.

'It's been a while,' she said.

He swallowed hard, unable to say anything.

She strolled out of the building. Her pace was slow. She probably wanted him to follow. He did so, a few steps behind her. They walked through the car park and passed a few shops before she led him to a small Western food kiosk.

Turning to face him, she asked, 'Have you had lunch?'

'Not yet,' he said, stopping to maintain the gap between them. He'd come straight to Youko's workplace after checking into the hotel, without even showering or changing.

Youko ordered two portions of fish and chips. Before Shouji could reach for his wallet, she took a few notes out.

He came closer. 'Let me pay.'

Ignoring him, she paid and moved to a quiet corner. He followed her and they stood side by side. This time, they were so near their hands were almost touching. He stole a glance at her. How strange it was for them to be close to each other again. Looking at her shoulders, he wanted to reach out to her, but his hands felt heavy. There was an invisible wall separating them.

Youko handed a portion of fish and chips to Shouji. The tips of their fingers touched, and he registered a tiny jolt in her expression. She moved away from him. The distance between them grew.

'You should eat it while it's still hot,' she said.

He opened the wrapper. Steam escaped. After waiting for the food to cool down a little, Shouji took a huge bite. He wasn't sure if it was because he hadn't had his lunch, or because the weather was chilly after the rain, but the food was delicious. Lightly battered snapper loin with chunky potato chips. The fish was fresh and the batter wasn't oily.

'I buy fish and chips from this kiosk at least once a week,' Youko said. 'There's a vending machine selling drinks around the corner. No Asahi Super Dry though. Can I get you a Coke?'

'Uh-huh.'

Youko went to the vending machine and bought two cans of Coke. She threw one at Shouji. He caught it just before the drink touched the wet ground.

'Getting slow, aren't you?' she teased him.

He gave a thin smile. 'I'm getting old.'

She avoided his eyes. Looking down at the damp asphalt, she shuffled a little in her canvas shoes. 'Why did you come here?'

Shouji swallowed hard. He'd wanted to say these words for so long: 'I miss you.'

She looked at him.

'I miss you so much, Youko,' he said.

He waited for her response, but she said nothing.

'I always thought you were in Tokyo, or somewhere nearby,' he said, trying to break her silence.

'I've been living in Kisejima for years.' Youko took a sip of her drink. 'How did you find out I was here?'

'It's a long story.'

He recounted how he'd managed to leave Akakawa, and how he'd met Liyun at the reunion. Holding her unopened Coke, Youko listened to his story without saying a word. Only when it came to the part where he had found Mizuki in Tokyo did she finally comment, 'So that was her real name.'

He nodded. 'Surprisingly, yes.'

'I'm glad she managed to get away from her husband,' she said. 'I'm sure you're relieved too. She was someone important to you, wasn't she?'

'Mizuki was more than just a customer. I saw her as a friend.'

Youko rolled her Coke between her hands. 'You had a crush on her.'

'You're mistaken.' Shouji shoved his left hand into his pocket.

'Nah, you did. You're easy to read, Shouji. Too easy, sometimes.' She averted her eyes. 'I knew you didn't realise it, which was why I never brought it up.'

He wasn't sure if he agreed with that. 'About Mizuki, I empathised with her. I had a difficult relationship with my father. He was really strict, and ...' Shouji cleared his throat. 'He could be violent.'

Youko turned to Shouji. 'You never told me that.'

'I never told anyone.'

Shouji still didn't want to talk too much about his father so he continued where he'd left off. An hour had probably passed by the time he had finally finished.

'Is that everything?' Youko asked after he had stopped speaking.

'Yeah,' he mumbled. 'From your passport, I learned that you'd changed the way you spelled your name when we first met.'

She didn't respond.

'Why did you change it into the character for sunshine?' he asked.

'It was my mother's name,' she said. 'Not many people know, but we had the same name, but spelled with different characters.'

'I see.' He turned to her. 'But why change it at all?'

She avoided his gaze. 'I had my reasons.'

'Were you running away from your past?'

Youko turned to Shouji.

He looked into her eyes. 'Am I right?'

She shook her head. 'It's true that I was trying to distance myself from my former life. But now I've learned to live with it. I came here to confront the past that was haunting me, to face it rather than avoid it.'

'And what about me?'

'What do you mean?'

'Why did you leave Akakawa alone? Why didn't you wait for me?'

'I thought it would be safer for us to go separately,' she said. 'Mr Satou said the same too.'

Wait a minute. 'Did you just say Mr Satou?'

She was quiet for a moment. 'You didn't know?'

•

That morning had started like any other day, except that Shouji had decided to skip work so Youko had gone to the tearoom alone. She was getting off the bus when a gloved hand grabbed her arm. Surprised, she turned around. Mr Satou was looking at her, his index finger over his mouth, signalling for her to keep quiet. Before Youko could fully grasp what was happening, the older man had pulled her away from the tearoom.

They turned into a small alley. The street was quiet and narrow, lined with small shops that were not yet open. Finally, Mr Satou let go of her.

'Why are we here?' Youko asked.

'There's no time to explain,' he said. 'I need you to trust me.'

She frowned.

'You're Youko's daughter, aren't you?'

Youko's heart skipped a little. 'You knew my mother?'

'Listen.' Mr Satou stared into her eyes. 'We've been ordered to eliminate you and Arai. You need to get away from Akakawa.'

'But …' Her voice was shaky. 'Why?'

'Arai broke the company's code of secrecy.'

'That must be a misunderstanding. How could he —'

'I'll explain later. We can't stay here any longer. I'll help you escape, but you must listen closely to what I say. You understand?'

•

An image of the well-dressed man in white gloves flashed into Shouji's mind. Could Mr Satou have been the mysterious man on the phone? Shouji had always wondered why the man hadn't come after him, but maybe he'd been on his side the whole time.

'He told me to leave town,' Youko said. 'We rushed back to the apartment. You were gone. I wanted to wait for you, but Mr Satou said we didn't have time. He promised to get you out safely later.'

Shouji shook his head. 'And you believed him?'

'I didn't have much choice. I was in a panic. I didn't know what was going on.' Youko bit her lip. 'I thought it was safer for us to go separately. But then you never came to find me. I assumed you'd decided it would be better for us to be on our own until things settled down.'

'How could I find you? You left without a word. You could have written me a note.'

'But I did,' she said. 'I left you a note on the table. You couldn't have missed it.'

•

After packing hastily, Youko took a notebook from her drawer.

'What are you doing?' Mr Satou asked. 'We need to go now.'

'Just a moment, please. It won't take more than a minute.' She grabbed a pen from the desk. 'If you can't wait, you can leave first.'

The older man sighed. 'Just be quick.'

She nodded and scribbled as fast as she could.

*Shouji, the people in the company are after us. It's not safe
to remain in Akakawa. I'm heading to Kuromachi. I'll wait
for you there. After that, we can return to Tokyo together. Mr
Satou is helping us. I have a feeling he is someone we can trust.*
– Youko

•

Could it be ... Shouji's heart skipped a beat. 'You don't know about
the fire?'

Youko's eyes widened.

'On the day you left, there was a fire at the apartment. I knew
the company was after me, so I couldn't come back.'

'No.' She covered her mouth. 'Then ...'

'I never saw your note.'

Youko was silent. She looked down for a long time, then she
started to shiver. Was she crying? No, she was laughing.

Shouji became flustered. 'What's so funny?'

'Don't you think everything is hilarious?' she said. 'I waited
so long, thinking you had left me to fend for myself. You probably
thought the same about me too.' Youko's laughter was getting louder.
She covered her face with her hands. Tears seeped through the gaps
between her fingers.

'Youko ...' he whispered her name.

'I thought you'd abandoned me,' she said, still covering her face.
'Or worse, that they'd managed to get you. I was worried. I tried
calling Jin's apartment, but he had moved out. I contacted some
of your friends too, but no one knew where you were. I even tried
asking the university for your phone number in Fukuoka, thinking

perhaps you might have gone back to your family, but of course the staff wouldn't give me your personal details. I was about to go to the police, but Mr Satou advised me against it. I was so scared. I didn't know what to do. I —'

He reached for her and hugged her.

'What are you doing?' she asked.

'I don't know,' Shouji said, whispering into her ear. 'I have no idea what I'm doing.'

She circled her arms around him and sank her head into his chest.

Looking at her, he was taken aback. He didn't remember her being so small. She seemed to be trying hard to suppress her emotions. He rubbed her back, hoping to calm her down, but her sobs grew louder.

Her tears brought him back to the morning they had first met, in the old apartment Shouji had shared with Jin. Back then, she'd also been crying.

●

After Youko had calmed down, they sat on a metal barrier in silence. Shouji took another sip of the Coke. Too sweet and too gassy. He craved a good cup of coffee.

'I've no idea what got into me,' she said. 'This is embarrassing.'

'It's all right,' he said. 'Each of us has our moments of weakness.'

'Are you trying to make me feel better?' She looked at him. 'I bet you have a lot of questions.'

'Yes, I do.' He paused. 'You said you went to Kuromachi?'

'That's right. I waited for a week in a house owned by a doctor acquaintance of Mr Satou,' Youko said. 'Mr Satou called every day to tell me he couldn't find you. I wanted to believe that you'd managed to get away safely. Perhaps you'd returned to Fukuoka. That would probably have been for the best.'

'You went to Okinawa after that?'

She nodded. 'I took the train from Kuromachi to Narita, and then I flew to Kisejima. Mr Satou told me to lie low until things calmed down. Anywhere is fine, he said. Just stay hidden for a while.' She stopped for a moment, her eyes narrowing. 'While I was waiting for you, I'd been doing a lot of thinking. I had to make amends with my past. Mr Satou gave me a number so I could call to update him on my whereabouts, but after a few months he became uncontactable.'

If Mr Satou was the one who had helped her, most likely he was also the mysterious man Shouji had spoken with. 'Why did he help you?'

'He said he knew my parents.'

'I see,' he mumbled, remembering the hostility he'd felt from Mr Satou when they'd first met at the tearoom. Had he been trying to be protective, to take the place Youko's parents had never filled? That said ... 'All these years, did you keep looking for me?'

'At first I did. I went to Tokyo a few times. But we had been separated for long. After a while, I felt like it was time to move on. I had no idea where you could be, and you would probably be seeing someone else, or —'

'Youko,' Shouji said, cutting her off. He took a deep breath. 'I've never been able to forget you.'

A gust of wind blew and shook the water off the trees.

Droplets of water fell on their skin, but neither of them wiped them away.

CHAPTER 35
SLEEPING LOTUS

Shouji sat on the edge of the bed, fidgeting with his fingers and listening to the sound of boiling water. He glanced at the clock on the wall. It was only 4.50 pm. Youko wouldn't finish work so early, but he was still anxious. To calm himself, he paced around his villa, which he hadn't fully explored.

The accommodation he had booked in a rush had turned out to be luxurious and a lot larger than he had expected. Rather than a room in a hotel, the place was a spacious three-level villa that could house up to six guests. It was located far from any public transport, so perhaps that was why the rate was still affordable.

The ground floor was an open-plan living, dining, and kitchen area. He climbed the staircase to the first floor, where the master bedroom was. A king-sized bed perched in the middle, a quirky rattan lampshade hung from the ceiling, and there was a wooden desk by the window with a coffee machine on top. The en-suite bathroom had a rain shower and a deep bathtub. The final level was a loft with ladder-style access, furnished with two sets of bunk beds.

Returning to the ground floor, Shouji opened all the curtains. The blue water sparkled in the distance. A pair of seagulls came and went, screeching.

He checked the time again. A quarter past five. How long would it take for her to get here? Just then, the doorbell rang. He went to answer it. Youko was there, standing on the porch.

'Can I come in?' she asked.

He pulled her into him and encircled her shoulders with his arms.

'The door is still open,' she whispered.

Shouji let Youko slip out of his embrace. She made her way in and he closed the door, feeling the coldness of the metal handle. Once the doorknob had clicked, Shouji rushed to Youko. He reached for her hand and took her in his arms.

Sinking his nose into her neck, he whispered, 'I miss you.'

Youko kept silent. He took a step back to look at her. She had a sad expression on her face, and his heart grew heavy. He ran his fingers through her hair, touching her chin and bringing her lips to his. The moment they kissed, he was overwhelmed with emotion.

Shouji led Youko to the bedroom and they undressed each other. Before long, he was deep inside her. He brushed her hair from her face and kissed her again. Her nails dug into his shoulders.

He stared at her. Her face was flushed, her breath heavy.

'What are you looking at?' she asked, cupping his face in her hands.

'You,' he said. 'It took me a long, long time to finally find you. I'm sorry you had to wait so long.'

He put his hands on hers, holding them tight. He would never let her go again. He wouldn't lose her again. Climbing on top of her, he turned her body around and saw her bare back.

'You got a tattoo,' he said.

'Yes. It was done by a local artist.' Youko turned her head to face him. 'Are you surprised?'

He gave the tattoo a closer look, tracing it with his fingertips. There was no mistake. It was the same design as the one he'd seen in his dream. How could that be possible?

'Why did you choose an open heart?' he asked.

Her eyes widened.

'The tattoo,' he said. 'It's an open heart, isn't it?'

She laughed. 'What are you talking about? No matter how you look at it, it's a flower.'

'What kind of flower?' He ran his finger over her skin. 'A lotus?'

'Very close. It's a sleeping lotus.' Youko got up and walked to the window. The afternoon sun illuminated her skin and the tattoo on her back. 'What do you think? Does it suit me?'

He looked at Youko and held his breath — her messy hair, her jutting collarbone, her tiny wrists, her smooth back, now inked with an illustration of a sleeping lotus. She looked so gorgeous.

'Yes,' he said. 'It really suits you.'

She closed her eyes, and a smile drifted across her face. The sun sunk lower and the room gradually darkened. The two of them had finally found each other. The years of separation seemed to evaporate.

•

The morning sun crept through the open window, shining on to Shouji's exposed skin and warming him. He squinted until his eyes adjusted to the brightness. Next to him, Youko was sound asleep. Not wanting to disturb her, he got up quietly and went to the bathroom to freshen up. When he returned, Youko was awake. She sat on the bed, staring at the sea.

'Good morning.' He went over to her. 'Did you sleep well?'

'I did.' She turned to him. 'This is a rather fancy place, don't you think?'

'I've got no complaints. Are you leaving for work?'

Youko glanced at the clock. 'It'd be late even if I made a move now.' She folded her legs in front of her chest and hugged them. 'What about you, Shouji? Where do you work now?'

'I'm an assistant editor.'

'Isn't that what you always wanted to do?'

'Kind of.'

'Do you enjoy it?'

'It's all right, and it pays the bills.'

'That's great,' she said, and chuckled. 'It feels strange asking you all these questions. It makes me realise how little I know about you now.'

'All the more reason to ask me,' Shouji said. 'What would you like to know?'

Youko smiled at him. 'All right, but give me a couple of minutes. My brain freezes in the morning.'

He walked over to the counter. 'Do you want coffee?'

'Sounds good.'

Shouji took out a white porcelain cup from the pull-out drawer. Listening to the soft humming of the coffee maker, they waited for the drink to be ready. A rich aroma escaped when the dark liquid streamed out. Shouji felt his senses awaken.

He brought the cup to the bedside table and sat next to Youko.

'Unsweetened,' he said. The way she liked it.

'Thanks,' she murmured, and looked out of the window. 'The view is amazing.'

'Uh-huh,' he mumbled in agreement.

She bit her lip. 'Now that I'm here, I don't know where to start.'

'Then tell me everything. What do you want to say? What's on your mind? I'll listen to whatever you want to say.'

Youko was silent.

'I want to hear everything,' Shouji said. 'I want to learn more about you. There are so many things I want to know. We have so much to catch up on. I think I'll have to spend my entire life with you. Even then, we may not have enough time, so you'd better start now.'

Still staring off into the distance, she gave a thin smile, 'You're so kind, Shouji, but our time has passed.'

'What do you mean?'

'We had a great time, but it was in the past. I've moved on. You've got your new life too. Of course, I have my regrets. We didn't have the chance to say goodbye. But this time, we can finally have the clean break we deserved. A proper farewell.'

'What are you talking about?'

She looked at him. 'I'm happy to see you, and I'm thankful for this chance to end our relationship properly.'

Her words hit him hard. 'I don't understand. Why can't we return to the way we used to be? Are you saying you no longer love me? Then why did we ...'

She shook her head. 'Shouji, you don't understand.'

'Then tell me. Make me understand.'

'Look at me,' she pleaded. 'I've changed. I'm no longer the same person I was when I was with you. I can't go back to the way I was before.'

'But you still love me, don't you?'

'I do. I still love you, and you're still someone precious to me, but I have my own life now, and you do too. Just because we still love each other, doesn't mean we have to be together. People come and go, but we can treasure the good memories that we have. Isn't that what life is?'

No, he wasn't buying it. Why couldn't they be together?

'Let's not hurt each other anymore,' she continued. 'I want us to part on good terms.'

Shouji sighed. 'You don't honestly think I'm going to accept that, do you?'

He looked into her eyes, but she averted hers. He took a deep breath to calm himself. It wasn't the time to argue.

'Would you listen to me first?' Shouji asked.

Youko didn't answer.

'Let's have a fresh start, all right?' he said, reaching for her hands. 'Today marks the beginning of our new relationship. I promise I'll be honest with you. No more secrets. I trust you, and I want you to accept me for who I am. The good, the bad, everything … and …'

'Shouji …'

He gave her hands a gentle squeeze. 'I want to know everything that happened in your life, but you only need to share it with me when you're ready. I won't force you, and I want you to know that I'm here for you.'

She kept quiet.

'Youko, there are still so many things I want to tell you, and there are so many things I want to do with you.'

'What else is there to do?'

'A lot,' he said. 'For instance, I want to go to the aquarium together. I live in Tokyo. We can go to the Shinagawa aquarium every weekend if you want to. I also want to take you to my favourite restaurant. They serve a great smoked beef brisket. And I have my own apartment now. We can drink coffee and talk into the night, the way we used to. Maybe eat crisps and laze around all day.'

He waited for her to respond, but she remained silent.

'Just come back to me, Youko,' he continued. 'We'll find our way forward together.'

Taking a deep breath, he brought her closer to him. They embraced in silence. How he wished they could stay like this for ever. They belonged to each other. It wasn't too late. When they were separated, time had stopped, and now that they were back together, it had finally begun to flow again.

On the bedside table, the coffee Shouji had made remained untouched.

Dear Youko,

You told me you couldn't see me off at the airport. When you said that, you were averting your eyes. You were never any good at lying, were you? But I know you must have had your reasons.

You said we couldn't move on if we didn't let go of our past. I do agree with you, but I never said I wanted to move on. I don't want to let you go.

If I could turn back time to when we started going out, I would do so many things differently. I would talk to you more about my past, and my feelings too. I would insist that you shared whatever was troubling you, instead of letting you carry it on your own. If I'd done that, perhaps we would still be watching that small television in our old apartment in Akakawa, both of us cradling a cup of coffee, yours unsweetened.

Those days were the happiest in my life. We were young and carefree. We didn't worry about much. Was I in love with you? At that time, I wasn't certain. But now, I know that I did love you. Yes, I loved you and I still do. I always will.

I believe that, in life, the things that are meant to be will eventually happen. If something slipped away from me, then it wasn't supposed to be mine. Because of that, I've never asked anyone to stay in my life. This is the first time I've done this, but now I know I must.

Youko, will you come back to me?

If you're still worried about the company, we could go to the police. I know they had men inside the Akakawa section, but the Tokyo force is bigger and my senior has connections there. I will contact them when I get home. Whatever happens, we'll figure things out together.

Even if you don't yet trust me, please believe in us. Take a leap of faith.

If, somewhere in your heart, you can find space for me, I've included my address in Tokyo.

I'll be waiting.

Shouji

CHAPTER 36
SINK OR SWIM

Shouji tried to open his eyes, but he couldn't. His eyelids felt heavy. His head throbbed as if it were going to split open. What was happening?

The last thing he remembered was taking the letter he'd written to Youko to the hotel reception to post. He had just got back to his villa when the doorbell rang. He went to answer it. No one was outside. How odd. He stepped out of the villa. It was then that something heavy hit the back of his head.

Shouji cursed. So that was what was causing the pain. He must have passed out. But who had attacked him? A burglar? He had nothing valuable to steal.

Eyes still closed, Shouji heard footsteps getting closer, followed by the sound of a string orchestra. The tune was familiar. Had he heard it on the radio? Or was it a movie soundtrack? Someone was whistling along to the melody. A man? A woman? Why would a burglar put music on?

Shouji tried to move his arms, but they wouldn't respond. He couldn't feel his limbs. Had he been drugged? He gritted his teeth. At least he could still do that.

A moment passed before Shouji managed to open his eyes. He blinked a few times. His vision was blurred. It took him a while to make out the rattan lampshade. He was still in his villa, but the ceiling looked far away and his back felt cold. He must have been lying on the marble tiles.

Slowly, Shouji regained some control of his body. He tried to wriggle. His arms were under his back, and his ankles and wrists were bound. Who had done this? And why? The whistling sounded close by now. If he could turn around, he'd be able to see whoever it was. But Shouji was paralysed.

Clenching his fists, he dug his nails as hard as he could into his skin. The jolt of pain woke him up a little and he managed to turn his head slightly.

A man naked from the waist up stood nearby, ironing a white shirt and whistling. He had white hair and wore black trousers held up with a black leather belt. Countless scars marked his heavily tattooed back. Not far from where he stood, a black jacket hung from the top of a wardrobe door.

Shouji held his breath. *Mr Satou*, he wanted to say, but the words disappeared in his throat.

The man turned and their eyes met.

'Mr Arai, it's been a while,' Mr Satou said. He went to the wardrobe and took out a hanger for his freshly ironed shirt. 'Do you remember me? We used to work for the same company.'

'What did you do to me?' Shouji asked, his voice small and hoarse.

Mr Satou hooked the shirt in front of the jacket. 'You're feeling numb and paralysed because of the drug I injected you with. Don't worry, the effects should wear off within a day. The actual time differs for each individual, but you'll be like this for the next couple of hours at least.' He turned to face Shouji. 'I hope you don't mind me borrowing the iron. I hate crumpled fabric, and it wasn't easy carrying you up to the first floor.'

'You were the one who spoke to me on the phone, weren't you?'

Mr Satou laughed. 'Yes, I've been lenient but, unfortunately, you didn't deserve my generosity. Why couldn't you do as you were told?'

A chill ran down Shouji's spine. Calm down, he told himself. He had to assess the situation. Was Mr Satou planning to kill him?

Mr Satou pursed his lips. 'I read the heartfelt letter you wrote, though, my apologies, I had to get rid of it. You're a fine writer.'

The letter ... If Mr Satou had read it, he would know about Youko.

'I can't have you going to the police, telling them about the company. Not when I told the boss you had already been taken care of.'

Shouji swallowed hard. 'Why are you here? What do you want?'

'I'm just doing my work.' Mr Satou took out a pair of white gloves from his trouser pocket and put them on. 'I am a cleaner. You know what I mean?'

'I don't care what you do to me, but please spare Youko.'

Mr Satou chuckled. 'Mr Arai, if you're trying to negotiate, you should bring something to the table.' He rubbed his gloved hands. 'Shall we?'

Before Shouji could protest, Mr Satou had dragged him off the floor. He tried to thrash around, but he could only manage to wriggle a little. Mr Satou pulled him into the bathroom and threw him into the tub. *This was it*. Mr Satou was planning to drown him.

Shouji thought about his mother and how he had dismissed her concerns over and over. He could swim, but not when bound and numb. This time, it was over.

No. He couldn't think like that. He had to survive this ordeal. It was too early to give up.

First, he needed to stay composed. He had to stall Mr Satou while trying to think of a way to get out.

'How did you know I was here?' Shouji asked.

Mr Satou smirked. 'I always know where you are. I'm always watching you. I've been following you ever since you took shelter at the Katsuragi Hotel.'

All this time, he hadn't been able to evade their clutches. 'Why didn't you kill me then?'

'Because I wanted to make up for a debt from the past. After all, you did shoulder a price I should have paid. You might not believe me, but I'm a man of principle.'

'I don't understand.'

'Of course you don't. That was your defence mechanism, wasn't it? You couldn't forgive yourself for the grave mistake you thought you had made, so you locked the memory deep inside you and threw away the key.' Mr Satou looked at Shouji kindly. 'I tried my best to help you. I thought I could silence you with threats, but I was wrong. You're planning to stir up trouble again. You should've stayed quietly in Tokyo, then we wouldn't have needed to have this conversation. Instead, you came to Kisejima to look for Youko Sasaki.'

A thought crossed Shouji's mind. 'You've never wanted me to be with her.'

Mr Satou gave Shouji a satisfied smile. 'You're starting to get the picture now. Yes, she's better off here, away from you. You know too many secrets, and you tend to ignore the rules. You're a ticking bomb. Being with you would only endanger her life.'

Something was off with the way Mr Satou was talking, Shouji's instincts told him. He could do this. He had to find an opening and use it to his advantage.

Think, Shouji. Think.

'I know you love her, but you're not strong enough to protect her,' Mr Satou continued. 'I'm the only one who can watch over her.'

That. That was the odd thing. Mr Satou cared about Youko. He hadn't said a word about harming her. In fact, it was the opposite. He'd always helped her. Back in Akakawa, he had warned her about the impending danger and facilitated her escape. He wanted to keep her safe and had gone to great lengths to do so, but why?

'Youko told me you know her parents,' Shouji said.

Mr Satou paused. 'Let's just say that we do know each other, well. Too well, in fact.'

Shouji sensed hostility in his tone. They weren't good friends. Mr Satou hated them. But then, why was he helping Youko? That didn't make any sense. Could it be …? No, that couldn't be it. But if his guess was correct, then a lot of things would make sense. He had nothing to lose. Even if he was wrong, perhaps the accusation alone could throw Mr Satou off guard.

'You're Youko's father, aren't you?'

Mr Satou's eyes widened. He stared at Shouji, not saying a word. And then he laughed.

'You must be a good journalist,' Mr Satou said. 'I have to give you that. Yes, she's my daughter, and you're the first person to find out.' He paused and adopted a solemn expression. 'I was serving my time in prison when my girlfriend gave birth to her. She decided it was better for her daughter not to have a father like me.'

There … he had him. 'If you knew the company was dangerous, why did you arrange for your daughter to work there?'

Mr Satou shook his head. 'You're mistaken. I found her in Tokyo, already working for the company. Before that, I was in Fukuoka.'

'You used to live there?'

'For a number of years, yes. There was another woman there too.' He tilted his head, seemingly reminiscing about the past. 'I had to move there because there were men searching for me all over Iwate. I lost track of my daughter, until I heard she was in Tokyo. I followed her into the company. A huge hassle, you know, to move over to another group in another city. I had to take on someone else's identity.'

Shouji swallowed hard.

'After being in Tokyo for a while, the company placed me in Akakawa, where I slowly climbed the ranks. Eventually, I managed to pull some strings and got my daughter transferred there too.' He looked at Shouji, chuckling. 'What I didn't expect was that you would follow her. Imagine my surprise when I learned it was you she was seeing, of all people. Fate has a funny way of toying with us.'

Shouji clenched his fists. He was slowly regaining control of his body. He had to keep up this conversation, find a way to untie himself, and subdue Mr Satou. 'Were you the one who set the apartment building on fire?' he asked.

Mr Satou cocked his head. 'What do you think?'

Shouji wiggled his fingers. Good, he could move them. Just a little longer. 'Youko and I love each other. You don't need to do this. We can work something out.'

Mr Satou laughed. 'What are you? A schoolchild?' Leaning down, he looked into Shouji's eyes. 'Your naïveté troubles me. Ever since you were young, you've had a gift of attracting misfortune to yourself and the people around you. And then, you conveniently forget.'

What was he talking about?

'You justify your actions by saying you have good intentions,' Mr Satou continued. 'Tell me, what's the use of that? Do you think your intentions matter? Look at what has happened to the people around you because of you.'

Shouji thought of Mizuki, and then, 'Mr Odagiri …' he mumbled the name softly. 'Did you kill him?'

Mr Satou tilted his head. 'Was that the name of that blackmailer? It's been so long I can't remember. But don't feel too bad about him. He was a leech, nasty and hard to shake off. Even if I hadn't dealt with him, sooner or later someone else would have. He should be thankful I was the one who cleaned him up. I hope he liked classical music.'

That reminded Shouji of the odd soundtrack. 'What is this song called?'

'It's Handel's 'Suite in F Major', also known as 'Water Music'. My favourite,' Mr Satou said with a hint of pride. 'It was composed for King George I, to be performed by a huge orchestra on the River Thames. The first performance involved about fifty musicians. Can you imagine how majestic that must have been?'

Shouji discreetly moved his wrists, but the binding was too tight. Or was it because he hadn't fully gained his strength? He yanked at the rope again. Still no use.

Mr Satou glanced at his watch. 'Looks like we're running out of time.' He turned on the tap. 'How's the water? Is it too cold?'

No. He had to buy more time. 'Do you need to do this? I won't go to the police. I'll keep quiet.'

'It's too late, Mr Arai.'

'Are you just trying to cover yourself, or are you being overprotective of a daughter you've never called your own?'

'Enough.' Mr Satou's tone was stern.

'She's an adult now. She's capable of making her own decisions. And if she wants to be with me, you can't stop her. She deserves to choose her own path to happiness. How long do you plan to keep her safe using your warped sense of protectiveness?'

'You're not wrong, Mr Arai, but you don't understand the position you're in. One day, Youko might settle down with someone, but that person can't be you. You're too problematic. You and your constant need to save others.'

'Why can't you admit that, in your eyes, no one would ever be good enough for her?'

Mr Satou paused before answering, 'Probably. You can never understand a father's sentiments.'

Shouji desperately tried to free himself. 'Youko will never forgive you for this.'

'Not if she never finds out.' He inched closer. 'Do you know what I love most about dead people?' He lowered his voice to a whisper. 'They're the most discreet creatures. The dead don't talk.'

Shouji felt the water filling up the tub. 'Even if you got rid of my letter, there's no guarantee Youko wouldn't look for me in Tokyo.'

'I know,' Mr Satou said. 'Which is why I've left a message at her workplace.'

'What do you mean?'

'She'll be the first to discover your dead body. That will spell a clean end to your relationship.' He sighed deeply. 'It's always difficult when you don't get proper closure, isn't it? We both know that.'

The water had now reached Shouji's ears. He started to panic. 'Let me go!'

'Ah, there is one more thing I want to tell you,' Mr Satou said. 'Listen carefully. That incident you tried so hard to erase, it wasn't your fault. You just happened to be unlucky. But don't be afraid. With your death, you'll finally be released from the guilt you've been carrying all your life. You'll find the peace you've always longed for. This old man will bear that burden, just as he should've done from the start.' He stood and looked down at Shouji. 'I don't like what I did, but it had to be done. I was just following orders. Try to consider this a privilege, Mr Arai. Not everyone gets to die listening to music fit for a king.'

Chuckling, Mr Satou walked away.

Once the sound of his footsteps had faded, Shouji frantically tried to pull his hands free.

The rope was still too tight. His whole body remained numb and the water continued to fill the tub. He didn't have much time. If he could sit up, he would survive this. But he couldn't move. Was there nothing he could do?

Shouji closed his eyes. His mind drifted, and he recalled his conversation with Mizuki.

They were in Professor Gouda's office. Shouji was on the sofa, while Mizuki stood near the window. The morning sun highlighted her long hair.

She turned to him and asked, 'Do you know how long it takes to lose consciousness under water? As little as two minutes. In four to six minutes of drowning, a person can sustain permanent brain damage.'

He watched her running her fingers along the window frame.

'By contrast, a human can hold their breath for more than five minutes. Interesting, isn't it? The key is preparation. Breathe slowly for several minutes and, before you dive in, take a deep breath.'

Mizuki's soft and calm voice was all he needed. He would survive this.

Shouji braced himself and began to control his breathing. One … Two … Three … The water level rose, but he forced himself to stay calm. Four … Five … Six … He continued to count, keeping his breathing as slow as possible.

Finally, time ran out.

Air. He needed air.

Shouji took a deep breath before the water covered his nose.

His whole body was now submerged. He could see the surface, but he couldn't move. He struggled. He yanked at the rope but, under water, his movements became laborious. Yet he didn't stop. He wouldn't allow it to end like this.

Air bubbles slowly escaped from his mouth. He clenched his lips together. He had to last as long as possible. His movements were getting more pronounced. The drug was wearing off. Shouji kept struggling, tossing, and thrashing around.

A little bit more. Yes, a little bit more.

His lungs hurt. He was in excruciating pain.

Help. Somebody, help. Was he going to die?

In his haziness, he heard a different tune. Had Mr Satou changed the song? No. This clear, precise sound was resonating inside his head. The delicate sound of a koto, and not just any koto. It was Shouji's mother's beloved seventeen-string koto. How had he not recognised it at once? The melody he had long forgotten came flooding in.

●

He heard his mother's pitch-perfect voice. He saw her elegant posture and her black hair, perfectly styled into a smooth bun, which suited her beautiful beige kimono. Her slender fingers danced on her instrument. Everything was so vivid. But where was he?

Oh, there he was, standing not far from her with a look of admiration on his face. He was still a little boy. The boy wished he could remain there forever, listening to his mother's beautiful music, but he didn't stay for long.

He was now dressed in black. He stared at his mother, but she was no longer playing the koto. She had changed into a black kimono. She was sobbing. *What happened, Mother? Who made you upset? Was it Father?* He was standing next to her, also dressed in black.

Not far from them, a man kneeled next to a small coffin with a stoic expression. Uncle Hidetoshi. What was he doing there? Whose funeral were they at?

Everything blurred. When he could finally focus, he was in the backyard of his house.

Before he could move, his father came to him. He shoved him to the ground. He took a wooden rod and hit the boy over and over. From the corner of his eyes, the boy saw his mother, standing still at the corner. His gentle, beautiful mother. Tears flowed down her face and her trembling hands were clasped in front of her chest.

I'm okay, he wanted to say, but no sound came out.

The man yanked the boy and dragged him into the shed. The man shouted something. He was asking a question. The boy shook his head. The man shouted again, but the boy shook his head once more. He couldn't remember. He didn't know what had happened. The man shoved the boy and the child landed in the corner.

'Stay there until you remember what you've done,' the man said, this time his voice audible. He slammed the door and secured it with a lock.

The boy shivered and cried. No, he wouldn't remember. He didn't want to remember.

And then something flashed into his mind. A red dot?

No. It was a red balloon.

Finally, he remembered.

EPILOGUE

The sun was at its peak as the boy rinsed laundry alone in the backyard. Despite being under the shelter, Shouji was melting in the heat. Sweat tickled his face as he dipped his hands into the giant plastic bucket. He wiped the sweat off with the sleeve of the old T-shirt he was wearing.

'Brother Shouji,' a small voice called. A toddler, walking unsteadily, came towards him. He held a red balloon in his hand. 'What are you doing?'

Shouji looked at his young cousin. 'Washing the laundry. Mrs Sakamoto is away visiting her family, so I need to help out with the housework. Where is your father?'

'My father is talking to your father.' The little boy peered into the bucket. 'Is it difficult?'

'Not really, but it's tiring.' Shouji stared at the balloon. 'Who gave you this?'

'The white-gloved man.'

Shouji frowned. 'Who?'

'A man who wears white gloves. He said today is a special day.'

'Oh ...' What was so special about it? Perhaps the man had said that to make his cousin happy. Ichirou, with his chubby cheeks, looked adorable in his denim dungarees. But white gloves? How odd. Why would anyone wear a pair of gloves in such hot weather? Perhaps he was a taxi driver.

The summer breeze carried over the sound of a string

instrument. Each note had a high degree of precision. The composition was simple, yet captivating.

Entranced, Shouji stood. He left his chore unfinished and walked towards the house. His mother was sitting behind her seventeen-string koto, wearing a beige kimono. They exchanged smiles.

Shouji settled himself on the porch, leaning against one of the wooden pillars. He closed his eyes. The clear notes blended with the whisper of the wind caressing the leaves. He felt himself becoming absorbed into her alluring world.

When Shouji opened his eyes, he saw the cloudless sky. So calm, so peaceful. He lifted his right arm and squinted, staring at the sunrays that came between his fingers. The summer holidays were the best time of the year. Too bad he had to return to school next week.

The music was still playing when Shouji noticed a stray red balloon. It flew higher and higher, disappearing into the blue.